dreamland social club

tara altebrando

· D U T T O N   B O O K S ·

A MEMBER OF PENGUIN GROUP (USA) INC.

DUTTON BOOKS

A member of Penguin Group (USA) Inc.

PUBLISHED BY THE PENGUIN GROUP

Penguin Group (USA) Inc., 375 Hudson Street, New York, New York 10014, U.S.A.•
Penguin Group (Canada), 90 Eglinton Avenue East, Suite 700, Toronto, Ontario, Canada
M4P 2Y3 (a division of Pearson Penguin Canada Inc.) • Penguin Books Ltd, 80 Strand,
London WC2R 0RL, England • Penguin Ireland, 25 St Stephen's Green, Dublin 2, Ireland
(a division of Penguin Books Ltd) • Penguin Group (Australia), 250 Camberwell Road,
Camberwell, Victoria 3124, Australia (a division of Pearson Australia Group Pty Ltd) •
Penguin Books India Pvt Ltd, 11 Community Centre, Panchsheel Park, New Delhi—110
017, India • Penguin Group (NZ), 67 Apollo Drive, Rosedale, North Shore 0632, New
Zealand (a division of Pearson New Zealand Ltd) • Penguin Books (South Africa) (Pty)
Ltd, 24 Sturdee Avenue, Rosebank, Johannesburg 2196, South Africa • Penguin Books
Ltd, Registered Offices: 80 Strand, London WC2R 0RL, England

CIP Data is available.

Published in the United States by Dutton Books,
a member of Penguin Group (USA) Inc.
345 Hudson Street, New York, New York 10014
www.penguin.com/youngreaders

Designed by Jason Henry

Printed in USA • First Edition

ISBN: 978-0-525-42325-6
1 3 5 7 9 10 8 6 4 2

For Elena June

I'm at the beach but it's not the real beach; it's indoors and it's called the Ocean Dome.

A blue sky with some white puffy clouds is painted on the ceiling, which is closed because it's raining outside. Maybe it's raining on the real beach, too, wherever that is.

Far away, I think, but I'm not sure.

There are tall curly waves in a big pool and waterslides and even a volcano. The red-orange lava is pretty, like liquid candy. I want to touch it but my mother says, "You can't. It's hot." Then she smiles and says, "Or maybe it isn't. What do I know?" She shrugs a pale shoulder.

She is building sand castles but they're not castles like for princesses. She says that one of the things she's making—a square building of sand with a slippery-looking slide smoothed out on one side—is the Helter Skelter, and another building is the Monkey Theater. Even though I have just turned six years old, I don't know what either of those things is, but I'm going down into the fake surf with our square yellow bucket to scoop up wet sand whenever she needs more of it. Soon she's sculpting what looks to me like a low wall and not a very good one—she's says it's a boardwalk—on one side of her city of sand, and I ask her what this place is called.

"Coney," she says.

When she finds a broken shell in the sand, she picks it up and says, "Huh. Nice touch." Then she starts carving twirly-whirlies and stars and moons onto her buildings with the shell's sharp edge.

I go to get some more wet sand as she starts to work on something she calls Shoot the Chutes, which she says is sort of like the roller coasters my dad makes but way older, way more simple, dumping its cars down one measly hill into a lake, which she'll build with a buried bucket of water. "It was really just a primitive flume," she says.

"Mom," I ask her as I watch, "what's Coney?"

She dumps the bucket's wet sand out and it holds its form nicely. "Home."

"Can we go there?" I ask.

"No," she says. "Not anymore."

"Is it gone?"

She looks up as the roof of the Ocean Dome splits the sky in two, cutting a cloud right in half. The real sun has decided to come out after all.

"That's right." She puts on her sunglasses. "It's gone."

Part One

THE MERMAID'S SECRET

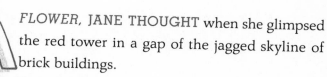 FLOWER, JANE THOUGHT when she glimpsed the red tower in a gap of the jagged skyline of brick buildings.

It looks like a steel flower.

Hundreds of metal sticks, stuck together this way and that, reached up to the sky, toward the tower's round bloom, where a light blinked brightly even in the midday sun.

"Dad," Jane said, "what's that?"

"That," he said from the front seat of the cab, "is the old Parachute Jump ride. But it's been shut down for years, so don't go getting any crazy ideas."

Jane couldn't think of a time when she'd ever had a crazy idea. "Like what?"

He turned and gave her a wink. "Like strapping on a bungee cord and jumping off it."

"Yeah." Jane's brother, Marcus—one year older and beside her in the backseat—shook his head. "That would be so like her."

About twenty minutes and a million degrees before, the Dryden family had stepped out of the hazy August air surrounding them at the JFK arrivals terminal and into an air-conditioned yellow cab bound for Coney Island. Jane was pretty sure that Queens, where the airport was, and then Brooklyn, where Coney Island was, were the top two most ugly places she had ever seen—and that was saying something, considering how much she had moved around over the years. Most recently, they'd done a yearlong stint in London.

Jane had hoped the scenery would improve when they left behind the highways and warehouses and marshland by the airport, but it only got worse as they followed signs that announced Coney Island, signs that said AMUSE-MENTS and BEACH.

Then she'd seen the tower—so pretty—and dared to hope.

"Why was it shut down?" she asked.

Her father shrugged, then said, "Parachutes on strings. Ocean winds. It just couldn't have been safe."

Jane closed her eyes and tried to imagine what the ride would have looked like with parachutes falling like petals in the wind and people dangling from them like long-legged spiders.

Probably not safe at all, no.

But fun?

Maybe.

Either that or completely terrifying.

When a building in the foreground blocked her view of the Parachute Jump, Jane's eyes finally returned to ground level. The cab wound its way through a maze of local streets where the gas stations and car washes and run-down shops seemed endless. The buildings were mostly high-rise brick apartments and, on a more commercial street, small white row houses with green bars on the doors and windows, even the second-floor windows. It probably didn't help Jane's first impression of Coney that the sky was dingy, threatening. Eventually the driver gave up on the AC and opened a few windows; Jane could almost smell the gathering thunderstorm.

The cab turned down Siren Street, and she felt her gut tighten at the blur of graffiti and soot stains on the brick of a row of abandoned houses. Dingy curtains still hung where there had once been windows; old rocking chairs sat eerily still on porches. Clearly, this was the wrong side of town.

The cab stopped.

They were right in front of a big old house that looked entirely out of place, like some tornado in Kansas had gotten carried away with itself. Jane's father looked at a piece of paper in his hand—"It's number two-thirteen"—and Jane found the crooked gold numbers near the door and confirmed that they'd found it.

Wedged between an ancient-looking bait-and-tackle shop and a fenced-in lot overgrown with weeds, the house was shingled and beige with weird peaks and small windows. An air conditioner in the second floor's right window was like a lone bucktooth; the uppermost window wore a top hat of black roof tiles. The front porch looked like it might fall off at any moment, and a gang of demented woodpeckers had apparently had their way with the glossy red paint on the front door. A waist-high chain-link fence surrounded the front yard, where two cement strips indicated a driveway that dead-ended at the porch. On the gate to the drive hung three metal signs—NO PARKING, DON'T EVEN THINK ABOUT PARKING HERE, and NEVER BLOCK DRIVEWAY. Next to *them* dangled a handmade wood sign that read, YES, ITS A DRIVEWAY. Jane had to fight the urge to add the apostrophe.

"This isn't exactly what I was picturing," Marcus said, and Jane would have laughed if she wasn't about to cry. It wasn't that she'd thought they'd be living in an amusement park, exactly, but her mother had *loved* Coney Island—*hadn't she?*—and Jane simply didn't see anything around to love.

"Your grandfather was what polite people called an eccentric," Jane's father said when he joined her on the sidewalk by the driveway signs, having paid the cab fare and gotten their luggage. "He went by the name Preemie."

"*What?*" Marcus laughed. "Why?"

"There was an amusement park here in the early nineteen hundreds. Dreamland. Incubators had just been invented." He wiped sweat from his forehead. "Your grandfather was part of a premature baby display when he was born."

Jane took a minute to process that: *a premature baby display.*

She had only had two weeks to process the fact that she and Marcus had inherited a house from a grandfather they had never known, that they were leaving England and moving to the place where their mother had grown up.

"That's pretty sick," Marcus said, and a thick drop of rain landed on his nose. Another one left a dark slash on his light blue shirt.

"Dreamland burned down, and your grandfather was rescued by nurses and the whole thing made him sort of famous." Their dad picked up a suitcase as the drops became increasingly, alarmingly abundant.

"What was his real name?" Jane asked. Her father so rarely—like ever—talked about her mom or her mom's family, and she wanted to keep him going.

He took a moment to think and then said, "No idea."

The heavens opened up then, and they all got soaked by heavy pellets of warm water in the short distance between the curb and the front door. Her father's wet hands struggled with the keys Preemie's estate lawyer had sent, until finally the front door surrendered with a click. Dust clung to every surface and the air felt thick; the grime on the floors muted Jane's footfalls as she stepped into the front hallway and put her dripping suitcase down. She swept water off her face with a wet hand and then wiped it off on her wet shirt. In the heat, her clothes had started to cling to her like a second skin.

"Crack some windows, but don't let the rain in," her father said, coughing and swatting at the air.

Fortunately, the squall had already blown past and the sun blared through a parting in the clouds. As light entered the living room, the air sprang to life with dancing dust, and items came out of shadow to reveal themselves. Faded black-and-white framed photographs lined the wall along the main staircase; a man whom Jane could only assume was her grandfather posed with famous people like Frank Sinatra, President Gerald Ford, Marilyn Monroe. Every end table and bookshelf—the fireplace mantel, too—boasted weird figurines, like a small Siamese totem pole in a glass case and a pewter statue of a two-headed squirrel.

There was a wooden horse, like from a carousel, in one corner of the living room. Jane went for a closer look. It was white and shiny, with a fiery red mane, pale pink gums, white teeth, and a gold-and-orange muzzle. A piece of purple armor shielded its chest, while red tassels dangling from its pink-and-green saddle seemed to have been frozen in mid-leap. Its glassy brown eyes were so lifelike they gave Jane the creeps, but she soon found herself distracted, instead, by the thick metal chain that was wrapped multiple times around one of the horse's legs and then looped over and under its red tail before snaking across the floor to twist around a radiator. It locked onto itself with a rusty padlock.

"My word," her father said from across the room, "it's like a museum."

"Yeah," Marcus said. "A *crap* museum."

"Why do you think this carousel horse is chained to the radiator?" Jane asked.

Her father shook his head. "I can't even begin to imagine."

As they uncovered old sofas and chairs, Jane's father told stories about Preemie, whom he had only met a few times. Like how his skin looked like worn brown leather from sun exposure; how he had famously *never left Brooklyn*—not even to go into Manhattan—and how he made his living harassing people on the boardwalk into playing a carnival game where you shot into clown mouths with water guns, trying to explode balloons to win inbred-looking stuffed animals.

"Trust me," her dad said, "he made an impression."

Jane felt like a portal had opened in a formerly impenetrable wall. She'd never heard any of this before.

"He actually harassed me into dessert once." He attempted a Brooklyn accent: *"Go on and eat it, whatsa matter? We got a Looky Lou here. Doesn't know what to do with a piece of tiramisu."*

"What's a Looky Lou?" Jane asked.

"Oh, it's somebody who basically just sits on the sidelines and stares. Though usually not just at a piece of cake.

Your mother thought it was the worst thing a person could be." He opened a window shade and released a new cloud of dust. "If she saw me rubbernecking when we passed an accident, or staring at someone with a big birthmark, she'd tell me that there was nothing worse in life than being a Looky Lou."

Jane was fairly certain she was a Looky Lou through and through.

She stepped up close to the wall by the stairs to look at more photos as her father moved on to his next topic: her grandmother.

"Her stage name was Birdie Cusack," he said. "That was her sideshow act, pretending she was part bird."

Jane studied a picture of a woman in a feather headpiece and a bodice that gave her a pear-shaped, birdlike body as her father went on. "She was in a famous movie about freaks in the nineteen fifties. Totally weird stuff."

Jane spotted a framed poster for *Is it Human?* and moved over to study the ghoulish cartoon drawings of the cast, which included a pair of female twins joined at the hip and a man who had hands coming out of his shoulder sockets. She found a drawing of a woman with a feather on her head, wearing a bird bodysuit, and whispered softly, *"Grandma."*

"Why didn't you ever tell us about them?" she dared, turning to her father. She'd had *grandparents*. Her grandfather, at least, had been alive until recently. She could have *met him*.

"Yeah." Marcus looked up. "Did you contact them after Mom . . . ?" He trailed off.

They'd all spent ten years trailing off. . . .

"Of course. I mean, someone notified them. So it must have been me." He shrugged. "But as for talking about them, well, you know how she was about the whole carny thing."

But Jane *didn't* know. This was the first she'd even heard of "the whole carny thing." "What does that even mean?" she asked. "Carny?"

"You know," her dad said again. "Carnival people. Sideshow types. Like Preemie and Birdie. They're like their own community. Like a different ethnic group, practically. And they've always been drawn to Coney Island."

"And Mom didn't like being raised that way?"

He shrugged. "I think your mother struggled to belong."

All Jane could think was, *Who doesn't?*

Jane claimed a third-story bedroom that looked out on a death's-door garden. Sun-bleached pink and purple blooms hung on browning hydrangeas, and some overgrown rosebushes held a few wan, yellow buds. Jane was no expert, but the yard desperately needed a trim, a drink; that freakishly short thunderstorm had clearly been no help at all. A small patch of grass was long and speckled with dry, brown blades, and a few white statues—*Were they ducks? Gnomes?*—needed to be saved from imminent weed suffocation.

She stood at the window for countless silent minutes, studying the view. Raindrops clung like white pearls to the black electrical wire strung between the house and a wooden pole at the end of the yard. Other buildings loomed there, with their fire escapes zigzagging between windows, and Jane thought of the countless Brooklynites who lived there, unaware that there was a new kid on the block. She could see the Parachute Jump in a sliver of sky between buildings and kept returning to the window to peek at it as she dusted.

Leathery wallpaper with bubblegum pink roses and army green vines covered the walls. Even though Jane couldn't imagine her mother had a hand in picking such a pattern, she had done a quick check of the other rooms in the house and knew that she'd chosen her mother's child-hood room. The only actual evidence she found, however, was tucked away at the back of a high shelf in the closet with some old pillows and blankets—a small mermaid doll. Jane took it down and blew the dust out of its curly red hair and its crown of pearls, and off the orange-and-white-striped tiger fish it held in its tiny hands. She still had a book of mermaid pictures, *The Mermaid's Secret*, her mother had given her. A note inside said: *My dear daughter, I used to be a mermaid once, so I know that mermaids are good at a lot of things, like keeping secrets. I hope your life is full of them. Love, Mom.*

The doll had to have been her mother's. She was sure of it.

Further examination revealed a silky tag that read

"Plays 'By the Beautiful Sea,'" hanging from the mermaid's sparkly green bottom. Jane wound the small metal handle next to the tag and released it but nothing happened, no music, and she set the doll down on the dresser.

Marcus ended up across the hall in a room that looked like it had most recently been used as a study or guest room: a desk, a bed, some old books. Her father took over the second floor, claiming the master suite and the room across the hall as his office.

Without conspiring, they'd all three unpacked—Jane had only really brought clothes and books, including that old mermaid book—then lay down and napped on dusty bed linens. She drifted off easily, into a memory of a day at the Ocean Dome, a memory that had long been locked away. . . .

two

"GO GET SPIFFED UP A BIT," Jane's father said when they all had woken up and reconvened in the kitchen. "We'll go for a walk up to the boardwalk and then we'll have dinner someplace nice. As a treat. A celebration."

"Of what?" Marcus asked with a stifled snort. "Our year of slumming it?"

Jane looked at her father, to see if he'd take offense, but he didn't. He just said, "If you want to think of it as 'slumming it,' sure!"

"It's only for a year" had become her father's mantra in the previous few weeks, and now Jane sensed that her father, at least, hadn't been surprised by the state of their new home. She got the distinct impression that he'd known it was going to be sort of a dump. Still, it was probably a better home than he himself could provide for them right now. He'd had a bunch of small structural engineering jobs in Europe and Asia for the last ten years—they'd even done time in Michigan and California—but nothing that amounted to the career he used to have, designing world-class roller coasters. His job in London had recently ended and he had no other prospects.

Another mantra: "We'll just move in, clear it out, clean it up, sell it, and move on."

And: "It's just until I get back on my feet."

They changed clothes and went out on foot as the setting sun cast long shadows on their street. They walked toward the beach—their block appeared to dead-end into sky—and past a series of abandoned lots, one of which was decorated with banners that said THE FUTURE OF CONEY ISLAND HAS ARRIVED.

"What do you think that means?" she asked.

"Just some snazzy builder talk," her father said.

He laced his fingers through the fence around the lot, and Jane and her brother exchanged a look. A look that said, *He used to be the one talking the snazzy builder talk. Before Mom died and everything fell apart.* But Jane looked away. She was afraid to hope that things could be different this time, that *something* about being here, where her mother was born, could change the way things were and get her father's career back on track.

When they reached the boardwalk and she saw the ocean's dark blue blanket stretching to the horizon, she felt a lump in her throat—some combination of hope and sadness and fear caught up in a sticky ball.

And the crowds.

The crowds!

They were the sorts of people Jane had expected to see in Brooklyn: black, white, everything, loud, laughing, terrifying. She just hadn't expected—and this was silly, she now knew—quite so many of them to be right there on the beach and on the boardwalk all at once.

Hundreds upon hundreds.

Thousands, even.

Then she saw that the Parachute Jump was lit by thousands of tiny lights, and their twinkle made her giddy. Giddy, and something else, too. She pushed the lump back down and looked out at the beach and promised herself she'd go down onto the sand one day and build a small Coney in her mother's memory. She would wait and watch and watch and wait until the tide came in and washed it all away.

What had she even meant, *It's gone*?

It's right here.

There was a rowdy crowd outside an open-front bar, where some white plastic furniture sat wobbly on the uneven planks of the boardwalk. The sign on the front spelled out *The Anchor* in dirty pink fluorescent script, and a long bar on the left stretched way back into darkness, high stools lined up all the way. Everyone outside was watching a guy do one-handed push-ups. He counted them off in a thick Brooklyn accent—". . . faw, five"—and when he got to ten, he got up and wiped his hands together and said, "Yeah, baby, told you so." Jane wasn't sure she'd ever seen a stranger scene, a dumpier bar.

Then she saw him.

A tattooed boy.

A beautiful tattooed boy.

He was standing on the boardwalk in front of the bar, pointing out elaborate tattoos on his forearms. A particularly terrifying crowd—in part because they looked to be around Jane's age, her *peers*—surrounded him. One of the boys must have been seven feet tall; one girl was a dwarf who also looked like a goth; another girl, a brunette, had a faint mustache and beard; and Jane would have sworn the brown-skinned girl with curly hair bent her knee the wrong way to scratch her calf. Through a parting between their bodies, Jane saw serpents on Tattoo Boy's skin, and mermaids and a seahorse and the same clown face she'd seen in those dreams about burning Ferris wheels, drowning roller coasters, and her mother still alive. His hair was black and soft-looking, and his eyes were marbles of blue. She'd never seen a more beautiful boy in her life.

"I like it," the giant said, and the dwarf in black said, "Bend down, let's see what you've had done to yourself now."

"I wouldn't mind a beer," Jane's father said, and Marcus said, "I'm starving, Dad."

"Well, then I'll get it to go." He ducked into the bar,

and Marcus shrugged and followed. Jane turned to follow him but not before taking one more look at Tattoo Boy. The crowd had dispersed, but he was still there, looking at her looking at him, and his tattoos felt familiar in a way that filled Jane with a sort of excited dread. He was rolling down the sleeves of his night-black shirt and he was still staring at her and smiling, too. "Whatsa matter?" he said. "Never seen tattoos like these?"

"No, actually," she said, studying the curves of the sea-horse again and feeling a kind of vertigo in her heart. "I have."

"Come on," her father said, appearing with a small brown bag in his hand, and Marcus on his heels. "Let's keep moving. And stay close."

They passed a small fenced-in amusement park called WONDERLAND—its entrance marked by a big sign featuring Alice herself and the Mad Hatter. The hat-wearing troll—*Was that what he was? A troll?*—was pouring tea as if to light the letters of the sign with neon green liquid. Jane watched the whirl and twirl of lights on the rides behind them. It was a crammed array of kiddie rides (planes, trains, ladybugs, elephants) and ticket booths and bigger rides like bumper cars and pirate ships—all the sort of rides Jane knew could be folded up and rolled up onto a truck in a matter of minutes. Not real rides—permanent rides—like her dad used to build. Still, people didn't seem to mind. She could feel the collective buzz, like a mosquito by her ear, of families having fun.

Past Wonderland, there appeared to be a gap in board-walk amusements, but then Jane spotted the banner hanging in front of a lot splattered with paint. SHOOT THE FREAK, it read, and a few people with guns were firing paint pellets into a sort of obstacle course of trash. There, a target—a real live person wearing padded gear and mask, all of which gave him the look of an intergalactic umpire—swayed back and forth, halfheartedly moving his painty shield, which looked like the top of a trash can.

"What on earth?" her father said. And Marcus said simply, "Cool." Which was pretty much how Marcus reacted to everything, a fact that infuriated his sister no end.

A massive blue Ferris wheel with lit pink letters reading WONDER WHEEL at its center came into view when she turned to follow her father again, its red lights blinking in a pattern extending from the heart of the wheel to its outer edges. For a second, she thought about suggesting they go on it. But they didn't do that kind of thing anymore.

They walked on, and then Jane heard a clack and cascading screams and turned and saw an old white roller coaster.

The Cyclone.

Marcus had made her watch an old B movie, *The Beast from 20,000 Fathoms,* right after they'd learned about Preemie's house. In it a frozen carnivorous dinosaur is thawed by an atomic explosion at the North Pole and starts to travel south, leaving a path of destruction along the Atlantic coast. The mayhem culminates at the fictional Manhattan Beach amusement park, a stand-in for Coney, where the beast is injected with a radioactive isotope and dies a fiery death among the hills and valleys of the Cyclone.

Had there maybe been a seahorse in that movie?

No, she didn't think so.

A car started clanking up the coaster's first climb and then went plummeting, and Jane could almost feel her own stomach drop.

They walked maybe one more block, and then her father stopped and turned around to head back in the direction from which they'd come. Jane looked farther down the boardwalk, not wanting to turn around, and saw the crowds thin out. There were no lights, no more amusements, no nothing. "That's it?" she said with some irritation.

This was *Coney Island.*

A place that was supposedly famous.

A tourist destination.

There had to be *more.*

"Yes," her father said. "I'm pretty sure that's it. I was only ever here a few times with your mother, but there was never much going on. Less so, even, back then."

"What a shithole," Marcus said.

"Watch it," her father said, then: "If I remember correctly, it's this way."

Back in the thick of the amusements again after a few minutes of walking, her father turned off the boardwalk and led them down a wide street with cars parked perpendicularly down a center aisle, past some delis and a big Coney Island Gift Shop with an assortment of Coney T-shirts in the windows. They were heading toward a sign for Nathan's Famous hot dogs, and Jane, who was starving, thought, *Hot dogs? We're celebrating with hot dogs?* She studied the long lines trailing out the restaurant doors, and saw people standing around eating dogs and thick crinkly fries, and desperately hoped her father had other plans.

He did. They crossed the street away from Nathan's. Jane heard the rumbling clack of a subway train and figured they were leaving Coney for dinner. The station had big arched windows and looked newer, shinier, than everything around it, almost like it was promising you that there were nicer places at the other end of the line. But her father turned away from the station and turned down a different street and approached a creamy stucco building. The name, Mancuso's, stretched across the threshold in tiles by their feet, and the wooden front doors featured stained glass that highlighted the letter M.

Inside they waited as a hostess seated another party: a laughing family of four. It was a busy restaurant and sort of fancy—high ceilings, big windows with rich-looking drapes, linen tablecloths, fancy dishes—but all Jane could see was a huge octopus clinging to the ceiling beams. When it was their turn to be led to a table, Jane had to be careful not to trip and fall. *What was it made of? Had it ever actually been alive?*

"This place is sort of famous," her father said, and Jane looked away from the octopus and said, "What for?"

"I don't know." The hostess handed them menus as they sat down. "Just being here, maybe. And surviving."

"Surviving what?" Jane asked, and her dad said, "So much time. So much change."

He turned his eyes down to look at his menu, but Jane just looked at her brother, wondering whether he wanted to say what she did: *What about us? Are we going to survive?*

"God, it's weird to be here." Her father put his menu down and sighed. "Your mother was planning on bringing you two here—we both were—right after the coaster opening in Tokyo. She hadn't wanted to come back for a long time but finally decided you should meet your grandfather, at least, and get to know Coney Island, and her friends and all."

He shook his head and said, "We had the plane tickets booked and everything."

Jane looked at him with raised eyebrows. This was the first she'd ever heard of this supposed big family vacation, and she absorbed the news as a sort of loss. Her mother had wanted to bring her here to show her around—maybe even show her off—and now that would never happen. Her grandparents were dead and her mother's friends—well, who even knew who they were or if any of them were still here.

"Do you remember any of her friends' names?" Jane asked, afraid that at any moment the portal would close again. "Anything?"

"I don't." He shook his head. "I wish I did." Then he

said, "I wish I'd known your grandparents better, too—at least I think I do. But there was never any time."

Jane's parents had met when her mother was in art school in Manhattan, and they'd eloped to Paris just a few weeks after she graduated. They'd honeymooned in the French countryside, and her mother had fallen in love with France and they'd decided not to go back to New York right away. So they traveled for a while and then Jane's father, who already had his engineering degree and a few ride designs under his belt, got a job at the company that was designing the rides for Euro Disney. Her mother got hired as a caricature artist at the park, and then after that they'd jumped around the world for ten years before deciding—finally, in their mid-thirties—to have kids. At which point, they *all* followed her father's coaster design work wherever it took them, until it didn't anymore.

"Anyway," her father said. "It's just for one year."

Jane's eyes found the octopus on the ceiling again, and she felt a sort of empathy. She'd read somewhere that the average life span of an octopus was only one year. With the way her family moved around so much, she felt like she'd lived her own life in octopus years—each of her own sixteen years so distinct from the others that they might as well have each been lived by different people entirely. She'd be spending this one in her mother's childhood home, though—and starting school at her mother's high school the very next day.

Would Tattoo Boy be there?

It dawned on her that this was the chance she'd always hoped for without even realizing it, to get to know her mother better. Maybe there'd be old photos in glass cases and old yearbooks to flip through, maybe even some that would lead to friends, people who knew her. The very prospect made her so giddy she knew she wouldn't sleep.

three

ARE YOU ONE OF THE TRANSFERS I'm supposed to hand-hold?"

Jane turned from her new locker, where she was struggling with her combination lock, and saw swarms of kids milling in the hall but no one who was speaking to her. She'd been to the office to meet Principal Jackson—a tall, all-business African-American woman wearing a red suit—and to get her schedule and locker assignment, but no one had said anything about hand-holding.

"Down here."

The goth dwarf came up to Jane's waist. Her ears were pierced more times than it seemed an earlobe could sustain. Her charcoal-lined eyes were a fierce turquoise, the color of the ocean near the equator. This girl had been there, outside the bar, with Tattoo Boy the night before. Unless there were two goth dwarfs kicking around Coney Island, which, at this point, Jane realized wasn't entirely unlikely. The goth's tiny black T-shirt had a white silhouette of a girl's profile, with teardrops falling from her eyes. For a second Jane felt like that girl; she wanted to jump into the shadows of the shirt.

"Are you done yet?" the small girl said, and Jane shook it off and said, "I'm Jane Dryden, if that's who you're looking for."

"I wasn't really paying attention but yeah, Dryden sounds right." She put on a fake smile and said, faux-cheery, "Welcome to Coney Island High!"

Jane turned to her brother for saving, but Marcus had already struck up a conversation with a kid who looked a lot like him: floppy hair, broody eyes behind geeky-cool glasses. They were leaning against a row of lockers, deep in conversation. That quickly, that easily.

"*Yoo-hoo.* I'm Babette."

Jane snapped to attention.

"And it was my understanding that you had a brother."

It was a simple statement of fact, but it made Jane sad. That had been her understanding, too—for her whole life—but her brother had never been particularly brotherly.

Jane looked at Marcus again, and this time he looked back. He raised his eyebrows, and Jane gestured at Babette and he turned to his new friend, shook hands, and said, "See you later, man." He came over to his sister's side.

"I'm Babette and I'm supposed to show you to home-room."

Marcus said, "Excellent. I'm Marcus." He had spent two seconds deciding what to wear on this, their first day at their new school, while Jane had been obsessing over her own outfit—namely which gray skirt to wear—for days.

Babette said, "Well, come on then," and led Jane and Marcus down the hall and around a few corners to a pair of double doors. She threw them open with small arms and shouted over the din of the crowd inside the cafeteria: "It's an experimental new homeroom approach. Based on some Quaker thing, or so they say. It's supposed to teach us about community or how to be accountable for our own actions or something. You just sign in over there"—she pointed to a long table—"and sit wherever you belong." She studied the Drydens and said, "Honestly, I have no idea where that could possibly be."

Hundreds of students were talking in clusters, sitting at long tables. Marcus waved across the room and said, "I'm good," and took off toward the guy he'd met in the hall. Babette jolted a bit, then said, "I guess that just leaves you."

Story of my life.

Babette took a deep breath and surveyed the room. "Here's my parting advice. That table over there?" She pointed to a table of big, loud guys with shaved heads and, in some cases, big holes in their earlobes. Jane didn't even want to imagine what they had those holes for, or how they'd been made.

"Those are the wannabe geeks, and not *geek*-geeks like smart. But geeks like *sideshow* geeks. Total wasters. They won't give someone normal, like *you*"—she looked Jane over again—"the time of day if you're lucky. In other words, stay off their radar."

"Okay," Jane said. "Thanks."

Babette nodded solemnly and went to a table near the windows where she was greeted excitedly by a few of the other kids Jane had seen the night before, like the girl who could bend this way and that. Tattoo Boy, again in jeans and a black shirt, was sitting at the table in front of a large doll dressed in a tiny T-shirt and jeans, which seemed odd for all the obvious reasons, but then the doll turned around and started talking to Babette, and flipped her long curly blond hair. Was she some kind of genius toddler?

They were like something out of a movie—a special effects extravaganza—and the way they laughed so easily made Jane wish she had a second head, or a tail, or claws for hands.

Right then a black boy who had no legs slid past her on a skateboard. Dizziness swelled inside Jane's head as she watched him give the crowd at Babette's table a quick salute—a tap of the finger to the forehead—and stop to chat. It had to be some kind of optical illusion, a trick of the eye.

His body just . . . *ended*.

Having never really fit in anywhere, Jane had hoped she might here, in Brooklyn, a place known around the world for its diversity, its lack of pretense. And if she wasn't destined to suddenly morph into a cheerleader or class president, it'd be nice to fit in among the misfits.

But she'd never seen misfits like *this* before.

Looking around the room for a potential in, a place to sit, Jane was as stumped as Babette. Frankly, there weren't that many white kids; maybe three tables of them, all clustered near one another, a fact that Jane found sort of sadly predictable. From the Indian kids in London, the black kids in Ireland, and the white kids in Bahrain, Jane knew that minorities usually stuck together. She'd often been among them. But what would it mean if she just strolled over to the white kids here, assuming they'd accept her?

She watched the guy with no legs slide on his skateboard away from Babette's table across the room, where he joined a large table of other black kids. Climbing up onto the seat bench, he shook hands with the guy next to him, then they laughed about something and he did a sort of weird pop-and-lock move with his arms. Jane couldn't help but think he looked like he was sinking in quicksand, and had to resist the urge to run over and pull him up. Watching him and his friends, she wondered again: What would it mean if she walked over to *his* table? Or Babette's?

There were only a few minutes before the first bell anyway, so she went back out to explore the hallways, to see if there were any old trophies or photos in glass cases. When she found none, she studied a bulletin board on one of the walls. There were signs for a math club and a science club, which had been her extracurricular staples all along the way. But there were some signs for clubs she'd never heard of before. One advertising the meeting of TEENS FOR THE REDEVELOPMENT OF CONEY ISLAND had been vandalized with a black marker; someone had scrawled CAPITALIST PIGS across the printed type. Another sign read, simply,

dreamland social club
TOMORROW AFTERNOON, ROOM 222.
You know who you are.

Whatever that meant.

Jane was barely in her seat, way in the back of classroom 231, behind the giant she'd seen in homeroom, before a hip-looking older guy wearing jeans, a boiler hat, and suspenders got up from one of the student desks, walked to the front of the room, and said, "Okay, field trip! Let's go."

The writing on the blackboard said "Topics in Coney Island History with Mr. Simmons," and Jane thought it strange. She'd never been to a high school with a local history class before, but then she'd also never been to school with a giant and a goth dwarf and a kid with no legs. The room was decorated with old postcards and photos having to do with Coney Island—some news clippings, too—but now was clearly not the time to try to explore it.

Feet shuffled and squeaked as everyone got up to follow Mr. Simmons out the door. Jane spotted Tattoo Boy in the chaos and her heart pounded harder. He was in her first class, a junior like her. And the seahorse tattoo was just as familiar today as it had been yesterday. It was more cartoonish than his other tattoos, like it was based on something fake, but that didn't help Jane to place it.

Babette was there, too, and Jane wasn't sure yet how she felt about that. Her assigned escort seemed sort of like a know-it-all, but then maybe that was exactly the kind of person Jane needed to befriend.

It was early, barely 8:00 a.m., and fine mist clung to the air as they walked along the boardwalk past shuttered amusements and closed-up clam shacks. Mostly, Jane just kept her head down, watching the warped and splintered boards under her feet, until they arrived at a building marked CONEY ISLAND MUSEUM. She trailed her classmates up a narrow staircase and then into the reception area.

Mr. Simmons led them into the main room—past walls of old posters for something called the "Mermaid Parade" and photos of human oddities who'd performed in Coney's famous sideshows over the years and of beachgoers in different eras. In a far corner, some old beach chairs and metal lockers sat below a bunch of old signs for different bathhouses. Jane wanted to linger on every item, every detail, sit in every chair—maybe even look for her mother in the pictures on those parade posters, because maybe that had been what she'd meant in her note about having been a mermaid once—but Jane didn't want to get left behind.

Finally, people started to gather around Mr. Simmons, who had stopped near a large television.

"We came here today to talk about Topsy," he said. "She was an elephant that worked at Luna Park, one of the great amusement parks of the turn of the century here on Coney, where she killed three men before she was sentenced to execution. That third victim, mind you, tried to feed dear Topsy a lit cigarette."

Tattoo Boy said, "Ouch," and some of the boys around him laughed. Jane closed her eyes and saw his tattoo in her mind's eye.

"Ouch indeed." Mr. Simmons stroked a goatee that didn't look like it had the nerve to be a beard. "Now, the death penalty for men had very recently been changed from hanging to the electric chair, so hanging Topsy was deemed cruel and unusual."

Mr. Simmons started to walk among his students. "Enter Thomas Edison, who was competing with George Westinghouse and Nikola Tesla for the contract to build the nation's electric grid. He decided to use his competitor's alternating current to execute Topsy, in order to show how deadly AC electricity could be.

"*And*"—Mr. Simmons paused dramatically here—"he decided to film it so he could show it to audiences around the country."

"Now"—he waved an arm toward a bunch of chairs set up in the middle of the room, facing the TV—"those of you who would like to can take a seat and view Edison's film. Those of you who don't want to watch such a disturbing thing—again, we're talking about *the electrocution of an elephant*—can step back out into the hall."

Jane had never been on a field trip this odd and thought she should probably bolt, but then Tattoo Boy said, "I've seen it before; I'll bite." He sat beside Mr. Simmons, and then his disciples moved to fill in seats around him.

A bunch of kids walked out into the hall and a bunch of others sat down and then Babette took a seat beside Tattoo Boy. Under the glare of the museum's overhead spotlights her black hair took on a bluish sheen, while her skin looked so white that Jane wondered whether she had somehow bleached it. She looked extraordinary right then—like a rare orchid or endangered bird. Jane only realized she was the only person left in the room standing when Babette shook her head, leaned toward Tattoo Boy, and said, "Five bucks says she won't do it."

There was something *wrong* with wanting to see such a thing.

Wasn't there?

Tattoo Boy looked up at Jane, took a moment to study her, and said, "I'm not so sure I'd take that bet."

The words "ELECTROCUTING AN ELEPHANT, A film by Thomas A. Edison" appeared, white letters on black, along with the year, 1903, and some kind of reference code: H26890. The type itself seemed to shiver on-screen, but Jane wondered if it was actually she who was shaking. Then Topsy—an elephant-shaped shadow in a mostly white shot—appeared, but the quality of the film was so bad that it was hard to know what was even going on. It looked like footage of an elephant in a blizzard, all white-washed and chilling.

There seemed to be a cut then to another shot of Topsy, walking up closer to the camera. Then puffs of what could only be smoke—*yes, smoke*—appeared under Topsy's feet and started rising to engulf her. She fell—forward, toward her right eye—as the smoke started to dissipate. A dark figure of a man rushed through the front of the frame as if in a panic and then it went to black.

It was over before Jane had even realized what was happening, before she could even work up the cry that had started to form deep in her gut.

"That's it?" someone in class protested.

The lights came up and Tattoo Boy said, "That is some fucked-up shit."

"Watch it, Mr. LaRocca," Mr. Simmons said.

So his last name, at least, was LaRocca.

Mr. Simmons looked at his watch, then led everyone out into the hallway where the rest of the class was wait-ing. "Tonight I want you all to write two hundred words about why you felt compelled to watch—or not watch—what you had to know would be a disturbing film. If you hesitated in your choice, and I know who you are"—Jane averted her eyes from his gaze—"I want to know why you did that, too."

The mist had lifted, unveiling a clear, hot morning. The ocean was churning up some white breakers right near the shore, and Jane stopped for a moment to watch and took a deep breath of salty air. It felt weird to be so close to the sea on a school day; putting a high school barely half a block from the beach seemed somehow cruel.

There was a fake palm tree on the beach right in front of her and it turned on: water sprayed from it, scattering a few startled birds. Jane tried to imagine wearing a swimsuit, dancing under the palm's spray, but couldn't yet wrap her head around it. She hadn't been swimming in what felt like a lifetime—not since the Ocean Dome, not since her had mother died—and she wondered whether and when she'd ever do it again. Noting the cigarette butts and soda cans in the sand, she thought that this hardly seemed the place.

Jane trailed behind everyone else, looking for Tattoo Boy and thinking it wouldn't be that big a deal to just ask him about his seahorse tattoo.

Would it?

But there was no sign of him, so she just watched some of the other kids joking around and felt a strange sort of longing. Then one of them said, "Check out the new chick," and nodded his head toward Jane. A few people turned, and Jane froze. A seagull landed on the railing a few feet away and seemed to study her to determine whether she was edible, peck-able.

"She looks like she's been dipped in gray paint."

A guy with a skull tattooed on his neck stepped out of a crowd, and Jane recognized him from the table of geeks that morning. He had piercings in his nose and eyebrows and huge, draping holes in his earlobes. Jane still wasn't sure what a geek was, exactly, but figured she'd find out eventually. He said, "What were you doing at Preemie Porcelli's house this morning?"

"I live there," she said, and the geek started to circle her. Her legs had begun to vibrate but she didn't think her fear was showing. Yet. She could see a few people in her peripheral vision, coming closer and listening in.

"You gotta be kidding me." The geek turned and snorted at one of his friends. He smiled.

In that second, Jane dared to hope that maybe she was about to find a lead. Because if this guy knew Preemie, maybe someone he knew—someone older—knew her mother. Heck, for all she knew Coney Island High had a Preemie Porcelli Appreciation Association and she just hadn't seen their sign on that bulletin board. Standing tall, with eyes clear and open, she said, "He was my grandfather."

The geek looked at Jane, then spat not at her but in her general direction and said, "Your grandfather was a piece of shit."

Tattoo Boy pushed his way up to the center of the action and said, to no one in particular, "What'd I miss?"

Jane had read a story the night before—in an old book

in the living room—about an elephant that swam five miles from Coney Island to Staten Island, escaping from Luna Park, where he'd been part of some kind of circus-sideshow attraction. It had given her the creeps, that story, because what on earth would be so bad about a place that an *elephant* would swim five miles to escape it? But that had been before she'd seen Edison's film. That had been before she'd started school. After barely an hour at Coney Island High, she looked out at the shimmering water and at the lump of land across the bay to the right. She wondered whether she could survive the swim herself.

"Come on," Marcus said at day's end. "I'll take you on the Wonder Wheel."

Jane had been fighting a sick feeling all day, but this brightened her mood considerably. So they headed out into a sweltering afternoon and over toward the Ferris wheel's entrance and wound their way through a short series of metal barriers—like a corral for cows—and then a man working the ride said, "Swinging or stationary?"

Marcus looked at Jane, shrugged, then said, "Swinging" just before Jane got to say, "Stationary."

The guy working the ride opened up the door of a big yellow-and-blue metal cage for them and they got in, sitting facing each other on hard benches, also painted yellow. They were locked in from the outside and soon floated way up high over Brooklyn. Jane saw the big brick buildings her father had warned them to stay away from—

"Those are the projects," he'd said, and Jane had nodded understanding though she'd never really understood that usage of the word—and she saw the Manhattan skyline—a small gray silhouette on the far horizon. She'd read in that book the night before that people used to say that you could see the Eiffel Tower in Paris from the top of the Wonder Wheel. You couldn't, she saw now, and she felt foolish for being slightly disappointed.

"I don't remember much," she said finally. "But I remember her talking about this place like she loved it. Do you know what I mean?" She looked out at the water again and thought about life back in Tokyo so very long ago—the Ocean Dome, the funeral, the rest—and how it all seemed like a dream, too. But not even her dream, somebody else's.

Marcus shrugged. "Sort of. I guess."

In that moment Coney didn't look as awful as it did from street level. From way up high in the sky, you could almost imagine it was cleaner, better.

Jane said softly, "I was thinking of trying to, you know, find some of her friends or something."

Suddenly, their car unhinged, and it felt like they were going to plummet to the ground and crash to their death. But after a second it stopped dropping and it just swayed back and forth, back and forth. It had slid down a rail to another part of the wheel.

Swinging.

Marcus's fingers were laced through the metal cage

of the car when he said, "It's just for one year, Jane."

"I know," she said. "But still . . ."

A teeth-deep sound crunched the air as they walked home. They cautiously approached a crowd that had gathered around the noise. Only a few people were wearing black. No one was holding flowers or crying. But they had the look of a funeral about them nonetheless. Beyond them, on the side of a building, a mural advertised a circus sideshow with large paintings of a snake charmer wearing a python like a necklace; a "human blockhead," shown with a nail in his nose; a Rubber Man with his legs hooked behind his neck; a geek with a bowling ball hanging from his tongue; and a bearded lady who called herself "The Dog Lady of Coney Island."

No wonder her mother had ditched her carny past.

Jane tore her gaze away as the sound started again and watched a huge clawed machine chew up a small red car. She stopped and stared, silent, like the others.

Metal crushed metal.

Wood splintered and split.

Small Go Kart cars in bright red, yellow, blue, surrendered to crushing one after the other. Just beyond them, a huge shark-mouthed machine bit up black chunks of track that tore in curvy sheets like giant melting vinyl records.

Someone in the crowd started booing, and then more people joined in and the boos became increasingly loud and angry. A man picked a bottle out of an overflowing trash can and threw it at the claw. It hit the side of the yellow cab and shattered, spraying caramel-colored flecks into the air. Tattoo Boy appeared and stepped over to him and said, "Easy, man," and the controller stuck his head out a small window and shouted, "Asshole!"

"What's happening?" Jane asked, and Marcus answered, "Don't know, don't care," and started to walk away.

CHAPTER

four

JANE'S FATHER HAD THE LOOK of a mad professor about him, all windblown and out of breath, when he came home with pizza that night. Jane was starting to think that living on Coney put you in a permanent state of windblown-ness. Her own hair, typically painfully straight, had actually never looked better now that it had a little salty body.

"So!" he said. "How was it?"

Marcus didn't bother to stifle his snort. "It was a total freak show."

"Jane?" their father said, and her mind was suddenly a blur of tattoos and earlobe holes. She said, "I guess it was a little . . . strange."

"Strange?" Marcus laughed.

"Strange how?" Their father put the pizza box down, pulled paper plates out of a yellow cabinet, and tossed them onto the table. He took a slice and bit off a piece, creating a long, thin trail of cheese.

"Dad," Marcus said seriously, "they could remake *Is It Human?* with the kids at this school."

"You mean *actual freaks*?"

Marcus nodded. "A small but highly freakish group of them, yes."

"Really?" He took another bite and pushed the box toward Jane. "Pizza?"

She pushed the box back. "No thanks." She found the tone of the conversation unappetizing.

Marcus said, "Apparently, the sideshow that came here a few years ago brought this little group of carny families with them, and you add that to some geek kids who have been here forever plus one kid without legs who just happens to live here and it's a complete freak show. Your poor shrinking violet of a daughter was accosted by a geek who told her Preemie was a piece of shit."

"What?" Her father was more than halfway through his slice.

"How did you know?" Jane snapped. "How do you know *any* of this?"

"I have my sources." Marcus shrugged. "And word got around."

"Well, that'll blow over." And now her father's slice was gone. "And anyway, it'll be good for you two. You'll learn a little bit about your heritage, your mother's family history. The whole carny thing."

There was that word again.

"No thank you," Marcus said.

Their father just shrugged. "It's the school we're zoned for," he said. "We can't afford private school and it was too late for you to apply to other public schools. And remember . . ."

Jane and her brother joined in with "It's just for one year."

Her father slapped her on the back and said, "Come on! It can't be that bad!"

"I saw a girl combing her beard by her locker," Marcus said.

"Just hang out with the other normal kids."

Marcus brushed some flour off his fingertips. "Planning on it."

When their father went upstairs to his office, Jane just sat and listened to the shuffling of papers and then the shutting and locking of the door. He reappeared in the kitchen with a portfolio in his hands and said, "I'm going out. Don't stay up too late."

Down the hall, the front door slammed behind him, and a picture in the hallway, one of Birdie dressed as a bird, jolted crooked on its hook. *Were* they normal? Jane wasn't sure.

Her brother raised his eyebrows.

"Do you think he has a job interview?" Jane asked.

"At seven o'clock at night?" Marcus shook his head.

They each took slices and ate them in silence. Jane's thoughts returned to her homework, to her Topsy essay. Why *had* she watched that film? Was it the same reason people used to go to see premature babies in incubators?

"Why do you think that guy said that?" she asked her brother. "About Preemie."

"I have no idea." He took yet another slice and got up, picking his backpack up off the floor and leaving the room. "Maybe Preemie *was* a piece of shit," he called from down the hall.

The remnants of a hurricane blew through the city that night—rain pounded Preemie's shingled roof and rattled and whooshed all the windows. Marcus braved the weather to go off to meet his new friend and so, with her father also out, Jane alone set out to find more of Preemie's personal stuff and see if she could decide for herself whether he was a piece of excrement or not. Ideally, she'd find some stuff that belonged to her mom, something more interesting than a mermaid doll music box that didn't actually play any music.

So when she noticed the string dangling from the ceiling in the upstairs hall, she pulled it. A series of stairs popped down and she climbed slowly, frantically swatting away cobwebs, and then stepped up into the attic, barely lit by the glow of a streetlight coming in the small window. When she found another string to pull, light left her face-to-face—she gasped!—with a huge red demon with eyes as big as her face. Carved out of a large piece of wood and painted a menacing red and black, it leaned against the main wall at the back of the house, beside the window that looked out onto the yard.

What on earth?

The room the demon guarded was long and skinny, with exposed rafters and a peaked ceiling. The wood planks that made up the floor had once been painted gray but were now chipped to reveal their original oak color. There were boxes everywhere and books stacked into jagged piles, and an old movie projector appeared when Jane pulled away a dusty old sheet.

She sifted through a stack of books, then sat in a worn dark blue armchair and read everything she could find about Preemie and Dreamland and the doctor who had blazed the incubator trail. People apparently had thought he was a quack, but Jane, having also been born early enough that she needed some additional cooking, knew that wasn't the case.

Along the way she learned that the "preemie" display wasn't the only weird thing about Dreamland. There had also been a ride called Creation that took people through the events of the book of Genesis and the very creation of the earth. There'd been one called Fighting Flames, where people could watch a tenement fire be put out, which seemed a little bit twisted; then again she'd willfully watched the execution of an elephant. Guests could also watch a reenactment of the Boer War, which she was pretty sure had taken place in Africa. Or go to a Dog and Monkey Show, whatever that was. There was even an entire village, Midget City, populated by a thousand dwarfs.

She paused to think about that one.

Midget City?

They actually *lived* there? In the amusement park? And people went there to watch them go about their daily lives?

She suddenly didn't feel quite so bad about watching the Topsy film.

She found pictures of the demon against the wall guarding the entrance to an attraction called Hell Gate—a boat ride through a re-creation of Hades. So Preemie was either an amateur museum curator or a professional thief. Whether or not that made him a piece of excrement, she wasn't sure.

When she confirmed what her father had already told her—that Dreamland had all burned to the ground one night in 1911, on the eve of opening day of the season, never to be rebuilt—she couldn't help but wonder whether the midgets had had something to do with it.

Flipping to the index again, she hoped to find something about a Dreamland "social club," something she'd missed the first time around. Sure enough, there was a separate line entry, and she turned to the page.

The photo there, dated August 13, 1924, contained about thirty or so people—black, white, tall, small, normal-looking, freaky, the works—behind a sign, propped by their feet, that said DREAMLAND SOCIAL CLUB. A large woman had a miniature man propped on her shoulder, and a girl in a white dress and hat perched on a chair had no arms or legs.

No arms or legs.

Which meant no hands, no feet.

Limbless.

How could you even live?

Most of the people looked normal, though Jane had to wonder what oddities the picture simply couldn't reveal. The caption next to the photo said only, "Performers from the Dreamland Circus Sideshow gathered at Stauch's," so there were probably sword swallowers, fire-eaters, snake charmers, and more. Reading the text on the page, she found no more information about any "club."

Again and again she returned to that one girl's face—so pale and young—and studied the people sitting around her. Were they her friends? Had she had any? And was the Dreamland Social Club at school related to this one?

Jane read about another famous park, Steeplechase, where the signature ride was a track where you could race mechanical horses, like you were the jockey. There'd been a human roulette wheel, too, and Jane studied the pictures of people splayed out on a big disc and tried to imagine how it worked, how it felt to spin and spin. People who came off the wheel were then subjected to something called the Blowhole Theater, where a dwarf with an electric prong gave men a zap as the women stepped over a platform that blew up their skirts. A few hundred people could gather in the theater's bleachers to watch.

She started to read, finally, about Luna Park, which had boasted a million lights. *Electric Eden*, they'd called it. She closed her eyes and tried to imagine never having seen a lightbulb—like a lot of poor people of the time—and then seeing Luna, a glistening city of minarets and spires and promenades and fountains with slices of the moon glowing white by its entrance and a glittering heart-shaped sign out front that dubbed it "The Heart of Coney Island."

A million lights.

She couldn't imagine. She wondered whether people fainted, or cried, or *swooned*. Luna, Steeplechase, Dreamland. They sounded like the most amazing places to ever have existed and they were all . . . gone. Was *this* the Coney her mother had been talking about?

When she came to a drawing depicting an attraction at Luna called Trip to the Moon, she felt a sort of spark of recognition. The ride simulated a lunar voyage and, upon arrival, riders were greeted by moon people with spiky points on their backs who sang a song for them. Jane realized it all sounded eerily familiar, eerily sad. . . .

My brother and I are sitting in a cardboard box, and my mom is shaking it and making vroom-vroom *sounds from where she's kneeling beside us. She takes a sheet she's pulled from the bed in my brother's room—it has stars and planets and rocket ships on it—and she's waving it around, over our heads. Shaking the box again, she puts on a deep voice and says, "This is your captain. We are passing through a storm. We are quite safe."*

I grip the sides of the box tight and laugh, even though I'm a little bit scared. Then in her deep voice she announces that we're landing, and she puts on a headband with a few antenna-type things attached to it; she made them out of straws and cotton balls. "Welcome to the moon," she says, sort of like a robot, and I laugh. "I am a Selenite, and I would like to sing a song for you.

"My sweetheart's the man in the moon," she sings. "I'm going to marry him soon./'Twould fill me with bliss just to give him one kiss./But I know that a dozen I never would miss. . . ."

She kisses my brother all over his face and he says, "Yuck! Get away!" and then she kisses me, her lips warm and wet and full, and I start giggling and can't stop.

Jane—officially *Luna Jane*—had been named after Luna Park. She knew that in some faraway part of her mind, just as she knew that it had been her own deep desire to start going by her middle name a few years after her mother died, when they'd moved to places where "Luna" was just too weird, too hard to translate or explain. Her father and Marcus had happily made the switch, as if they'd both felt that the name had only ever felt right on Jane's mother's tongue anyway. But Jane hadn't ever known what Luna Park *was*, exactly—beyond being an amusement park—or that the games of her childhood had been inspired by it.

Games.

Plural.

There had been more.

She sat down with her journal and tried to write down the details of the memories as best she could, and then she suddenly remembered there'd been a game about a submarine that went to the polar ice caps, clearly inspired by Luna Park's Twenty Thousand Leagues Under the Sea attraction, and a battleship game that she'd never liked quite as much as her brother, something her mother called War of the Worlds. There had been toy ships made of Tupperware involved; the bathtub, too. Her heart suddenly ached for the mother she'd almost forgotten and was only now—ten years later—starting to remember. The very synapses in her brain seemed to be responding to her new surroundings.

Setting her journal aside and returning to a Coney book, she found a picture of a building shaped like an elephant—a hotel, the caption said—that used to stand on the land that eventually became Luna Park, and she realized that had been a game, too. Involving peanuts and trunks made of . . . what had it been, exactly? She couldn't recall, and she felt a sort of irrational anger at her own brain, for failing her, for not remembering more . . . or everything.

When she discovered a box of old film reels, she pulled out one labeled *Orphans in the Surf* and approached the projector. With a few adjustments it whirred to life and projected an image on the attic's far white wall. A group of little kids—they couldn't have been more than two or three years old, mostly boys—frolicked in the surf. Some were fully clothed, even wearing hats, but some wore only diapers.

For the minute the film played—and despite the gentle

whir of the projector—the attic seemed quieter than was possible, a black hole of sound. And in that painful silence, the grainy black-and-white images, herky-jerky on the wall, seemed to call out for some kind of mournful sound track. Jane could almost feel the sounds of strings hitting melancholy notes in her heart as a few kids pushed farther out into the water and then rejoined the group. They clasped hands and skipped in a circle, playing a silent game of Ring Around the Rosie.

Ashes, ashes. We all fall down.

It was only a minute or two and then it was over, and Jane sat back down in the old armchair and wondered where those orphans had ended up in life, if they were orphans at all, and whether or not they'd ever found a place to call home. In that same instant, she decided that Preemie couldn't have been as bad as the geek said.

A line of light escaped from under her brother's door. She knocked lightly and heard him say, "Come in."

Marcus was reading in bed by the light of an antique lamp on his night table. He put the book aside as Jane sat at the foot of the bed.

"Do you remember that game we used to play when we were little," she asked. "Trip to the Moon?"

He thought for a second and put on a deep voice. "This is your captain. We are passing through a storm. We are quite safe."

"Exactly!" Jane felt relieved that she hadn't made it up. "It's based on a ride at Luna Park. That's an actual quote."

"Weird," Marcus said, and Jane added, "And the Twenty Thousand Leagues Under the Sea game, where Mom would put on her parka and pretend she was an Eskimo taking us to the North Pole to see polar bears?"

Her mother had made an igloo out of white sheets and tickled their faces with seaweed made of green yarn when the submarine surfaced.

Her brother nodded.

"That, too." Jane's nose itched from the memory. She was pretty sure there'd been a whale made out of a pillow on the way to the North Pole, and some sea turtles made of upturned green bowls. Had there been seahorses, too?

No. She didn't think so.

"What are you doing, Jane?" Marcus said, his voice full of a strange kind of disappointment.

"Nothing," she said. "Why?"

He switched off the light and turned on his side.

five

JANE SHRIEKED AND SWATTED at the headless rubber chicken that had flown across the hall and smacked her on the head, then watched it fall to her feet, a soft sickly looking thing with fake blood drips on its severed neck. A bunch of geeks stood a few paces down the hall, laughing it up.

Suddenly, Babette's bendy friend picked up the chicken and hurled it at the geeks. "Grow up, assholes," she said, and they had to duck as the poultry pounded the lockers behind them with a deep *thwack*. She didn't stick around long enough for Jane to thank her, so Jane just hurriedly collected her books. Babette was standing *right there* when she closed her locker door and turned around. Jane said, "I thought you said they wouldn't give me the time of day."

Babette's tiny eyes went wide. "You really don't know?"

Jane had no idea what she could possibly not know. She shook her head. Whatever it was, it wasn't good. The geeks were still laughing it up by their own lockers.

"Stoop down or something," Babette said. "I can't talk to you when you're all the way up there."

Jane lowered to Babette's eye level, into a squat.

Babette looked around as if to make sure no one was listening. "Okay, so a long time ago, like in the twenties or thirties or some other time B.C., Grandpa Claverack built a carousel, and it was sort of famous and it was in Steeple-chase Park for years."

Jane hadn't been expecting a history lesson. For a second she was relieved, except then she remembered that this story was going to have something to do with her.

Babette could really talk: "After Steeplechase closed, they moved the carousel but some of the horses had to be taken off, since the new building was smaller. Preemie somehow got his hands on one of the horses and for years, the Claveracks had been asking Preemie if they could buy it off him. Since their grandfather *made it* and all. But Preemie wouldn't do it. And he used to taunt old man Claverack on the boardwalk, telling him to giddyup and neighing at him."

Now Jane thought she might be sick. "You're making this up."

"Afraid not. And apparently his grandsons"—she nodded toward the geeks—"know how to hold a grudge. Preemie used to neigh at Harvey—he's the one who confronted you. And Cliff, too, he's the one to the left." Turning back to Jane, she said, "I would have told you this yesterday *if you'd told me who you were.*"

Jane stood up and they walked in silence then, heading toward their first class. Jane pictured Harvey—the way his pores tore right through the ink on his skin—and then his brother, sort of a Harvey-lite, but still scary.

She could just give them the horse.

It would be that easy.

"People were taking bets on whether you two would even show up today," Babette said.

Jane looked at her blankly for lack of anything else to do. Crying, while tempting, was not an option.

"I lost ten bucks, but I'm actually happy I was wrong." Babette stopped short to let the legless kid roll by on his skateboard. "Because believe it or not, things had started to get sort of boring around here."

They entered the classroom then and Babette said, "And another thing." She waved her hand to indicate Jane should bend down again, and so Jane did. "You're brother's cute and I happen to be in the market for a boyfriend."

Jane looked for Marcus between classes that morning but couldn't find him anywhere. Luckily, she survived several hours without further incident and made it to lunch. Juniors and seniors were allowed to leave the school and eat on the boardwalk, and Jane thought a bit of air might do her some good. When she saw Tattoo Boy sitting alone on one of the benches right near school, she almost turned right back around, but she didn't. He was drinking from a bottle of water, and something about the fact that it was just water reassured her, calmed her.

He was *human.*

He drank *water.*

And just thinking hard about the seahorse wasn't going to help her figure it out. She waited a minute to make sure he was, in fact, alone, and then walked over. This close up, she noted the sharp line of his lips, the ski jump at the end of his long nose. His hair, as black as Babette could ever hope for, seemed to be constantly in motion, like the soft tentacles of a sea anemone.

"Hey," she said, and he said "Hey" back. The blue of his eyes swirled, like his irises had been tattooed to look like a lollipop. She looked out toward the ocean, counted ten people standing way out on a cross-shaped pier, and considered what to say. The sea was a dark gray that morning, and calm. With a strange sort of calm in her heart she said, "Where did you get the seahorse tattoo? The design, I mean."

"It's from an old postcard," he said. "You gonna explain what you meant? When you said you'd seen it?"

"It's just *really* familiar. Sort of like I dreamed it."

He looked at her funny, then shrugged a shoulder. "I can look for it if you want."

Maybe it was a postcard from somewhere she had lived. That would explain it. "Do you know where the postcard is from?"

"I'm pretty sure Florida."

Jane had never been to Florida, and she said so.

"Well, I'll look for it anyway."

She said, "Thanks," and was suddenly lost at sea in their conversation, afraid it was over.

"So Preemie Porcelli was really your grandfather?" He gave her this look, sideways and suspicious, like the whole story was too unlikely to believe, and maybe she'd have felt the same way if she'd been an outsider considering Preemie Porcelli on the one hand and Jane Dryden on the other.

"He was." Jane eyed the bench, pocked with flattened bits of gray gum and some bird crap, too. The paint was so chipped it was barely there and the wood looked soft, worn from the wind and the water. She decided to sit anyway, close enough that no one would sit between them but not much closer than that.

"What was *that* like?" His eyes lit with actual curiosity.

Jane knew the truth would disappoint. She practically sighed when she said, "I never met him."

"You never met your *own grandfather?*" Tattoo Boy crossed and then uncrossed his ankles, legs stretched out.

Jane shook her head, and when she thought she saw him look at her knee, she tried to cover it with her gray skirt, then felt dumb for doing that. "My parents moved abroad before I was born."

His eyebrows climbed up to meet his hair. "So you've never even lived in *America* before?"

His accent was sort of crazy: *befaw*.

"Twice." She shook her head. "When I was like seven.

In Michigan and California." She remembered that period right after her mom died only by the apartments they'd lived in while their father worked on some bridge or building, remembered missing being around amusement parks all the time, missing getting to go on rides for free, missing her mom. "It was a long time ago."

Tattoo Boy nodded and then smiled and said, "*I knew Preemie.*" He turned to her. "I mean I played his game a few times—the water gun game—and got yelled at by him a few times. And I used to see him all over the place, you know. On his bike. I think he's the only person I've ever seen smoking and riding a bike at the same time."

"He *did that?*" Jane almost laughed.

"It was a sight to behold." He looked back out toward the water. "My dad used to tell me stories about him, too. He'd always be placing weird bets at the Anchor, like how he could eat three pieces of Wonder Bread in a minute or smoke a whole cigarette in forty-five seconds."

"*Really?*" Jane felt a sort of thrill in knowing that she'd walked past a bar Preemie had been to, even if it was a dump. "I wish I'd known him," she said after a moment. "Or at least I thought I did until I met the Claveracks."

Tattoo Boy nudged her with an elbow and said, "It'll blow over." Then he raised his eyebrows. "Is it true that he had a ton of great old Coney stuff in the attic? That's what my dad said."

Jane nodded. "Yeah. I've only made a dent, but there's all these old films and books and"—Jane wasn't sure she should be talking about this, considering the situation with the carousel horse, but she wanted to impress—"he's got a big demon face that I think used to be at Dreamland."

"The one from *Hell Gate*?" Tattoo Boy asked.

Jane nodded.

His eyes went wide, and he let out a plummeting whistle. "Holy shit."

The surf had picked up—a storm must have been churning off the coast—and Jane tried to picture the submarine that she'd read was shipwrecked somewhere off the coast of Coney. She imagined swimming down to it with Tattoo Boy, and hiding out there while they told each other their life stories, why they both felt like they'd always known each other.

"I'm Jane," she said, "but you already knew that." And for the first time in a long time, it felt wrong to use her middle name.

"Leo," he said. "Nice to meet you."

Then he smiled and said, "I think."

During study hall, in a far, dark corner of the school library, Jane found the school's old yearbooks—years and years worth of *Coney Island High Tides*. She pulled out the one from 1978, the year her mother graduated, and flipped through to the "Seniors" section, and then flipped through pages and pages of alphabetical student photos until she found her.

Clementine Porcelli.

Her mom had long, straight hair in the photo and was wearing a T-shirt with some kind of writing on it, though you could only see the tops of the letters and thus couldn't read what it said. She was smiling with her mouth closed, and had a look in her eyes that said she really couldn't be bothered. Still, she looked pretty.

Under her name appeared the words "Founder, Dreamland Social Club."

"*No way,*" Jane whispered to herself.

Heart thumping with the thrill of discovery, she compared her mother's entry to some others. Most of the seniors pictured had long lists—Math Team, Drama Club, Editor-in-chief of *The Siren* (which she gleaned was the school paper, though she hadn't seen it yet) and on and on—underneath their names.

But not her mother.

It made sense on some level that her mom was a non-joiner—the woman had practically un-joined her own family—but she had *started* the Dreamland Social Club? And it was still going after all these years? Something about discovering a legacy, even if Jane had no idea what it actually *was*, made her happy.

When the section for club photos turned up no picture of the Dreamland S.C., she went back to the beginning of the alphabet and started looking for other people who'd listed it among their extracurriculars. But the whole thing proved more time-consuming than she'd realized and, by the time the bell rang, she'd only gotten to the D's and hadn't found any other members.

The second she stepped out into the hall to head to her next class, a voice said, "Well, look who we have here."

She turned to face Cliff Claverack, whose face was red, as if from a workout. He said, "We are going to make your life a living hell."

As nonconfrontationally as she could manage, Jane said, "I didn't know about the horse."

He leaned in close to her, so close that she could see the pores on the face of the dragon tattooed on his neck. For a second she half feared that that tattoo was going to open up and breathe a stream of fire at her.

"Doesn't matter whether you did or didn't," he said. "He was a piece of shit and shit runs in families."

"But I never even met him!"

He's not even really my family! she almost added. But of course he was.

He covered his ears and said, "Not-listening-not-listening-not-listening," then pulled his hands away and said, "Just turn over the horse and we'll leave you alone."

Fine, Jane almost said. *I will!*

But a voice came from down the hall—"Giddyup, Claverack"—and Cliff looked up and over Jane's shoulder. Jane turned and saw a black kid walking down the hall. She recognized him as the guy who had no legs, but here he was. Walking. Wearing jeans and shoes.

"None of your business!" Cliff sang in a sort of singsong.

"Is if I make it." He was standing beside Jane now, taller than her by several inches. His teeth were straighter than any Jane had ever seen, and his arms were tight with muscle.

Cliff backed away. "That's how it's gonna be?"

Jane didn't understand how it was possible, kept look-ing at those jeans, those shoes.

He said, "That's how it's gonna be," with a crooked smile that made the teeth look even straighter.

Cliff clomped away then, and she turned to her savior and said, "Thanks." But confusion must have tinged her features, because he bent to knock on his thigh and said, "Prosthetics."

"Oh," Jane said.

"I'm H. T. Astaire." He held out a hand, which Jane shook. It was calloused, rough; felt the complete opposite of how the skin on his face looked.

"Officially Henry Thomas," he said. "Unofficially, Half-There." He hit his prosthetics again.

Jane put it together. "Half-There Astaire."

"I dance"—he held up his hands—"mostly on these. Which might be the reason Claverack is scared shitless of me. You gotta use what you got, you know?"

"Well, thanks," Jane said, not sure she had anything to use at all.

"He's just a big, dumb bully." He shook his head. "I got no time for that. And yo, do *not* give them that horse."

"But their grandfather made it."

And it's my ticket to freedom!

"Doesn't matter who made it. Doesn't belong in their grubby mitts."

A late bell rang, and Jane consulted her schedule. When she saw that she was expected in gym, possibly her most dreaded class in the history of the world, she thought about hiding in the bathroom. Then again, she'd need to be fit if she was going to survive that five-mile swim.

After school that day, Jane studied a bulletin board for information about *The Siren*, then found the offices, located in a far corner of the school's basement, and dared to knock. She poked her head in after someone called out, "It's open!"

She walked into a cement-walled room with rectangular windows and exposed pipes running along the ceiling and heard only the buzz of a printer or scanner. At a desk in a far corner, one covered with piles of papers, the giant stood up from his chair. A shadow fell over Jane as he blocked the lights like a big cloud in front of the sun.

"Hey." He held out an oversize hand. "I'm Legs Malstead."

She went to shake it but her hand barely covered the span of his palm; it was more of a high-five than anything until Legs enclosed her hand in his other hand to hold in there long enough to have a proper shake. Jane was grateful he had a system.

"I'm Jane," she said. "Dryden."

"I know."

"Oh." She figured she should just cut to the chase. "I was wondering, do you keep archives?"

He bent down on one knee and, irrationally, Jane thought he might propose. Instead he said, "We do." And then he seemed a little bit irrationally excited when he said, "What are you looking for?"

Jane felt her cheeks tighten at the thought of having to say any of it out loud, so she kept it short and sweet. "My mom went to school here." Talking about her mother out loud, with a stranger—and a giant, no less—took the wind out of her. She had to concentrate hard in order to speak again. "I wanted to see if she was ever written up in the paper."

And of course the founding of a new school club seemed potentially newsworthy, but she didn't feel the need to elaborate. Not until she knew more, anyway. Not until she could breathe again.

Legs nodded quickly and said, "Just give me one minute to finish something up. . . ." He handed her an issue of the paper. "Read while you wait."

Jane's eyes landed on a Faculty Q&A in a box on the first page of the paper. It definitely offered up some interesting facts about Coney Island High's chemistry teacher—like that he worked at the Coney Island Sideshow during the summer, as Garth the Human Garbage Disposal—but the reporter hadn't asked the questions Jane would have asked. Then again, she probably wouldn't have chosen a teacher to shine her spotlight on. She wished for a spotlight on H.T. or Leo, even one about Babette. Because she couldn't just flat-out ask her new classmates things like "What's the best thing about being a goth dwarf?" and "What's the worst?" Or "Why do you get tattoos?" Or "Do you envy people with legs?" She'd be tagged a Looky Lou forever. And besides, the core question behind every question she wanted to know the answer to was unanswerable. It was "What's it like to be you?"

And not me.

She sort of felt like it was the only question ever worth asking anybody. Not where are you from? Or what do your parents do? Or what do you want to be when you grow up? Or any of the usual bunk. Just what is it *like*? What are *you* like?

It was a question she couldn't answer.

You know who you are.

Or you don't.

"Okay," Legs said finally, putting some papers in some sort of courier bag. "So. Archives. They're definitely not complete. Come this way. . . ." He walked toward a door at the far end of the room and opened it. Boxes upon boxes filled tall metal shelves. "But you're welcome to have a look."

Right then the genius toddler came through the office door, walked over, and jumped up onto Legs's knee and kissed him. So, apparently, she wasn't a toddler.

"Oh, hey," Legs said, almost falling over. He indicated Jane. "This is Jane Dryden; Jane, this is Minnie Polinsky."

"His girlfriend," Minnie said, in a high-pitched voice. She gave Jane a smug look, then turned to Legs and said, "Come on. We're going to be late."

"Oh," Legs said, then he looked at Jane, then back at Minnie, and said, "Jane here wants to look through the archives. Isn't that interesting?"

"Yeah," Minnie said, sort of slowly and suspiciously. "Sure. I guess. But we still have to go to . . . you know."

Legs sighed. "Jane? Can you do this another time? There's someplace I have to be and I can't leave you here alone. We can set a time. I can help."

"Sure," Jane said. "No problem." She nodded. "That'd be great."

She followed them out into the hall, then said goodbye and started walking away down the hall in the opposite direction. When she heard them open a door and disappear into a classroom, though, Jane doubled back.

Muted laughter came from Room 222, and she stopped near the closed door.

The Dreamland Social Club was meeting.

She walked by the room a few times—back and forth, back and forth, as casually as she could—and caught glimpses through a small window in the door of Legs and Minnie and H.T. and Babette and some others—was Leo there? She couldn't be sure—but then the bearded girl came into the hall and Jane panicked and rushed down to the main floor and out the front doors into a wall of hot, salty air.

CHAPTER

six

THE SPIDER PLANT THAT HUNG by the one window in the painfully dark living room seemed to be straining toward the glass for survival. On the TV in the corner a black-and-white woman pointed at a man with no arms or legs and screamed, "But is it *human*?"

"Look," Marcus said. "It's a movie about our school."

"Not funny," Jane said. "Where *were* you all day? I looked for you everywhere."

He shrugged.

She plopped down on one of Preemie's old couches. The cushions were less cushy than she'd expected and she'd plopped too hard. It hurt. "You've got an admirer," she said. A dwarf had just appeared on-screen.

"Oh yeah?" Marcus didn't even look up.

"Babette," Jane said.

Marcus frowned. "Not my type. Now that other little one, I could maybe . . . well, never mind."

"Anyway, Babette told me something weird." She tried to get more comfortable on the couch and puffed up some dust; she sneezed, then rested her head against the sofa back. "That Harvey guy and his brother, Cliff?"

Now Marcus looked up.

"Their grandfather had this long-standing battle with Preemie about that horse."

She nodded at the horse, and a car alarm sounded on the street: *Woo-oooh-ohhh-ohh.*

Marcus's face scrunched up. *"What?"*

Eh-eh-eh-eh.

"Their grandfather made it. He built the carousel. And he wanted to buy it from Preemie but Preemie wouldn't sell, and he taunted the Claveracks about it for years."

Beep-eeeep-eeep-eeeep.

Marcus shook his head and paused the movie. "That's ridiculous."

Waheeee, waheeee.

"Is it?" Jane said. "What do we know?"

Whoop-whoop. The alarm clicked off.

Marcus tossed the remote aside, got up, and went into the kitchen, and Jane followed. "It's chained to the radiator, Marcus. Doesn't that strike you as a little bit *strange?*"

"Jane," he said sternly as he opened the refrigerator and then closed it, having found nothing worth eating or drinking. "Didn't Dad say it enough times? We're just here for *one year.* So just go make some friends who are into what you're into, whatever that is, and suck it up and keep your head down and then we'll be on our merry way."

"You're not even a little interested in the fact that our grandfather had a mortal enemy whose grandkids are in school with us?" Jane followed him over to the cabinets by the sink, which didn't reveal anything worth his stomach's attention either.

He closed the cabinet doors, looked at his watch, then headed back toward the living room and sat down. "I just don't know if I'd believe everything a goth dwarf told me. And I mean, whatever. They can have it, right? I seriously couldn't care less."

He started the movie again, and Jane settled in to watch. A woman dressed like a bird—big, pear-shaped costume and feathered headdress—walked on-screen. "Is that Grandma?" Jane asked.

Marcus gave her a look. "That's Birdie, yes."

"What?" she said defensively. "She *was* our grandmother. Where'd you find it?"

"Around."

Jane tried to focus on Birdie alone—tried to study her countenance and manner for signs of some kind of family relation—but it was hard not to be distracted by the man who was just a torso. She wondered whether this man with no limbs had ever met the girl with no limbs from the Dreamland Social Club. She thought about telling Marcus that their mom was listed in her yearbook as the founder of their school's Dreamland Social Club, but if he didn't care about the history of the carousel horse, he'd hardly care about some dopey club.

The conjoined twin brunettes who kept doing interstitial song and dance numbers, their voices all warbly from the warping of the tape, gave Jane the chills, and when the final scene played out and the new sideshow act, a person with a skull that turned pointy at the top, a "pinhead," was revealed to be Martian—*not human after all*—the credits rolled and Jane sighed with relief. Black-and-white movies always made her queasy, and she decided it must be because everyone in them—every actor and actress she'd seen, every name on the final credits, every orphan in the surf—was dead.

When the film ended and Marcus left the room, Jane approached the horse and ran a hand down its long mane. She thought about climbing on, but it seemed disrespectful to treat it like a toy, even though that's basically what it was. Instead, she bent to study the lock. Picking it up—and wow, was it heavy—she tugged at the closure but it wouldn't budge. She'd have to look around for an old key but wasn't very hopeful.

Based on what she'd learned of Preemie, he sounded like the kind of guy who would have taken the key to his grave as a sort of final F.U.

Giddyup, Preemie, she thought. *Neigh yourself.*

When she heard her father come home, Jane got up from the uncushy sofa, where she'd fallen asleep, and went into the front hall to greet him. He looked windblown again. More like soul-blown, really. "Everything okay?" she asked.

"I'll tell you," he said. "This pounding of the pavement ain't fun."

"Any leads?" She relieved him of his portfolio, then put it on the hall's small table.

"Not a one." He kicked his shoes off in the hall and padded down to the kitchen and threw a newspaper onto the table. Jane could see some help-wanted ads that had been circled with blue ballpoint but didn't dare look at what kinds of jobs they were. It was all too depressing.

"Anyway." He tousled her hair. "Never you mind. Something'll turn up."

"Yeah," she said. "It always does."

She found the ensuing silence in the room so awkward that she decided to fill it with this: "Hey, did Mom ever mention something called the Dreamland Social Club?"

Her father furrowed his brow for a second, then shook his head. "I don't think so. Why?"

"It's a club she founded when she was in high school." She was trying to sound nonchalant but she wasn't entirely sure why. Maybe because this "talking about Mom" thing was still sort of new, skittish.

"Really?" He raised an eyebrow, and Jane nodded and said, "It still exists."

"What is it?" He opened the fridge and took out a beer.

"I have no idea."

"Are you going to join?" He took a swig.

"It's not that simple, Dad." Not when you considered the cryptic posters and the way Legs and Minnie had seemed so secretive about where they were going.

"Okay." He squeezed her shoulder as he left the room. "If you say so."

seven

MR. SIMMONS SAT CROSS-LEGGED in the middle of his classroom on a map of Coney Island in class that Thursday. It was comprised of large wooden puzzle pieces labeled THE GUT, MANHATTAN BEACH, WEST BRIGHTON, and a few more Jane couldn't read, in no small part because Mr. Simmons was sitting on them. He was a bit kooky, Mr. Simmons, but Jane was already fond of him and knew that, if she ended up in another school next year, she'd remember him and Garth the Human Garbage Disposal (whose class she hadn't even been in!) and possibly none of her other teachers here.

"All will be explained in time," he said as students came in and looked confused by the fact that he was sitting on a map and also by the fact that all the desks and chairs had been pushed to the back of the room. Jane waited next to Babette on one edge of the map and studied a bulletin board on the room's side wall. It was covered with old photos of Luna Park and Dreamland. She stepped up close to a photo of Dreamland's Creation ride, where an angel carved out of stone stood by the entrance, seemingly holding the weight of the whole building on its wings.

The bell rang and Mr. Simmons said, "The history of Coney Island is, at its most basic, a series of landgrabs. Meaning that whenever it was possible to take land away from someone else and claim it for themselves, that's what people did. And have continued to do. Over and over again. So!"

He stood and stepped over to his desk, gestured to the map, then held a whistle to his mouth. "When I blow, you grab!"

At the shrill sound, Jane pushed her way forward, dove straight for the piece marked CONEY ISLAND BEACH, and held on tight as people moved and grabbed around her. The bustle died down in a matter of seconds, and a few people shouted out complaints—"I didn't get anything!" "There's not enough pieces!"

Mr. Simmons said, "Not destined to be landowners, then."

He started talking about the different puzzle pieces then, but Jane just wanted him to get to hers. She hadn't been able to figure out where, exactly, the old parks had been, and she wanted very badly to have ended up with the right piece and for Mr. Simmons to tell her where, exactly, they had been. That way, maybe she'd be able to walk on hallowed ground.

Finally, he said, "And who had the good fortune-slash-misfortune of getting Coney Island Beach proper?"

Jane raised her hand, held up her piece.

"Ah," he said. "Jane. You hold in your hands one of the most coveted and embattled pieces of property to ever exist in the world." He strode around the room. "So, what are you going to do with it?"

Time seemed to halt for a moment as Jane's mind traveled to the attic, so full of amazing old Coney lore, and took a Trip to the Moon, with Selenites singing, and to those grim apartments they'd had in grim cities while her father worked random jobs, and then she was back in the moment and she said, "I'd want to do two things."

Heads seemed to perk up in surprise that the new girl had an answer—in two parts, no less. "I'd rebuild the old amusement parks, just like they were, and—"

"Dude," Babette interrupted before Jane could get part two out. "That's blasphemy."

Jane turned to her, feeling like one of Preemie's water balloons that had just popped. "It is?"

"Midget City?" Babette's eyes sparked with agitation. "Ever hear of it?"

Jane felt foolish but, of course, she hadn't meant that *everything* would be re-created. She was pretty sure, for example, that a reenactment of the Boer War would bore people to tears. And shows like Fighting Flames were too gory, too dangerous.

Babette seemed to shiver. "Every once in a while I have a dream that I'm living in Midget City and I can't get out. That stuff's best left in the past." She shrugged. "Doesn't mean I want the place to turn into a shopping mall, though."

"Sorry," Jane said, not knowing what a shopping mall had to do with anything. "I wasn't thinking of rebuilding Midget City—or a mall. I just think a lot of the stuff that's here now, on the boardwalk, is so run-down. I think some new rides"—she couldn't stop herself—"maybe a new roller coaster or something, would be good. That's part two. A big new ride. A proper theme park."

Her father could design it!

Leo's hand shot up, and Mr. Simmons called on him.

For days Jane had been hoping for some kind of sign from Leo, some kind of acknowledgment that he'd found the postcard or at least looked for it, but so far none had come. He said, "I think it's important to remember that the people who have kept those businesses on the board-walk alive all these years shouldn't be locked out of new plans. I mean, what happened to the Go Karts just wasn't right."

Jane had almost forgotten about the first day of school, the bottle throwing, the shards of glass splayed in the air like confetti. A second ago she'd thought that people would absolutely want the sort of coaster her father de-signed, but maybe it was more complicated than that. The sick feeling she'd had that first afternoon came back.

"Unless they can't afford the rent," someone in the back of the class said, and Leo said, "Oh, screw you."

Clearly they weren't talking about puzzle pieces anymore. But Jane wasn't sure exactly what they *were* talking about.

Mr. Simmons returned to the head of the class. "Like I said . . ."

Everyone waited.

"Embattled."

Mr. Simmons changed gears then and went on to other areas, then circled back to assign homework. "I want you to write one sentence describing the most fun you ever had on Coney Island. Don't overthink it. Just do it. We'll talk more about the full assignment next time." He stopped by Jane's desk. "And Jane, I know you just got here. You can pick another place if you like."

"Hey," Jane said to Babette after class. "I didn't mean to offend you."

"No big deal," Babette said. "No pun intended."

"Still," Jane said, thinking of Preemie in his incubator, a neighbor of Midget City himself. "So did your grandparents work in Midget City or something? Did your parents grow up here?"

Of course Babette would have told her if her parents had grown up with Jane's mom, wouldn't she have? Still, the thought of it got her hopes up for a split second.

"Actually, *my* parents and grandparents are completely,

painfully normal. My father's a cop and my mother's a teacher in the elementary school in Brighton Beach. We only moved here like four years ago."

"Oh," Jane said. And then a more surprised, *"Oh!"* because she had been picturing Babette at home with a small family.

"It's just a gene mutation," Babette explained. "Straight-up dwarfism, unlike perfectly proportioned Minnie Polinsky, who has primordial dwarfism, which is like the rarest of the rare, and also the reason she's so darn cute like a china doll while I'm just"—she looked down—"like this. Anyway, my parents look happy in old pictures but they don't seem that way anymore, not since I came along. I try not to blame myself."

"You shouldn't!"

"I don't. Not really." Babette shrugged. "Just put in a good word with your brother for me, will you?" Her T-shirt today featured a drawing of an octopus—a yellow image on a gray base. "It's really only a matter of time before he drops his aloof act and falls under my spell. I'm small, but I have other charms."

"I'm sure."

"Oh, please." Babette punched Jane's thigh. "Like you're not going to bed at night thinking about getting tattoos that say 'I Heart Leo.'"

Jane shot her a look.

"I'm not blind. I see the way you look at him, all dreamy." Babette batted her eyelashes.

"I hate needles," Jane said.

"Well, this little plan of yours to knock stuff down so you can rebuild Dreamland or some slick new coaster isn't going to wow him either," Babette said with new energy that sounded like frustration. "His father owns the Anchor, you know."

That dump?

It would explain why Leo's father told him stories about the strange bar bets Preemie had made. It would explain why they'd all been outside the bar that night. Was it possible that Leo's father had known her mother?

Babette said, snarkily, "And his mother is only the *president* of Coney Islanders for Coney."

Even better. Maybe *his mom* had known her?

But before getting carried away with the idea, she asked, "What's Coney Islanders for Coney?"

"It's a local sort of activist group that's fighting the Loki plan."

It was like Babette was speaking a different language. "What's the Loki plan?"

"Dear naive Jane." Babette's eyes seem to glitter in the hallway's fluorescent lights, and her hair looked deep purple. "You really have to get a clue, or an act."

"An act?"

"Yeah, you know. An act? An angle? A shtick? Something that sets you apart from the rubes?"

Which was carny for losers, chumps, paying customers.

Jane said, "Why can't I just be me?"

"You *have* heard of *adolescence*, right?" Babette huffed. "Traumatic period of life wherein no one is free to just be themselves. Not without ridicule anyway."

Jane looked around at the hordes of normal kids, plowing through the halls, going about their typical high school day. She said, "Plenty of people here—*most* people here—don't have an act and no one cares."

Babette threw her little hands up in the air. "Fine, hang out with *them!*"

"Maybe I will!"

Babette sighed. "All I'm saying is I can't hang out with you unless you do something for your image." She put her hands on her small hips. "I mean, really. Jane. Have you looked in a mirror lately?"

Jane looked down at her blah outfit and wanted to tell Babette that it wasn't her fault that her mother must have taken any fashion sense their family had ever had to the grave. That her clothes had actually worked, she thought, in London.

Babette said, "Just promise me you won't wear *that* to the party next weekend."

"I'm not *going* to a party next weekend."

"Oh, yes you are."

They took back-to-back stools in biology lab—they'd been assigned neighboring lab tables—and Babette said, "You and your brother should both come. It's in the projects, so it's mostly gonna be project kids. But the project kids are cool."

"I don't know any of them," Jane said.

"But you know *me*. And I know H.T. And *he* knows Mike and Ike, who are the drop-dead gorgeous twins you will have already noticed if you're not a lesbian, and it's their party."

Jane couldn't say for sure that she'd seen them, but nodded recognition anyway. H.T., at least, she'd actually met.

"It'll be good for you," Babette said. "You'd be making a statement."

"What kind of statement?" Jane studied the cow's eye in the jar on Babette's table. It seemed to be looking at her skeptically, like maybe it had heard through the cow grapevine about her, about the way that she seemed to prefer the company of cows to people during that year she'd spent living in Ireland.

"I don't know," Babette said. "That just because people are talking trash about your grandfather you're not going to curl up and die."

"Why are you being so nice to me?" Jane asked before she even realized she was going to. Almost like the cow's eye had said, *Just ask her.*

But *was* she being nice? As soon as she asked, Jane wasn't so sure.

"I don't know. You seem cool." Babette shrugged with one tiny shoulder. "And you've got carny blood, even if it's obviously very highly diluted.

"Here's a tip, though." She dug into her book bag, pulled out a rumpled newspaper, and handed it to Jane. "You should really read the paper once in a while."

■　　■　　■

Something about biology labs had always made Jane a little nauseated, and this lab at Coney Island High certainly wasn't going to help matters. It had that smell she hated—of something antiseptic and half dead—and there were jars along the far wall that she dared not look at too closely. The cow's eye was bad enough. But when Jane's partner showed up and it turned out to be Venus Anders—a walking, talking tangle of red dreads and rose tattoos, the girl equivalent of Tattoo Boy (who was not, to Jane's disappointment, in this class)—Jane felt like the cow's eye might be the least of her problems. At least she only had lab once a week.

"So, what's your deal anyway?" Venus said as they started to line up a bunch of equipment they needed, though Jane had dared not read the full instructions on the handout in front of her: scalpel, magnifying glass, petri dish.

"No deal."

"Where are you from?" An ink vine with black roses on it climbed up her neck. More roses peeked out from under her black long-sleeved shirt, touching the knuckles on her hands.

"Nowhere, really," which was how it felt. "I mean, sort of all over."

"Your grandfather cheated me out of a stuffed animal once." In between words, she was chewing on a fingernail that had been painted black. "When I was little. He used to tell me to go play in traffic."

Jane knew she had to stand her ground. She'd been confronted by the alpha female in pretty much every school she'd ever transferred into, which had always seemed strange to her, as if she were any kind of threat at all. She said, "You don't seem like the stuffed-animal type."

Venus studied her, not sure how to react. After a moment, she said, "Not the point."

Jane was about to say, "What is?" but got distracted by the ink on Venus's skin, wondering how deep it went. Venus said, "So you think you've seen Leo's seahorse before?"

Jane fought to hide the sting of what felt like a betrayal. "That's right."

"What about *my* tattoos?" Venus rolled up her sleeves. "Have you seen mine before?"

"No," Jane said. "I don't think so."

All at once a dream she'd had the night before—a nightmare, really—came back. She'd been struggling to breathe underwater. The seahorse had been there, staring her down. For a second she had thought she'd be able to ride it up out of the water to safety, so she'd grabbed onto it, only to find out it wasn't real but was made of plastic, a toy. It wouldn't save her, couldn't save her, and she awoke as if gasping when breaking through to the surface of the sea.

"What about these?" Venus turned around and lifted up the back of her shirt, revealing a whole garden of ink. Wildflowers reached up toward her shoulder blades; lilies floated on what seemed to be a small pond. If you blocked out the red, shiny bra straps cutting across it, it was beautiful in a shocking sort of way. Jane couldn't help but think that you just shouldn't do that to skin. "Familiar?"

Jane, suddenly self-conscious about staring at Venus's bare skin and bra strap, said, "No, pull your shirt down."

"Yeah," Venus smacked her gum and fixed her top. "I didn't think so. Just Leo's."

"Right," Jane said. "Just Leo's."

Then Venus said, "Go figure," and the teacher, whom Jane had just met and had already forgotten, probably for good, called the class to attention as Jane reconsidered her dream. The seahorse wasn't going to save her, and if Leo was already blabbing about her questions, he was unreliable at best.

Only she could save herself. She'd have to go back to the yearbook, to the original plan of finding the names of other people who were in her mother's club. Of seeing if she could track any of them down.

Walking out onto the beach at day's end, after a quick stop at the library, where she had slipped her mother's yearbook into her bag undetected, Jane sat down on the sand. She thought about looking through the yearbook right then, but didn't want to get caught now, not after she'd successfully gotten it out of the building. So she took out some of the required reading for English Lit. Opening her book to a Wordsworth poem, she read,

I wandered lonely as a cloud
That floats on high o'er vales and hills,
When all at once I saw a crowd,
A host of golden daffodils . . .

But it was way too nice out for homework and besides, she'd already read that poem at least three gazillion times before, at three different schools. She pretty much felt like that cloud. But without the daffodils. The good news, she realized then, was that tomorrow was Friday. It appeared she would survive the week.

She put down the book and watched a group of older girls and guys—like in their twenties—sitting nearby on the sand. The girls wore pigtails and sunglasses half the size of their faces; one of the guys wore a T-shirt that said "Ithaca is GORGES." The boys were building sand castles while the girls read glossy magazines.

What *would* Jane wear to a party? She *did* look like she'd been dipped in gray paint—day after day after day—and for a second, she closed her eyes and dreamed that if she dove into the ocean, her gray clothes would all fall off and fade away and she'd resurface in lavish new garments in coral colors. What *had* her mother meant when she'd said she'd been a mermaid once? Probably nothing at all.

Spying Babette's newspaper in her bag, Jane pulled it out and scanned the page it was folded to. Her eyes landed on a headline that read **NO MORE GO FOR CONEY'S GO KARTS.**

Coney Island's beloved Go Kart ride was demolished earlier this week. The destruction of the Go Karts before the official end of the summer season next week marks a dramatic move on the part of Loki Equities, who until now has been the silent and mostly invisible landlord to various Coney mainstays, including the Go Karts, Wonderland amusement park, and more. The Regan family, who ran the Go Kart ride for thirty years, confirmed that they received notification by mail from Loki several weeks ago that their lease would not be renewed. The operators of Wonderland confirmed that their lease is up this spring, though they have not yet discussed terms with Loki.

This winter, a special New York City commission is due to review a proposal by Loki Equities, the largest landholder on Coney Island, to develop a controversial year-round Vegas-style theme park and mall. In the meantime, the city is moving forward with its own plans to develop several acres and is accepting bids from amusement park operators and designers.

She read that last bit again and thought she might burst.

Leo was suddenly sitting next to her. "What's up, Looky Lou?"

She looked at him askance as she put the paper back in her bag so she could show it to her father later. Who *was* this guy?

He nodded toward the sand castles. "You going to join the fun?"

Jane watched a bucket full of upturned sand crumble in a series of small landslides. "Wouldn't be a very good Looky Lou if I did."

They were quiet for a moment; a seagull walked closer, presumably to see if they had any food.

"What does that even mean?" she said.

"What?" Leo smiled. "Looky Lou?"

"No," she said. "Ithaca is GORGES."

"Not worth explaining," Leo said. "But suffice it to say, the hipster influx is not a good sign. It means the gentrification of Coney has begun."

Jane had never heard the word *gentrification* before. "What's that?"

"It's a good thing you've never lived here before and have a reason for not knowing this stuff," Leo said. "Otherwise I'd be starting to wonder right about now, whether you were sort of, I don't know"—he rooted around for a word—"daft."

Daft? It was one thing she most certainly wasn't. "Are you going to explain or not?"

"You're cute when you're pissed off." He smiled, then leaned back to rest on his elbows; Jane thought she might die from the *cute*. "It *means* that the hipsters and yuppies and rich people seem to have recently woken up and said, Hey, wait a second, Coney's *awesome*. Why is it so *working class*?"

"And that's bad?"

"Yes, that's bad." Leo was exasperated. "Because it means the price of everything is going to go up and the little businesses that have kept Coney alive all this time are going to get pushed out or bought out. It's the beginning of the end. The Go Karts were only the start of it."

Jane just looked out at the sun's white reflection on the waves and thought about telling him about her idea, how her father could maybe help turn things around by bringing more business to the area if the city bought one of his coasters—maybe even a whole theme park. But then Leo said, "Now that you're landed gentry you probably don't even care."

"It was just a dopey puzzle piece," she said, and Leo shook his head and said, "I'm talking about the house. Preemie's house."

"Oh." Of course. Maybe she *was* daft. "I don't technically own it yet."

"Ah, but you will. And when you do, someone will come along and offer you more money than you can refuse so they can make way for some big-box store or some other crap, and you'll take it."

Her head hurt. "Isn't that sort of how it works?"

"Doesn't mean it's right."

Jane couldn't argue with that, not on the spot anyway, so she said, "I'm sorry for what I said about the boardwalk today."

"What, you mean, how the Anchor should be knocked down?" He was smiling.

"Don't take this the wrong way," Jane dared. "But the Anchor sort of looks like it's going to fall down on its own."

He smiled and elbowed her. "I could say the same thing about your house."

"Touché," Jane said. But it was different. She didn't love the idea of Leo's father owning such a dump. She felt like it said something about the kind of guy Leo was, or would end up being, though she wasn't sure what.

Leo wiped sand off his hands. "Have you even *been* to the Anchor?"

Jane shook her head. "Of course not."

"We're going to have to remedy that situation one of these days."

"If you say so," she said with an edge of sarcasm.

"I say so." He ran a hand through his hair. "And shit, I have to find that postcard for you. Sorry. I looked around the house. I swear I've seen it recently, but I can't think of where. "

"It's no big deal," she felt the need to say, then wanted to take it back. She felt like she wanted to ask him to ask his parents if they'd known her mother, but then she felt like she was already asking too much. The guy barely knew her. Finding the postcard was good enough for now.

"Either way." Leo stood up and wiped sand off his jeans, and said, "So I guess I'll see ya."

"Yeah."

He turned to go but then stopped and said, "Actually, Jane?"

She looked up.

"Do you think maybe I could see it sometime, Preemie's old Coney stuff?"

"Of course." She looked at her watch, wondered whether anyone was home, whether it mattered.

Leo laughed and said, "I don't mean right this second, but you know. Just say when."

He backed away a few steps before turning away, before Jane had a chance to whisper *when*.

Like *Orphans*, this film—labeled *'King' & 'Queen' the Great Diving Horses, 1899*—was grainy and black-and-white, and when the projector whirred to life in the quiet attic, it was hard to believe, somehow, that the images were real.

Jane sat on the dusty floor in her pajamas and watched one horse and then a second one plunge off a high platform into a pool below, making a huge black-and-white splash. She tried to imagine what it felt like for an animal of that size to hit the water with so much velocity, and imagined it hurt. Maybe even a lot.

She watched the reel again, this time looking for a trainer with a prod, maybe something electrical and sharp. But the horses had jumped on their own. Seemingly, no one had forced them.

Jane felt like maybe she knew what King and Queen had been thinking, if they'd been *thinking* at all. Because Leo—who wanted to take her to a bar, who wanted to come up to the attic, who made her feel like *staying*—seemed dangerous, but all she wanted to do was dive in.

CHAPTER

eight

SMOKY AIR DREW JANE TOWARD the back window of her room on Saturday around lunchtime, and she saw her brother out in the yard, manning a small charcoal grill. Since she was up to the letter R in the yearbook and still hadn't found any more members of the school's original Dreamland Social Club, she set the task aside and went downstairs and out the back door—swirls of wrought iron with a screen that let cool air pass—and stepped over all sorts of old, dead foliage, then sat in a black metal chair near the grill. She stretched out her legs and said, "What's the most fun you've ever had?"

Marcus raised his eyebrows salaciously and said, "I

don't think you really want to know." He was wearing shorts and a sweatshirt, a combo that Jane guessed worked on only about three days of the year in New York weather. Today was one of them.

"Ew." A hydrangea plant next to her held some purple blooms in defiance of the decay around it. "And I don't believe you anyway."

"I don't know." Marcus flipped his burgers and each one sizzled. "I had fun at that big theme park in Germany, and that Ocean Dome place in Japan was pretty cool. Actually, they should build something like that here, you know?"

An indoor beach was certainly a better idea than a shopping mall, but Jane still wasn't convinced that day at the Ocean Dome was the most fun she'd ever had. She reviewed her memory of it all. The sand castles of Coney. The volcano erupting. The wave pool. It had been fun, at the time. But now she had a hard time thinking of anything she'd done with her mother as fun. "I'm supposed to write a sentence about the most fun I've ever had on Coney, or somewhere else since we just got here. I'm drawing a complete blank."

"One sentence?" Marcus shrugged. "Make something up."

But that wouldn't do. Something about the assignment was getting under Jane's skin. It was under there right next to this business about the city accepting bids for their new amusement park attractions. She hadn't had a chance to talk to her father yet. "Where's Dad?" she said, and Marcus shrugged again.

He pulled the burgers off the grill with a spatula, slid them onto a plate where two open buns awaited. "So are you going to that party next weekend?"

Of course he already knew about it.

"I don't have anything to wear," Jane said, because Babette had gotten under her skin, too.

"It's a party in the projects, Jane. Not a cotillion." He bit into a burger, nodded approval as he chewed, and presented the plate with the other burger to Jane.

"What do you care what I do?" Jane said. Then she took a bite of her burger and felt her body come alive from it, felt the warmth of it slide down to her belly.

"Eat fast," he said. "I want to show you something."

Five bites later their burgers were gone, and then Marcus got up and walked to a set of metal doors at the side of the house, built into the ground at an angle. He opened one of them and took a step down and said, "Follow me."

Jane did as he asked and then the lights came up on what appeared to be . . . well, she wasn't sure.

A huge fake stone facade covered the far wall, where a red leather bar sat on four small wheels. It had a fireplace on the front of it—replete with fake logs—and a wire running to a nearby outlet. Marcus plugged it in, and the fireplace glowed orange through a gray film of dust.

The rest of the room's walls were covered with red-and-gold wallpaper adorned with American eagles. Overhead, wagon-wheel lanterns dangled from a white stucco ceiling cut across with dark wood beams. Then Marcus switched on a light by the bar, and a neon sign that read "Birdie's Bavarian Bar" glowed red. On a shelf behind the bar sprung a liquid rainbow: liqueurs in bright green and cherry red, even electric blue.

"Wow," she said, and Marcus said, "Yeah. There's a bunch of Birdie's stuff here. Some clothes, even. I thought maybe . . ."

"Thanks," she said, trying to take it all in, since she hadn't found much of Birdie's stuff anywhere else in the house. "This is where you found the movie?"

"Yeah."

There passed a split second during which Jane was going to get mad that Marcus hadn't shown her the bar as soon as he'd found it, but she hadn't exactly gone running to show him the attic.

"I'll leave you to it," Marcus said, heading back up the stairs to the yard.

Jane found the clothes in a huge wardrobe in the corner. They weren't dresses and costumes, like she'd been expecting, but more casual skirts and tops, the sort which a girl like Jane could actually wear *to school*. This was good, but no help on the party front. There were drawers beneath the hangered section, where some old shoes sat waiting in pairs. Jane slipped them on and they fit. She liked knowing she took after her grandmother physically, even if it was just a shoe size.

She approached a large wooden chest that sat on the floor in the farthest corner of the room. *Please, please, please,* she said—to herself, to God, to no one, but mostly to her dead grandmother—as she knelt and opened its dusty top.

First came the hats—five of them—and then a sequined green bird costume. She couldn't exactly go to the party wearing only a hat or dressed as a bird, so she tossed it all aside, only to pull out still another bird costume, this one gold, and then another in a fiery pink and another in a neon blue. The last one was a sea-foam green.

She kept digging, though, and finally found a dress, and then another dress, and then another; they had been pressed and folded and individually wrapped with tissue paper like someone had actually hoped they'd be worn again someday. She pulled out a gorgeous deep blue, almost black, dress that was just way too nice for a high-school party. But soon she found a burgundy dress with an overlay of lace on a silken shift. It was a little ornate in its details but still managed to seem subtle, almost casual. She stripped down to her bra and underwear right there in the basement bar to try it on and said another silent prayer. Looking at her reflection in a mirror that had taken on a gold sheen with age, she saw that the dress fit perfectly, made her body look better than anything in her current wardrobe. Birdie Cusack had saved her life, and Jane would never be able to thank her.

Digging through in haste to make sure she'd found the best dress of the lot, Jane rammed her nails into something and pulled a small wooden box from the chest. Putting the dresses aside so she could open it, she found that it held a few old trinkets: a small cross on a chain, a silver rattle, and a small silver cup, the kind they make for babies, with the name *Clementine* engraved in it. She set it all aside to take upstairs and turned her attention to a manila envelope full of old photos. Flipping through jagged stacks of sepia-toned squares, she found pictures of Birdie as a young girl riding a bike, as a young woman smoking a cigarette in a director's chair, and then pictures—rectangular and color—of her mom as a little girl, by a lake with Preemie and Birdie—all of them in square swimsuits. There were baby birthday parties and Christmas trees and then— a shock—a picture of Birdie, in her bird costume, next to a man like H.T., legless, also wearing feathers and a headdress. They were smiling cheek to cheek thanks to a pedestal. Two birds of a feather. She set that photo aside, too.

After packing the costumes back up, she approached another large piece of furniture—a sort of tall cabinet. She ran a finger along the metal plate on the front that said "Victrola," then lifted its top lid to discover a record player. Nearby on the wall, a shelf held what had to be several hundred old records, in a size Jane had never seen before, a little bit smaller than Marcus's handful of collectible LPs but not by much. She thought about putting one on but then saw there was already a record on the turntable. Jane spun it so that she could read the title: "Meet Me Tonight in Dreamland."

She placed the needle on it and then hit a button that looked like a power button, but nothing happened. Opening the front door of the cabinet, she found a crank, so she removed the needle from the record, wound the crank a bunch of times, then put the needle back, hit the power button, and, *voilà*, orchestral sounds flowed into the room. Then a warbly female voice followed, crooning, *"Dreaming of you, that's all I do,/Night and day for you I'm pining,/And in your eyes, blue as the skies,/I can see the love-light softly shining . . ."*

And then Jane wasn't hearing the lyrics anymore but was concentrating on a memory, trying to re-create it in sharp detail. But it was fuzzy, like the edges of sleep. . . .

I'm not tired. I don't want to go to bed. I want to play more, but my mother says, "No, it's time."

I say, "But I miss you when I sleep."

She smiles. "Well, then I'll meet you tonight in Dreamland."

"Where's that?"

"You go to sleep, and I'll go to sleep, too, a little later, and when I do, I'll find you there. Okay?"

"Is it nice there? In Dreamland?"

"Oh boy, is it! And there are angels there, waiting for us."

She tucks me in and now I really want to fall asleep, can't fall fast enough, because the sooner I do the sooner I get to meet her in Dreamland. . . .

She hums a song, a tune I'm sure I'll never forget, and I drift off and wait and wait until I forget I'm waiting. . . .

Turning off the Victrola, and then the lights, Jane took the burgundy dress and a few of the skirts and tops and went back out into the yard, then into the house.

"Find anything good?" her father asked when she appeared in the kitchen. He was sitting at the table eating a sandwich with one of his old sketchbooks in front of him, pencil in hand.

"I don't know. Just some baby stuff of Mom's." She held up the rattle. "Some of Grandma's clothes." She indicated the dress.

He nodded, put his pencil down, and closed his book, then held out a hand for the rattle. "I should send you back down with a couple of trash bags. And up to the attic, too." He examined the rattle, ran a finger across the engraved letters, then shook it, releasing the jangle of a hollow bell, and handed it back. "This place isn't going to get cleared out on its own."

"I don't mind doing it," she said, but it wasn't her top priority. Her top priority right at that moment was seeing what her father was sketching in that notebook. Because from the tiny glimpse she'd stolen, it looked like it might be the beginnings of a coaster design. "Whatcha working on?" she asked with a nod toward the book.

"Nothing," he said, and he pulled it toward himself protectively.

"Okay," she said. "If you say so."

"Touché," he said.

She crossed the room to the hall, where her bag lay, and pulled out Babette's newspaper. "I thought you'd want to see this," she said. "The city is accepting bids for attractions."

"Oh, Jane." He sighed. "If only it were that easy."

"Maybe it is," she said, and he let out another sigh and started to read as Jane spun on her heels and left the room.

SHE HAD COMPLETED HER EXAMINATION of the yearbook that Sunday and had, infuriatingly enough, found no other mentions of the Dreamland Social Club.

Not a one.

But she *had* noticed a female student who looked an awful lot like Babette's bendy friend at school. Like a twin. So when she found herself walking with Babette into homeroom, which she had mostly been avoiding to avoid the issue of deciding where to sit, Jane said, "Hey, I want to thank this girl, I think she's a friend of yours, for helping me out with the Claveracks last week." She nodded toward Babette's usual table, where the girl was already sitting.

"Rita?" Babette said.

"I guess so."

"*She's* got an act," Babette said pointedly. "Rubber Rita, aspiring contortionist extraordinaire. She's double-jointed. The Claveracks call her Rubber Rican—racist losers."

Jane didn't know what to say except "I don't have an act!"

"Well, come on, then," Babette said, and led the way. At the table, she introduced them. "I wanted to say thanks," Jane said to Rita, "for what you did last week. With the rubber chicken."

"No problem," Rita said, and Jane and Babette took seats across from her. Legs and Minnie were at the table, too, talking to each other intensely, and Jane did a quick comparison of Babette's body type with Minnie's now that she knew there was an explanation for how they could both be so small in such different ways.

She felt weird flat-out asking Rita if she was born here and if her mother had grown up here and maybe had known Jane's mother, so she asked, instead, "So what extracurriculars do you guys do?" That was a normal question, wasn't it?

Babette and Rita exchanged a look so quick that Jane would have missed it if she hadn't sort of been anticipating it.

"I don't do much," Rita said. "I spend most of my spare time at a gym, doing gymnastics and stuff."

"Cool," Jane said, feeling terribly uncool.

"I do the occasional piece for the school paper," Babette said. She set about eating her brown-bag breakfast.

So they weren't talking about the Dreamland Social Club. They weren't going to be any help in that regard. The fact of it irked her, and she decided to just dig in. Trying to sound casual, she turned back to Rita and said, "So were you born here?"

Rita nodded.

"And your parents?"

Another nod.

Jane leaned in toward Rita. "Did they go to school here?"

Rita looked up and spoke through a mouthful of bagel. "You got a lot of questions."

"Well, my mother went here, so if your mom did, too, maybe they knew each other."

Right then Marcus walked over and sat down and Jane wanted to scream, *What do you think you're doing? It took me more than a week to get a seat here!* She said only, "This is Marcus. My brother."

"I know who you are." The curls of Rita's hair seemed to spring to life. "Everyone knows who you are."

Turning back to Jane she said, "How old's your mother?"

Marcus said, "She's dead," and Jane wanted to smack him.

"Oh," Rita said, curls deflating some. "Sorry."

Jane said, "But if she were alive she would've been, like, fifty, fifty-one?"

Rita shook her head. "My mom's not that old."

Jane didn't understand. "But there was a woman in the yearbook that looked *so much* like you."

"I look a lot like one of my aunts," Rita said. "She's older."

Babette pinched Jane's arm. "Why didn't you tell me?"

Jane shrugged and Babette sighed, then said, "How?"

"Brain aneurysm," Marcus said. "Here one minute, gone the next."

He looked at the second half of Rita's sandwich, untouched on a piece of waxy white paper. "You going to eat that?"

She pushed it his way and Jane noted the gold rings on her fingers, matching the hoops peeking out from those curls. She couldn't believe Marcus could be so nonchalant about things sometimes.

"Can you ask her?" Jane pressed. "Your aunt?"

"Yeah," Rita said. "Sure, I guess."

Marcus was chewing, but Jane could tell he was also subtly shaking his head.

They were all quiet for a moment and then Babette, apparently taking her tact cue from Marcus, turned to him and said, "So, did you hear about the party on Saturday?"

He nodded while he chewed, not looking up from his half sandwich.

"You should totally go."

Jane felt embarrassed on Babette's behalf.

"Hey, I just heard about the headless chicken thing." He turned to Jane as he brushed his hands together—the sandwich was gone—and got up. "You okay?"

"Yeah." Jane was annoyed that he was playing the part of the good big brother when he never did it without an audience. "It was a lifetime ago. And anyway Rita helped me out."

Marcus turned to Rita and said, "Thanks for the sandwich," then got up to throw out his trash. Rita crumbled the waxy white paper into a ball and threw it about ten feet to land in the same can a second later. She stood and pumped her fists in the air, revealing the brown skin of her taut belly. Marcus turned and smiled. Babette looked like she might cry but only for a second, only until Rita turned back to the table, pulled her shirt down. She had some serious breasts in there.

"So really," Babette said brightly to Jane, "what are you going to wear?"

The next morning a naked baby doll hung from the door of Jane's locker in a noose. The Claveracks were hovering, as usual, and Jane decided to just leave the doll there. At least for now. Maybe even all day. What did she care? It was just a doll. So she gathered her books, closed her locker, and walked away, leaving the baby hanging.

"You forgot your grandfather," Harvey said. "He looks like he could use an incubator right about now."

"That's just not funny," she said.

"You know what's really not funny?" Cliff said. "You keeping our grandfather's horse when he *made* it and has the right to do whatever he wants with it."

"And what, exactly, does he want to do with it?" she snapped.

"Sell it," Harvey snorted. "What else?" He elbowed his brother. "Ride it around the living room?"

"How much is it worth?" she asked. It wasn't like her family couldn't use the money.

"Like we'd tell you," Harvey said. "You know what, Cliff? That old house of Preemie's doesn't look that hard to break into."

"You know, Harv, you're right."

Jane said, "Breaking into the house isn't the problem. The problem is the horse is chained to the radiator and the radiator and horse combined probably weigh, I don't know, a ton? So good luck to you."

They backed away, snorting useless comebacks—"I could probably bench-press the freakin' thing"; "F.U. and the horse you rode in on"—and Jane walked back to her locker, pulled the baby off it, and walked down the hall toward Principal Jackson's office, fully prepared to register an official complaint. But when she found the office empty, she lost her nerve, tossed the doll into the trash can by the door, then hurried to Topics in Coney Island History, where Mr. Simmons was handing out postcards in see-through plastic sleeves.

"Americans bought seven hundred and seventy million, five hundred thousand postcards in 1906," he said, giving Jane a solemn raise of the eyebrows since she was officially late. "And imagine this: on one day in 1906, over two hundred thousand postcards were sent from the post office right here on Coney Island. One day. Two hundred thousand postcards."

Jane gingerly held the card Mr. Simmons handed her right then, but she also tried to bore her thoughts into the back of Leo's head.

Seahorse, seahorse, seahorse.

Postcard, postcard, postcard.

"Ms. Dryden," Mr. Simmons said. "If you will. . . ."

"Johnny," she began, then took a breath. "I'm having the time of my life here on Coney. The bars are rowdy. The women are mad."

People started laughing, and Jane felt herself start to blush. She read on: "Hope you're holding down the fort. Cheers, Geoff."

"Thank you, Ms. Dryden." Mr. Simmons nodded. "Anyone think their postcard is particularly worth sharing?"

Leo raised his hand.

"Mr. LaRocca," Mr. Simmons said. "Let's have it."

"Billy. You wouldn't believe me if I told you half the things we've been up to," Leo began, in an Irish accent.

Everyone laughed again and Jane smiled and had to resist the urge to doodle her name and Leo's in a heart. She'd dearly loved Ireland, and was impressed with the accuracy of his accent.

"Was picked up last night for drunk and disorderly behavior. Turns out the copper has a taste for the Irish; we'll have to send him a case when I return. 'Tis a mad place, this Coney. Who knew the States were so liberated? Best, Jimmy."

"Excellent," Mr. Simmons said. "Now can anyone point

out something that these messages have in common?"

In the silence that followed, Jane heard the flutter of a bird and looked out the window. A pigeon had landed on the outside ledge, and for a moment she studied it because it seemed to be studying her. She looked hard into its round pigeon eyes, wondering if maybe it was Birdie reincarnated?

"The people are having fun," Babette called out.

"Bingo," Mr. Simmons said, and he turned and wrote the word FUN on the board. "Coney was known during this era as the 'Playground of the World.' So let's talk for a minute about fun! What is it?"

Luckily he didn't seem to actually expect a response. He just kept talking. "Is fun by definition bad? Sinful?"

Now he waited.

"Not necessarily," Legs said. "If you think things like the human roulette wheel and the Shoot the Chutes are fun. Or riding wooden horses at Steeplechase Park."

"Good," Mr. Simmons said. "That's what I believe we call good clean fun, right. But Coney Island has also been called 'Sodom by the Sea.' And not by some religious fanatics or anything but by a reputable source: *The New York Times*. Who can tell me what Sodom is?"

Jane waited for someone to answer, but everyone's faces seemed blank. For the first time she wondered whether her education to date—while scattered about the globe—was actually better than she'd realized. She raised her hand, and Mr. Simmons called on her. She said, "It's a city that was destroyed by God for being so full of sin."

"Exactly," Mr. Simmons said, and Jane thought, *Thanks, Mrs. Chester,* who had taught her religious studies class in Ireland. "And it was considered sinful back in the late eighteen hundreds and early nineteen hundreds for women to cavort in the surf with their skirts pulled up, or to wear swimsuits in public. There were, let's face it, brothels here on Coney and bars—lots of bars—where people were free to overindulge."

"Sounds awesome," Leo said, and people laughed.

"How's this for fun?" Mr. Simmons said. "When Fred Trump bought Steeplechase Park, he threw a demolition party where guests were handed bricks and encouraged to destroy windows, rides, whatever, at Steeplechase. Does that sound like a fun party?"

"It sounds like a party for assholes," Leo said, and everyone laughed again and Mr. Simmons did, too. "You do have a way with words, Mr. LaRocca."

Back at the bulletin board, Mr. Simmons said, "What about executing an elephant? Or watching it? Fun?" He picked up the stack of Topsy essays and started handing them back with grades. "Some of you thought so. Others, not so much."

Jane was a little bit disappointed that she'd only gotten a B+.

"Before we meet again, I want you all to turn that sentence you wrote last week"—he winked dramatically and said, "And I know you all did it"—"into a postcard. A postcard from the place and time here on Coney where you had the most fun of your life. And I want you to send it to me."

He pointed to an address written on the board, the school's address. The class groaned.

Mr. Simmons just kept talking. "Be creative. Have fun with it. Bust out your crayons or markers if you must!"

Jane studied the main word in question—the hard corners of the F, the symmetrical curve of the U, and the jagged rise and fall of the N—but nothing was clicking. There was nothing fun about this assignment at all.

A tightly folded piece of paper landed on her desk as Mr. Simmons went on with his lesson, and she held it down low and out of sight to open it. Probably from Babette.

It said: "Still looking for that damn postcard. Want to go to the Anchor after school on Thursday?"

She looked over at Leo and he raised his eyebrows. Jane just nodded and then the bell rang.

Babette asked, "Where is your postcard going to be from?" as they headed out of the room.

"I'm not sure." It was hard to talk to Babette while walking—*and* while freaking out about Leo's invitation—but she had to try. "What about you?"

Babette looked up. "The Mermaid Parade last year. Hands down."

"What, exactly, *is* the Mermaid Parade?"

Babette's eyes widened into large blue pools.

"Sorry. But I don't know," Jane said.

Babette shook her little head. "You, my dear, are in for a treat."

"How many Preemies does it take to screw in a light-bulb?" a geek said as he passed them in the hall. Jane and Babette both braced for the punch line.

"I don't know, but it only takes one of me to screw a Preemie."

"I swear," Jane said to Babette when the geek had passed, "I'm just going to give them the stupid horse."

"And let them win?"

"They're already winning!"

"What did I tell you about reading the newspaper?"

"I read it!"

Babette stopped and huffed so that her black hair lifted off her forehead for a second. "Here's the thing about newspapers, Jane. They have *news* in them. Like *every day*. *Different* news."

"Just tell me what you're talking about."

"The city just announced that it's going to restore the Claverack carousel as part of this whole redevelopment that's happening. It's like a landmark, and they're moving it to like Ohio this winter to have it fixed up. Maybe they'd want the horse, since it was part of the original."

So the carousel was *still here*? Which meant the Claveracks were probably looking to sell the horse to the city, which wasn't the worst idea in the world, not if the horse could take its rightful place back on the original Claverack carousel. Maybe Preemie had guarded it for all those years awaiting just this sort of project. He must have had a reason for keeping it, right?

"I just want them off my case," Jane said finally, having no idea how to go about seeing if the city even wanted the damn horse.

"You think that'll happen if you hand it over?"

"It's worth a shot!"

"I see you didn't inherit Preemie's spine." Babette shook her head and walked away.

Rita, whom Jane found in the hall heading for the cafeteria at lunch that day, looked at her apologetically, then said, "So my aunt remembers your mother."

Jane's body jolted. "She does?"

"Yeah." Rita made a wincing face. "But that's all. She knew *of* her. She wasn't friends with her. She's not sure they ever actually talked. It's a big school, you know. Was then, too."

"Oh." Jane's mood deflated. "Well, thanks for asking."

Rita chewed her lip for second, then said, "Legs said you were going to try to find her in the school paper, but then you never followed up."

"He told you that?" It seemed a weird thing to share.

"You should do it." Rita shrugged, then said sadly, "I guess you don't remember a lot about her."

Jane could only shake her head, holding back tears. "I need to go in here," she said, indicating the girls' bathroom, then she ducked in with a small wave. She sighed with relief when the other girl in there went on her way, leaving the room in silence. She went into a stall and just stood there and wondered how long she could stay without being missed.

One hour? Two?

One day? Two?

The stall's thick pig-pink paint was carved up with graffiti, and Jane started reading it, wondering how old it was and whether any of it might date back to her mother's high school years. She hadn't seen any trophies. There were no old photos in glass cases. Nothing.

SAVE CONEY, she read.

Followed by: SCREW CONEY.

And then Coney crossed out and replaced by YOU.

Next to that someone had carved out CARNY ISLAND HIGH.

To which had been added SUCKS.

Looking farther up, some newish-looking writing made her want to hide out forever: PREEMIES MUST DIE.

She might have just turned up for the meeting of the Dreamland Social Club that week if it hadn't been for Venus, who found her in the hallway after school and said, "What are you still doing here?"

"Oh," Jane said. "Nothing."

Venus had her hand on the doorknob of Room 222 and twisted it before saying, "I think it's lame of you to not give them the horse, by the way." She opened the door, and Jane heard voices and laughter all mixed up together. "I know that's not the popular opinion, but there you have it."

"Thanks for sharing," Jane said, surprising herself, and Venus said, "Are you giving me attitude?"

"Of course not," Jane said, and she headed down the hall.

Any club that Venus was a member of was not a club for Jane, even if her mother *had* founded it.

There were keys in the drawer next to the sink, keys in the small drawer in the table in the front hall, keys in a dusty red glass jug on a shelf in the living room, keys on hooks inside a kitchen cabinet. None of them worked on the lock on the carousel horse.

"Whatcha doing over there?" Jane's father said from the hall when he came in and found her on the floor by the radiator, surrounded by keys. "Planning on riding off into the sunset?"

"Something like that."

Her father started down the hall toward the kitchen but Jane said, "Dad?" and he came back.

"There are kids at school whose grandfather made this horse. Carved it and painted it, the works."

"Well then, they had quite the artistic grandfather."

"Yeah." Jane hadn't really thought of it like that. "But they're sort of, well, mean. And scary. And Preemie refused to give it back but now they want us to."

"Fascinating."

Not the word Jane would have chosen, but that sure was another way of looking at it.

"So why not give it to them?" he said. "We've got to clean this place out anyway."

"That's what I thought, too. At first. But it's just, well, they're so *mean* about it. Threatening to break into the house and stuff."

"Well, I think they would've done that by now if that was their big idea." He sat on one of the couches. "I mean, the place was empty before we got here."

"True." The idea that the Claveracks were all talk was sort of appealing.

"Well, anyway." Her dad got up. "I trust you to decide what's best."

"Why would you do that?" Jane snorted.

"Because you inherited your mother's good sense."

She was down to the last key. It didn't work. "She doesn't sound to me like someone who had a lot of sense."

"Well, at the very least, she had the good sense to leave Coney."

Jane studied one of the horse's hooves. The detail really was amazing. "Why do you think Preemie even has it? I mean, why did he bother?"

Her father shrugged and said, "I don't suppose we'll ever know."

ten

THE TABLES OUT IN FRONT of the Anchor that Thursday afternoon were crowded with people, but Jane was trying to avoid eye contact with any of them lest they see how wildly underage she was. So as Leo snaked through the tables, she saw only flashes of tongues licking beer-frothy lips, and fingers sandwiching white cigarettes, and teeth chewing on puffy hot dog buns. She soon found herself standing inside next to Leo, who was beside two empty bar stools. He nodded at the shirtless man behind the bar, who nodded back. The man was opening bottles of beer for two men a few feet away, then he turned to the ancient register with some bills and Jane saw the huge serpent tattoo on his back. She softly asked, "Is that your dad?"

"I'm afraid it is," Leo said, and then his father came over. "Dad, Jane. Jane, my dad."

Jane reached out her hand when Leo's father extended his to shake. He said, "Name's Jimmy."

"Nice to meet you," Jane said, and then Leo said, "What happened to your shirt?"

His father reached across the bar and pinched Leo's face. He walked away and said, "What can I get you?" to two more people who'd just come to the bar, then slapped coasters onto the bar in front of them.

"I'm not really sure I could tell you the last time I can be certain that my father wore a shirt." Leo seemed genuinely embarrassed.

"Shirts are overrated," Jane said, and Leo said, "That's what *he* says!"

She took a seat on a high stool beside Leo and looked up at a collection of nautical-themed signs and figures hanging on the wall above the bar. There was a small cluster of "Gone Fishin'" signs next to a cluster of beach-themed ones: "Life's a Beach," "Life Is a Beach: Watch Out for the Crabs"—and then a bunch of signs like "Thataway to the Beach," pointing in the wrong direction. There were handwritten signs—things like "No Credit. No Exceptions" and "Not Responsible for Lost or Stolen Items"—and official ones, like one about how pregnant women shouldn't drink. The rest of the wall was covered in post-cards—some with the picture facing out, some with the message out—from all over the country and the world.

The jukebox must have been between songs when

they'd walked in, because right then a Beach Boys song filled the air. Jane turned to see if she could see the person who'd put on "Surfin' U.S.A." and took a guess that it was the guy wearing a green-and-yellow-checkered swimsuit who was pretending to surf on one of the bar tables—also shirtless. It was hot out. And in—since in wasn't really *in* with the bar open onto the boardwalk like that. Jane sort of wished she could be shirtless, too.

Spotting the sign for the restrooms, she excused herself, then walked toward the back of the bar, where a cracked wooden door decorated with a wooden mermaid—a fisherman for the men's room—hung on a dusty hinge. Inside, Jane examined three locks on the door, none of which inspired confidence. She opted to lock them all because the toilet was far away, on the opposite side of the long narrow room. The mirror was fogged with age, the toilet seat cracked, and water trickled in a trail of drops—like ants marching—down the pipe below the sink. Tiptoeing across the room, she made a mental note to hose her shoes down later. So far the Anchor was living up to expectations.

When she was done she looked for soap but found none, so she rinsed her hands and patted them dry with a coarse paper towel. She went back out to join Leo and saw he'd gotten them Cokes.

As soon as she sat down Leo spun away from her on his stool. There was an old man whose face looked like a baked potato sitting on the next stool down. "Hey," Leo said to him, "tell my friend here why you come to the Anchor."

"What's so great about the Anchor?" Mr. Potato-head barked back.

"Yeah," Leo said, laughing. "What's so great about the Anchor?"

"The beer's cold, the women are loose, and no one ever gets kicked out." He raised his beer and then drank heartily.

Leo's father walked by then with a big bin of ice and said, "How's my boy?" but he wasn't looking for an answer.

"I know it doesn't look like much," Leo said. "But it's just a great, low-key place. If they keep jacking up the rent, though, my father's done for."

Leo's father bounced a quarter on the bar and it landed in one of his patrons' beer mugs; people cheered. Jane had no idea how much rent on a place like this would be but had to hope for Leo's sake that his father could keep paying it.

"Your father, I trust, has a respectable job?" Leo turned to Jane, toying with a quarter in his own hand on the bar.

She knew she should come clean and tell him that her father was a roller coaster designer, but then he'd want to know more—people always did—and she didn't trust herself to not tell him that it was her secret wish that her father design a new ride for Coney.

"He's a structural engineer," she said. "But he's unemployed."

It wasn't a lie.

After a moment's silence, Leo said, "I heard about your mom."

Jane just nodded and studied the wall behind the bar until her eyes landed in a most unexpected place. It took her a minute to process what she was looking at, to jolt her body awake into the tingling state of discovery. "I found the seahorse," she said, and pointed.

He followed the line of her finger and said, "Holy shit." He got up and went around behind the bar and pulled the postcard off the wall, then handed it to Jane. On the front, a woman was kissing a toy seahorse underwater, the same seahorse that was inked into Leo's skin, the same seahorse Jane had seen in her dream. The type said "Wish you were here . . . in Weeki Wachee!"

Weeki Wachee.

It actually did sound vaguely familiar.

Leo lifted her hand so that he could see the flip side of the photo and said, "It's to my mom from somebody named Tiny."

"Tiny's *my* mom!" Jane nearly shouted. "Clementine." Then she turned it over and saw that it had been addressed to Beth Mancuso.

"Like the restaurant?" she said, turning to Leo, who nodded and said, "Family business." He looked around. "The *other* family business."

Returning to the card, Jane read: *Dear Beth: It's not the same here without you. Do you think my mother ever regretted keeping me from my true calling here in the tanks? LYLAS, Tiny.*

There were tiny drawings surrounding the writing. A mermaid smoking a cigarette while sitting on top of some kind of little round submarine. A curled ocean wave. A lobster drinking a cup of tea. She felt like she might cry.

Leo said, "I got a tattoo based on a postcard that your mother sent to my mother."

She could barely process it. "What does LYLAS mean?"

"Don't know. So wait." He got back on his stool. "Was your mother a mermaid, too?"

"What do you mean was she a mermaid?" For a second she felt like this was going to be some cruel joke.

He pointed to the swimmer on the card. "They call them mermaids. The swimmers. My mom went to some camp there when she was like fourteen. Mermaid camp."

Jane wanted to strangle him. "Why didn't you *say* so?"

He matched her in intensity when he said, "I didn't know it mattered!"

"Can we go talk to her?" Jane asked, and Leo said, "Yes," and got up. Jane thought the excitement might kill her, but then he said, "No, wait. Shit. She's in the city this afternoon. Until late. I'm sorry."

"It's okay."

"But tomorrow. After school? She's usually at the club by four."

"The club?" As in *Dreamland Social*? No, it wouldn't make sense.

"My mother runs the lounge upstairs at Mancuso's. The Coral Room. With mermaids like these." He indicated the card again. "Swimmers."

Jane couldn't find words to speak, just studied that mermaid and her cigarette and nodded.

"Come on," he said. "I'll walk you home."

"Anybody here?" Jane called out in the dusty foyer. When there was no answer, she invited Leo in.

"So there it is," he said immediately upon entering the hall, then he approached the Claverack horse and stroked it, as if it were real.

"Climb on if you want." Jane turned a lamp on; it glowed gold.

"Nah," Leo said. "I shouldn't." He stepped back from the horse. "What do you think you'll do with it?"

"I honestly have no idea." She nodded her head toward the stairs. "The rest is upstairs."

She led the way to the attic, pulled the bulb light on, and stepped aside to let Leo up the final step. He crossed the room to touch the Hell Gate demon and said, "Incredible." He shook his head a few times in disbelief. "How the *hell* did he get his hands on this?"

"I don't know. But I found this in a box of stuff." She handed a small piece of cardstock to Leo; it was an invitation to Trump's Demolition Party at Steeplechase. "He must've been on a sort of mission to save stuff. It's possible he made off with the horse the night of the party."

Leo turned to take in the rest of the room. She just watched his eyes, the way the blue in there seemed to swirl with excitement over what he was seeing. She had uncovered a few other notable pieces in Preemie's collection: an old sign from Nathan's; a sign that said "Wonder Wheel 5¢"; and a pair of old signs, one "swinging," one "stationary."

Leo shook his head. "Crazy old dude was single-handedly trying to preserve Coney. Gotta love that."

Orphans in the Surf was on the reel, and Jane moved to the projector and turned it on. Leo swatted at the title card projected on his shirt, then laughed and moved out of the way. He turned and watched, and the only sounds in the room were the whir of the motor, the click of the film, and their breathing.

"It's so sad," Leo said as the film played, and Jane just nodded, watching the kids run through the surf.

Ashes, ashes. We all fall down.

The film ended and she turned the projector off. Leo said, "Do you think they were really orphans?"

She shrugged. "It's almost sadder if they're not. Because that would be cruel, you know?"

Leo stuck his hand into the box of reels and pulled one out. "What's on this one?"

It was a reel Jane hadn't watched yet. She'd been taking it slowly, savoring them, spreading them out over time. But Leo was there and he was asking, so she changed the reels, threaded the film. When the image of the entryway of Luna Park appeared on-screen—with its moon slices and towers and lights—she and Leo both sat cross-legged on the floor and watched.

It must have been a reel that they showed in movie houses, advertising Coney Island to tourists, because it was just a series of clips of amusement park attractions with people enjoying them. Jane recognized some of the amusements from pictures she'd seen, but to see them in action was another thing entirely. *There* was the human roulette wheel, with a bunch of people spinning round and round on a big circular disc, then being shot out off it when they couldn't hold on any longer. *There* was the crazy spiral roller-coaster ride. Who would have guessed that the whole thing spun like a top on one big axis while cars rolled down the track. She wished she knew what it had been called, longed for it to have a name.

"Do you think it's weird to be nostalgic for something you never even experienced?" she said, and Leo said, "No," softly, shaking his head in the dark. Jane was suddenly *this close* to tears for reasons she couldn't explain. Something about these images reached deep inside her, as if looking for a memory there, but it wouldn't come. Not yet. She pushed the emotion aside and just watched. Because maybe it was nothing, not a memory at all. Maybe it was just that seeing Luna Park in action was more powerful than seeing it in photos.

That Coney Island, *old* Coney Island, had been something worth saving. Only no one had.

When the reel ended, Leo said, "I'd give my right arm for a time-travel machine," and Jane felt like her heart might burst. Then when he said, "So tomorrow, you'll meet my mom," she was sure of it.

■　■　■

"I found something I want to show you," she said to her father later that day. He fixed himself a cup of tea and then climbed up to the attic behind her, and Jane felt at once like she was about to do something both potentially great and potentially dumb. "Sit," she said, and she reloaded the reel.

The images were no less magical the second time around, and Jane alternated between watching Luna Park come to life again and studying her father's rapt face, lit by the film's glow.

"Wow," he said when the film was done.

"Wasn't it amazing?" she said.

"It was." He nodded, then sipped his tea, swallowed. "And you know something? I gave your mother a hard time about wanting to name you after Luna Park. Now I sort of wish I hadn't."

Jane said, "It should be that way again, don't you think?"

He was quiet.

"You could help, Dad. It's what you do."

"Did," he said. "It's what I did."

"I know you're working on something," she said. "I saw you."

He got up, breathed hard, and said, "Well, come on then. I'll show you."

He led her to his office, which she hadn't entered since the day they moved in. There were books splayed across the floor and overgrown plants hanging from the ceiling by the window. The books and knickknacks on the shelves were crooked, knocked over, covered in dust. It was arguably the only room in the house that looked worse now than it had the day they arrived.

She followed her father to a desk in the corner by the window overlooking the garden. She could feel a cyclone in her gut when she saw a drawing of a roller coaster that shot out off the shore and over the ocean on a pier and then peaked and rode back in like a tidal wave. It appeared to plunge down through the sand of the beach into a tunnel and reappear out of the boardwalk. She saw the Coney Island skyline sketched in light strokes in a second drawing of the same coaster: the Parachute Jump was on there; so was the Wonder Wheel.

Her father was looking at it alongside her and said, "I had this basic concept years ago. I can't even remember where. But it was never quite right." He ran a hand over the page. "It's called the Tsunami."

The front door opened downstairs and then Marcus called out, "Hello?" Jane and her dad both said, "Up here," and then Marcus bounded up the stairs and came into the room. "What's going on?"

Jane pointed, and he came to her side and studied the renderings. "Wow," he said.

"Yeah," Jane said. "Wow."

It really was incredible.

Especially that spiral track that seemed to twist right up through the boardwalk. "Does it go underground?" she asked. "Through the beach?"

"That's the idea," her father said. "Yes."

"Cool, Dad," Marcus said.

"So you're going to submit it to the city?" Jane said.

"What's the city got to do with it?" Marcus said.

"They're accepting bids for new ride designs," Jane explained curtly.

"I don't know," her father said. "It still needs more work. And it's a bit over the top, budget-wise, I think."

"You *have* to submit it," she protested.

He shrugged, then looked at his own drawings. "I guess I can make a few calls."

"It's really amazing, Dad." She turned to give him a hug.

"Yeah," Marcus said. "Seriously."

"Thanks." He looked like he might cry, but then he said, "Oh, and not a word about this to anyone, okay? Because if nothing comes of it, well, you know . . ."

Jane considered right then telling her father and Marcus that she'd located a friend of Mom's. But maybe caution was in order there, too. *Because if nothing ever comes of it . . .*

"Sure, Dad," Jane said, barely able to contain her excitement about it all. "Of course."

When sleep wouldn't come—*Leo's mom, the Tsunami, Leo's mom, the Tsunami*—she climbed out of bed and looked out at the Parachute Jump and tried to picture one of her father's creations in its shadows. She imagined what the coaster's sign might look like, with a big blue-and-white wave hanging threateningly over the capital T of Tsunami.

She imagined lines of people, waiting for a chance to ride and then spilling out onto the boardwalk to talk about how amazing it was. No doubt some of them—a lot of them—would go to the Anchor for a beer. Leo's dad would be able to pay as much rent as he needed, and whatever Loki did just wouldn't compare.

She wished the mermaid doll on her night table would come to life and give her some tips on keeping secrets. Because she wanted to tell Leo and Babette and anyone else she could think of about the Tsunami.

Please let this happen, she begged. Though she wasn't quite sure who she was begging. She just didn't want to have to be there to pick up the pieces of her father if this didn't come through for him.

The old window rattled in the wind then, and she pulled the covers up against the empty house and whispered to herself, inviting sleep with three sentences on a loop:

This is your captain.
We are passing through a storm.
We are quite safe. . . .

eleven

SHE WAS GOING TO BE EARLY to meet Leo and his mother at the club after school if she didn't slow the hell down, so she stopped to look at one of the big vacant lots that had been plastered with THE FUTURE OF CONEY ISLAND HAS ARRIVED signs. She hadn't noticed the logo on the signs the first time she saw them, but she saw it now.

Loki.

The god of mischief. A shape-shifter.

(Thanks, Mr. Motamed of Introduction to Mythology.)

The *I* of the logo took the shape of a serpent.

She wasn't sure that was the best kind of name—or logo—for a company that was coming into a neighborhood and causing so much trouble; it was almost like they were bragging. But maybe there was no good name for a company like that.

At the gate to Wonderland, she looked up at that Mad Hatter. It had been a long time since she'd read *Alice's Adventures in Wonderland*, but she remembered that weird tea party, the way the Mad Hatter talked in riddles. *Why is a raven like a writing desk?*, he'd asked Alice at one point, and Jane had been boggled for days, constantly asking Marcus to tell her the answer. She couldn't remember how long it took her to understand that there was no answer. That question, too, was unanswerable.

She turned down the block that ran alongside the park and stopped by the Polar Express ride—a series of cars that ran around a circular track with hills—and studied the paintings on it, of skiers in goggles mid-jump and, of course, polar bears with big white hairy bellies. She remembered a joke her brother used to tell, about a baby polar bear who keeps asking his parents, "Are you sure I'm not a brown bear or a black bear?" They always tell him, "No, you're our own baby polar bear and we've loved you and cherished you since the day you were born." Finally, the parents ask their baby polar bear why he keeps asking this question. He looks around and says, "Because I don't know about you, but I'm *freezing*."

Walking farther down the side of the park, she stopped by the Pirate Ship ride—this park was pretty loosey-goosey with its theme—and wondered what would happen when the park's lease was up in the spring, as that article had said. In the meantime, she guessed the park would close for the season in just a few weeks, with their fate hanging in the balance. It wasn't the nicest amusement park she'd ever seen, but she felt a little sad, anyway, when she wondered where the Polar Bears and Pirates might end up. She closed her eyes and imagined walking a pirate ship's plank, falling off into choppy seas with an *Aarrrgh!*

There must have been a hundred fish in the tank at the Coral Room. And the tank must have been two stories high. Right as Jane walked into the empty club, a school of something gold swam by and turned in sync, and Jane nearly gasped with surprise. Resting on a seabed that appeared to be actual sand were coral clusters and sea anemones—waving gently like Leo's hair—and a treasure chest overflowing with costume jewelry.

It was absolutely dazzling . . . at first. But on closer inspection, the rest of the room was less so. The velvet curtains and couches looked a little nubby, and the floor appeared matted, scuffed. There were rips in the leather on some of the booth seats around the room's perimeter. Jane didn't care.

Leo and his mother were sitting at a table in a far corner and Jane approached. His mom wore a dress that was sparkly—almost bubbly—and made of something shimmery and pink. With straight blond hair cut to her chin and lips painted cherry red, she looked clean and crisp and inviting, like a cocktail. She was the exact opposite of Leo's dad, but sometimes, Jane guessed, that worked.

Leo said, "I'll leave you two alone," and Leo's mom

looked sad and happy at the same time. She pulled Jane into a hug, and she smelled as fruity and crisp as she looked. "I'm Beth," she said. "It's wonderful to meet you."

Jane just let herself be absorbed and waited, unnerved by how good it felt to be held just so.

"Birdie used to update me, whenever she got letters from your mother." She pulled away. "I can't believe it's you. I mean, you're *hers*."

Behind Beth, in the aquarium, seaweed swayed slightly as a tiger fish swam through it. Up close like this, the gravel sparkled like silver and the sea sponges looked like brains. Jane tried to imagine a woman, dressed like a mermaid, swimming around and waving at people sitting at the bar. It sounded sort of silly and also, well, fun.

"Sit." Beth sank back into her chair. "We were best friends, your mom and me. For a long time."

Jane had so many questions to ask, but the one that came to her lips was "What was she like?"

"What was she like. Gosh." Beth had a faraway look in her eyes. "What was she like." Her lips softened into a smile. "She was an absolute doll. Sweetest, most thoughtful woman you'd ever meet. And boy, could she tell a joke. And flirt. Oh, the woman flirted like a pro. But she wasn't fake about it. She just really enjoyed people, you know? She could talk to anyone about anything. I mean, anybody. All walks of life."

Jane nodded, waited for more.

"I don't know. She was just . . . fun. Fun to be around." *The very thing that I'm not.*

Beth reached across the table and squeezed Jane's hand. "It was an awful thing that happened to her." And released her hand. "To you. I still can't believe it. You look just like her, you know."

Jane felt the tears start to generate behind her eyes.

I can't believe it either. I didn't know. Or she *thought* she knew, just from the pictures she had seen. But no one had ever *told* her.

To keep her eyes from giving in, she focused them on another fish in the tank, this one a really small blue fish with a slash of white on its side.

Beth stood and seemed to shake something off, then said, "You hungry?"

Jane nodded.

"Let's get some food, hmmm?"

She summoned a waiter and they invited Leo back over, and they sat and ate in the empty lounge, in the rippling light of the aquarium's spotlights, while Beth told stories about Jane's mom. Like how they used to piss off the guy who ran the water balloon game that competed with Preemie's by only ever playing when they were the only two around, so that one of them was guaranteed to win. She talked about their terrible, terrible sunburns, how they would have to spray themselves down every fifteen minutes for hours with something called Solarcaine because it hurt so bad, before people knew how bad the sun really was for you. She talked about winters on Coney, how she and Jane's mom would eat piping-hot potato knishes from Mrs. Stalz's in Brighton Beach almost every day after school. She talked about mermaid camp, when they were fourteen. How Birdie had driven them down to Florida in her beat-up old car in a two-day frenzy, and how Jane's mom had had to be put in the car forcibly when camp was done. She had wanted to stay, had wanted to drop out of high school and train to be a mermaid for real.

"Your mother went back after high school. To audition." Beth shook her head. "But they didn't have any openings. That's when she sent that postcard. Then I went away to college and she went to art school and got married and took off, and we lost touch."

"What does this mean?" Jane pointed at the LYLAS.

"Love you like a sister," Beth said sadly.

They were done eating, and she sat back in her chair. "We used to do crazy things. Your mother was the troop leader."

"What kind of crazy things?"

"We used to break into the amusement parks at like two, three in the morning."

"You *did*?" Leo said. It was the first he'd spoken the whole time.

"Sure. We used to climb to the top of the Thunderbolt after dark and smoke cigarettes."

"What?" Leo said. "You're kidding me."

"What's the Thunderbolt?" Jane asked.

"An old roller coaster that got knocked down." Beth seemed to be enjoying the memories now. "And we'd try to climb the Parachute Jump, but we never got very far before we either got scared or got caught."

Leo was shaking his head and smiling.

"Your mother was a bad influence." Beth smiled. "In the best possible way. Sneaking beers onto the Wonder Wheel. She had keys to everything. I don't even know how." She turned to Leo. "But don't go getting any ideas."

Then sadness tugged at the corners of her eyes. She took the postcard into her hands and studied the little drawings. "She used to doodle all the time. She had this crazy journal she carried everywhere and she was always writing stuff down. Lyrics and quotes from poems, but mostly doodling. My God, the doodling."

A deliveryman had come in, carrying some boxes. "I have to take this," Beth said, and got up. Leo and Jane got up, too. "But please. Come and see me again. We'll talk more. Okay?"

Jane nodded, and Beth went to sign for the delivery.

Stepping up close to the aquarium now, Jane looked up at the tallest kelp plant, a deep orange underwater tree that stretched high to the top of the tank. Just above her head she noticed a starfish clinging to the glass and she put her hand up, pressed it against the glass, against the five points. She thought she saw one of them twitch.

Jane looked under the mattress and up on that high shelf of the closet and behind all the drawers in the dresser and then under the bed, by the springs, but didn't find a journal anywhere. She went down to Birdie's Bavarian Bar and looked in the chest of clothes, and still nothing. No journal.

She brought her mermaid book into bed that night and

reread the inscription. *My dear daughter, I used to be a mermaid once so I know that mermaids are good at a lot of things, like keeping secrets. I hope your life is full of them. Love, Mom.*

It was such a weird inscription. But mostly, it was a ridiculously weird book. A book full of pictures of mermaids.

The Mermaid's Secret.

Who *publishes* that?

Who, besides her kooky mother, would actually buy it?

The pages were mostly filled with illustrations, of course. Mermaids didn't really exist. And some of them were ridiculously over the top. Because would mermaids really find it practical to have hair that long? Would they really wear makeup? For the first time Jane regretted that this was the one book her mother had left her, the one book she'd come to cherish above all others. It was possible mermaids were good at keeping secrets, but this book held none. There were no life lessons to be learned in its pages, no inspiration to be found. It was story-less.

She flipped and flipped until she found what she suddenly knew she'd find: the same photo that appeared on the postcard her mother had sent Leo's mother.

The seahorse.

Being kissed by a mermaid.

Right there on page 45.

She remembered, when she was younger, not understanding why there were regular women in old-fashioned bathing suits pictured in a book about mermaids, but she'd never bothered to read the captions before. This one said "Mermaids at Weeki Wachee, 1959."

Setting the book aside, Jane picked up the mermaid doll and wound it and still no music came out.

Song-less.

Only then did she study the underside of the doll and discover the stitches—a rip that had been repaired. Thinking that odd, she got out a pair of scissors and snipped the thread away. Because maybe the doll could be fixed, made to sing, after all.

Reaching into the mermaid's innards, she felt something hard and was able to hook her finger on it. The keys she pulled out hung on a small silver hoop, and each one was labeled with a small taped-on piece of paper. One said "Jump," one said "Thunder," a third said "Wonder," and another "Bath."

We used to climb the Parachute Jump.

We used to smoke on the Thunderbolt.

She held them in her hand and felt a sort of completion in her heart, like her body had been trying to draw a circle for years and had finally connected two points.

Thunder. Jump. Wonder. Bath.

Mermaids were good at keeping secrets after all.

*U*nder the too-white lights of the Rite Aid, it's hard to know what time it is, let alone what kind of makeup will look good on me. At a party. Tonight. If tonight ever gets here. A check of my watch reveals that only a minute has passed since I last checked.

Time can be a trickster.

Memory, too.

Can I remember, for example, anyone ever teaching me how to apply makeup?

No.

Of course not.

But my mother. Now there was a woman who knew how to wear makeup. Though why I think that I'm not even sure. Except that I remember jars of goo, cases of tiny squares of shimmering colors, and soft brushes—big and small—wherever we lived. I remember her brushing makeup onto my cheeks and onto my eyelids when I begged. I remember looking in the mirror then and seeing nothing there and being a little bit confused but still feeling pretty. Like her, with her silver–dusted eyelids and ruby red lips. Now I know she was faking.

I pick up a pale shade of fleshy cover-up, some rosy blush, and a lip gloss that looks sort of like the color of my lips but with a bit of sparkle. I grab mascara but skip the rest of the eye stuff, since I don't know what to do with it anyway, and honestly have no idea how any person can pull off silver eyelids.

I swing by hair products and grab some of those: a pomade that claims to "Energize," a gel that smooths, a mousse that adds body. I've got all my bases covered.

Hands full, I head toward the register, surprised to see Halloween candy, since it's still only September. I consider buying decorations for the house—paper cutouts of pumpkins with demonic faces carved out of them and of witches with gap teeth on broomsticks—but decide not to. It's pretty much fright night at Preemie's house every night. I've all but stopped going downstairs after dark to get water lest my eyes fall on that horse, with its glassy eyes and bared teeth.

Shivers.

But the question of the horse is no longer the priority.

Thunder. Jump. Wonder. Bath.

These are the new priorities, as is not making a complete fool of myself at this party.

I recognize a guy from school a few spots ahead of me, already at the checkout counter, and I make the mistake of noticing that he is buying condoms. The thought that some of my classmates are having sex, will maybe be having sex tonight, fills me with dread and makes me a little queasy. I've only ever kissed a boy once. In London. So it wasn't even that long ago but it feels that way, and I have to work to remember his name, the way I've been working so hard to remember so many other things.

Martin.

Martin Booth.

It wasn't an especially good kiss and I didn't really care that much at the time; I just thought it would be nice to get that out of the way. The first. It was, after all, past due. But now I sort of wish it had been better. Or that I'd waited for someone else.

For, let's face it, Leo.

There is a problem with the line. An old lady is arguing about the price of a certain kind of toilet paper and the cashier is patiently explaining that the circular the old lady is holding is not the current one and that the sale was for the four-pack not the six-pack of rolls anyway. Nothing in the whole store seems to be moving except for their lips and even those seem so . . . very . . . slow. I hope I never become the kind of person who will keep a girl from party prep on account of the price of t.p.

Because I can't bear to just wait—it makes time go even more slowly—I double back to the hair products and put back the tub called "Energize," now that I've had ample opportunity to actually notice its exorbitant price. After that, I swing down the aisle that holds stomach remedies, but the queasiness has passed now that the guy from school and his condoms are no longer in the store.

I keep moving.

Movement makes time go faster.

The cashier calls for a manager through the store intercom, so I decide to wander a few more aisles. Maybe I'm forgetting something.

Toothpaste. Check.

Razors. Check.

Shampoo. Conditioner. A-okay.

On my way back to the cashier, eventually, I pass through the Halloween section again, this time noticing the costumes. A pirate. Mickey Mouse. Tinker Bell. And a mermaid. And then I am remembering that I am lying on my big, blue beanbag chair as my mother wraps a sheet around my legs.

We are playing mermaids, and the beanbag is supposed to be a seashell, my favorite place to lounge and watch the ocean go by. When my legs are wrapped and the sheet tied with some kind of scarf to help make a fin at the bottom, my mother wraps her own legs up, too, and lies down on the floor in front of me.

"We're not like other women," she sings as she starts to fan herself with a folding fan. "We don't have to clean an oven."

I'm giggling and pretending to fan myself, too.

"And we nev-er will grow old. . . ." she sings. "We've got the world by the tail!"

My journal is in the next room—the kitchen—and I

get up and shuffle over to get it because I want to draw a mermaid in it, but as soon as I turn to bring it back to my shell, my mother says, "Eh–eh–eh. It'll get wet."

"But I want to draw a mermaid," I say. I can't write a lot of letters yet, only the four that spell my name. So my journal is full of pictures, and I only keep it at all because my mother keeps one and it makes me feel grown-up.

"A self-portrait," my mother says with a laugh. "Great idea. But you'll have to do it when you're above water." She's still fanning herself and smiling.

"But we live down here."

She gets up and shimmies into the kitchen and comes back with a clear plastic Ziploc bag. "Keep it in here to keep it dry," she says. "And we'll find a good place to hide it."

"What about behind that shell?" I say, pointing to an ashtray on the coffee table.

"Let's look around," she says, and she uses her arms to pretend to swim around the room. "I bet there's a submarine around here somewhere or a shipwreck or a . . ."

I am struggling again in Rite Aid now.

With a word.

The word at the end of the memory that is missing.

And in a moment I am on line again and I am afraid to look at my watch.

———

Part Two

———

THE KEYS TO
CONEY ISLAND

CHAPTER

I N HER ROOM JANE PUT ON some cover-up, blush, and lip gloss. She put a little goop on her fingers and ran it through her hair, then slipped into Birdie's burgundy dress. She put some money, her keys, and her lip gloss into a beaded purse she'd found in Birdie's Bavarian Bar and looked for her father to tell him she was going out. When she couldn't find him or Marcus, she left a note on the kitchen table, then headed out to meet Babette.

Jane walked away from the boardwalk toward Surf Avenue and turned right, then walked past Nathan's and the Coney Island Museum and a bunch of stores. She stopped in front of Luna Park Furniture with a seed of excitement, but then all she saw inside were leather couches and ornate end tables and kitchen tables made of something mirrored and something black. It didn't seem fair that such an ordinary store could bear the name of Luna Park. Then again, she was named Luna, and she wasn't exactly a dazzling specimen either. She felt more like one than she had in years, though—only wished that it were a different night, a different era, that she were on her way to Luna Park—*Electric Eden*—and not the projects. She passed a few creepy-looking men and tried to push down her fear by imagining a dazzling world of lights, and shimmering lakes, and ladies in gowns and men with top hats, all on their way to Trip to the Moon or Shoot the Chutes, and suddenly wished her brother had come with her.

There was no sign of Babette in front of the McDonald's where they'd planned to meet. Big double arches came up out of the ground in front and then disappeared into the building's roof, and Jane peeked inside to see if the yellow structures, like huge, B-movie spider legs, continued there. The McDonald's definitely seemed like it was out of another era, just not the right one. Maybe built in the fifties. Babette pulled on her arm.

"Okay. I think I like." She twirled a finger. "Turn around."

Jane complied and Babette said, "A lot of people couldn't really pull if off, the vintage thing. But for you, it sort of works. It turns you from sort of boring into sort of, I don't know, edgy."

Now that was a compliment Jane could get behind. She knew she wasn't beautiful or pretty or, despite Leo's claim to the contrary, *cute*. But edgy had a ring to it. It was how she felt inside, too.

The projects didn't seem all that different from the other apartment complexes around Coney. All the faces they passed as they wound their way down a few paths between buildings were black, but that was the only difference Jane could see, and she still didn't really get it. What a "project" even was.

They got in an elevator, then came out an outdoor corridor where Babette rang the doorbell of Apartment 12-09. A gorgeous guy—Babette had been right about that, at least—answered the door and looked at Jane in confusion.

Babette said, "H.T. told us to come," and the guy looked down at her. She said, "You're Mike, right?"

"No," he said. "Ike."

"Shit," Babette said. "Sorry."

He shrugged and let them in. "H.T.'s in the kitchen."

"Cool," Babette said. "Thanks."

The apartment had an amazing view through huge windows facing the ocean. Jane walked right over to it and looked out at a cruise ship that was making its way into New York Harbor. She imagined its captain's view, wondered if he could see her tiny figure at the window through binoculars. Babette appeared at her side with two beers, though Jane took one sip and decided it would be her last. Too much booze and she'd probably turn to Babette and say what she was really thinking.

What are we doing here?

Why are we the only white people?

Is Leo coming?

That was the sort of stuff that was better left unsaid. That and things like *I found a set of secret keys inside a mermaid doll.*

That didn't mean she wasn't going to say it, though.

Leo was popular. He would definitely be coming.

Right?

The party seemed to take some kind of turn just a few minutes later when a big group came in all at once. Suddenly, the room felt electric, charged, and Jane felt buzzed without so much as a second sip of her beer. "Come on," Babette said. "Let's say hi to Debbie."

And so Jane was finally introduced to the bearded girl. Her hair was light brown, so her beard was, too, and it wasn't coarse-looking at all. Jane couldn't help but think it was actually sort of, well, pretty. When Babette ducked away to get another beer, Debbie blurted, "My mother's the bearded lady at the sideshow. I'm thinking about electrolysis, though."

Jane just nodded.

Debbie said, "You can touch it if you want," and stroked her beard. "It's soft."

"No," Jane said. "That's okay." She really had no interest.

"Oh, come on," Debbie said, then took Jane's hand and pulled it toward her face. Jane complied and stroked it for a second, then shrugged. "It's just a beard," she said. "My dad used to have one."

Debbie raised her beer can to toast. "Now you, I like. And your grandmother, for the record, was one cool lady." Debbie nodded her head approvingly and Jane said, "You knew her?"

"Not really, but I've seen her movies and I used to see her around. I asked her for her autograph once and she told me to feck off."

"*Feck?* Really?"

"Yeah, like in a funny way."

"Oh, okay."

They both just looked out at the room for a minute and Jane tried to think of something to say. Then Debbie said, "So are you thinking of joining any clubs or anything?"

"I don't know," Jane said, stiffening, then decided how to answer. "I move a lot. With my family. Maybe math club or something, though. What clubs are you in?"

It felt like a dare.

She'd seen Debbie in the hall near Room 222 after school that Wednesday.

"Oh, just the math team and science club." Babette was almost back. "Some others . . ."

Jane hadn't noticed the music equipment in the corner until Leo was up at the microphone, guitar in hand, with three other guys—one of whom was either Mike or Ike—behind him. The twin who wasn't in the band approached Leo, said something, and Leo stepped away from the mike.

The twin said, "Give it up for my boy, Leo. And check out my brother rockin' the bass. Here they are, for your entertainment . . . Cleon!"

A couple of people clapped and woo-hooed, then people started moving forward to watch as the band kicked in with a burst of guitar blare and bass booms. Jane had a weird angle on the stage and saw the seahorse on Leo's neck, where muscles and veins were shifting as he sang. She saw Venus across the room and thought, *Told you so. It* was *familiar,* then decided not to give Venus another thought.

The song was full-on, fierce, an assault on the ears but not in a bad way. And it was followed by another and another—and the room pulsed and sweat—and then the whole party seemed to inhale and wait when Leo put his guitar down. No one wanted it to be over, least of all Jane. But Mike or Ike—whichever twin wasn't in the band—handed a chair up to the stage, such as it was, and Leo sat down and picked up a saw.

Yes—Jane had checked again—a saw.

Like from a hardware store.

And with the barest of accompaniment from Mike or Ike—whichever one *was* in the band—on a keyboard set to sound like an old-timey piano, Leo started to play the saw with a violin bow. Jane closed her eyes and listened to the sound—it was uncanny how like a woman it sounded—and recognized the tune somewhere deep in her heart.

Meet me tonight in Dreamland . . .

Opening her eyes, she watched as each person in the room seemed drawn to Leo and his saw. She could only catch glimpses of him as the crowd moved forward to see what was going on, but he was there, working the saw, which bounced and bent and vibrated in his hands.

And even though it was a wordless melody, even though it was clearly not human, Jane swore she could hear the lyrics. Swore it sounded almost exactly like her mother's voice, humming her to sleep. . . .

She pushed through one room after the next when the band was finished, looking for Leo in the sweaty, drunken crowd—the keys gripped tightly in her hand—but when she found him, he was down the hall, pinned against a wall by Venus. She couldn't see their faces, but his hands were on the skin between her tiny top and low-rise jeans, their bodies pressed together tight.

Jane's gut retracted as if from a punch.

She turned away and decided to find Babette and go home, but then she heard Leo call her name. She turned back.

"Hey." He came closer, then nodded in the general direction of his performance. "What'd you think?"

"Oh." The moment, the magic, Dreamland was all gone. All she could think about was that shiny red bra, of his hands on Venus's waist. "You were great."

"Thanks," he said, but he looked sort of hurt, like she hadn't really meant it.

Her body jolted forward from a push, and the keys fell

from her hand as she fell into Leo and then recovered with the help of his strong arm.

"Hey," Leo said, pushing Harvey Claverack in the chest with both hands.

"Mike! Ike!" Leo called out, and immediately the twins and a few other guys were dragging Harvey away, telling him he was out of line, unwelcome.

"She's not giving you the horse!" Leo snapped as Harvey disappeared through the door.

I'm not? Jane wanted to say.

"You okay?" Leo said finally.

She worked hard to breathe and nodded, then realized the keys weren't in her hand or anywhere that she could see. Bending down to look for them, she heard Venus calling from down the hall, "Leo, come out to play," in a singsong, over and over.

Some kind of inside joke.

"Hey," Leo said softly, and he took her elbow and helped her up. "What did you lose?"

Right then she saw them and bent to snatch them up. She'd been so mad a few minutes before that she wasn't going to tell him, after all, but now, well . . . "So you know how your mom said that she and my mom used to break into places after dark and stuff?"

Leo nodded.

"I found these." Jane opened her hand and Leo took the keys, his fingers briefly brushing hers.

He flipped through them and examined the labels. "Oh. My. Garage."

Her pulse quickened at the phrase, which she was sure she'd heard before, from her mother's mouth. *This* was the kind of boy her mother would have hung out with, flirted with. *This* was the kind of boy who spoke her mother's language. He was exactly the kind of boy—no, he was *the exact boy*—Jane needed. She said, "Do you think any of them still work?"

"From the look in your eyes," he said, "I'd guess you were going to try to find out?"

Jane nodded and said, "I'd be afraid to do it alone." Which was true, but of course not exactly why she was asking.

He handed the keys back. "Is that an invitation?"

She nodded. "What are you doing later?"

He smiled again. "Isn't it already later?"

She shook her head. "Two a.m. Like our mothers did."

"You're serious."

"Very."

He nodded and said, "You're on."

"Well, you survived," Babette said when they cut up to the boardwalk to walk home. She patted Jane on the back of her calf. "I'm proud of you, kid."

"Thanks," Jane said.

She was about to tell Babette everything she'd been keeping to herself—about the postcard, about the fact that her mother and Leo's had been friends, about the keys—but the words that came out were "Is Venus Leo's girlfriend?"

"I don't think so." Babette shook her tiny head and seemed to be walking too hard in order to keep up.

Jane slowed her gait. "I think I saw them kissing."

"Well, either they were or they weren't."

"I couldn't be sure."

Babette's voice was small, like the wind had snatched her up and carried her far away, when she said, "It probably doesn't mean anything."

But Jane knew that wasn't true.

Everything meant something.

CHAPTER

two

IT WASN'T EASY TO SNEAK OUT of Preemie's house. Floorboards creaked. Doors whined. The staircase practically whistled "Dixie" when walked down. But Jane tiptoed and stepped on the stairs at their wall edge and opened the doors in slow motion and finally managed to get out undetected. The street was dark, abandoned, so she took off running to meet Leo outside the Anchor.

It was 2:00 a.m. and the bar was still open, still loud. But they weren't staying. No one even noticed as they moved away and sat on a bench to make a plan. Leo had a backpack hooked on one shoulder, and Jane suddenly regretted not coming more prepared, though she had no idea what she would have brought apart from the keys, which were in her jeans pocket.

"So." She took them out. "I'm guessing this one has to do with the Parachute Jump. And this one the Thunderbolt. The other two, I have no idea. Bath, no clue. And I guess this one's either the Wonder Wheel or Wonderland."

Leo nodded and said, "I say we start with Thunder."

"But I thought you said it was gone." She had already accepted that that key might be useless, that they all might be. But she wanted to be sure.

"It's gone," Leo said, and they took off down the boardwalk. "But we can still go there."

"I don't understand."

"Some stuff is never really gone." He led Jane down along the side of an abandoned lot that faced the boardwalk and a side street she'd walked down countless times before, right to a padlock on an old chain-link fence and said, "Okay. Try it."

Jane got the keys out, then took the lock in her hand and inserted the key. Sure enough, the lock turned.

"Unbelievable," she said, and Leo said, "Well, this may be the only key that does anything. This lot hasn't changed hands in like thirty years."

In they went, stomping over tall weeds and cracked bottle glass, eventually taking cover behind a small trailer that looked abandoned. Not that Jane got the impression anyone was there to see them or that anyone who saw them would care, but it felt like taking cover anyway, their backs leaning up against the metal wall.

"There's nothing here," Jane said.

"Nothing but ghosts," Leo said. "This land is owned by a fried chicken mogul. The same chicken mogul that wanted to try to rebuild Steeplechase Park in the eighties."

"For real?" Jane said. Clearly, this chicken mogul would have to be found, so that her father could pitch his coaster to him, too. She desperately wanted to tell Leo about it all, but she simply couldn't break her father's trust.

"Yup." Leo nodded.

"Why didn't it happen?"

"Same reason most things here don't happen. Money. Greed. Ego. Lack of follow-through. But this is where the Thunderbolt used to be." He unzipped his backpack, pulled out a photo album and a flashlight and then a small blanket. "I was there when they knocked it down. Want to see?"

"Of course."

He opened the blanket up and they sat. He handed her the album and moved closer, shining the flashlight on the first photo. There was Leo, as a boy, standing on the board-walk with the Thunderbolt—a long series of track hills and valleys—behind him. The coaster's support beams had been overgrown by shrubs and weeds and climbing vines, and Jane had to push away an image of Venus's viney arms around Leo. He said, "That was the day before we heard the mayor was having it ripped down. It was two thousand, so I was like five or six."

Jane turned the page and saw Leo again, next to what looked like a shack beneath the coaster. "People lived there," he said.

Uh-oh, I think I hear a train coming. Jane's hands formed fists, as if bracing for some kind of impact.

My mom is shaking the pot on the stove and saying, "Oh, no. Better hold on or we'll lose our dinner."

My brother and I are jumping around and he's making a rumbling noise. We're playing that we live under a roller coaster and every few minutes all hell breaks loose.

He stops rumbling and my mom stops shaking the pot, and she wipes her brow and says, "Whew! That was a close one!" She puts an empty pan in the oven and says, "I better get this in before the next coaster comes by."

"I'll help," I say. "I'll set the table."

My brother says, "You can't set the table, you idiot. It's all going to slide off."

"Marcus," my mother says. "Be nice."

I feel confused and left out and then my mother says, "Uh-oh. I think I hear another one. Everybody hold on!" She runs and grabs me and picks me up and spins me around and the rumbling—my mom and brother making deep rumbling sounds—starts again. . . .

Leo was still talking. "And before that, it was a hotel. They actually built the coaster around the hotel—like put steel support beams through the hotel—to save the building. People don't do stuff like that anymore." He shook his head. "They just knock shit down."

She wanted to tell him right then about the Coney games of her childhood, about her mother. But it felt like maybe it was too soon and too, well, heavy.

Together they looked through pages and pages of photos of the Thunderbolt after it had been turned into a pile of metal and wood and wire. There were lone coaster cars sitting in the middle of the field days later, and then the book ended with another shot of Leo, on the same spot on the boardwalk as in the first shot, but with nothing but sky behind him.

"This is amazing." Jane handed the album back. "Thanks."

"It's weird." Leo thumbed the pages. "I find myself looking at it a lot. I'm not sure why. Maybe to remind myself of what's possible. What's likely, even. I got this tattoo"—he pointed to a T struck through by a bolt of lightning on his calf—"because of the way my father always talked about the Thunderbolt and about Coney in general. I think I wanted something permanent, you know?"

"Was that your first one?"

"Nah, this was my first one." He pointed to an anchor on his arm.

"Why'd you get that one?"

"Things were weird." He shook his head. "*Bad* weird. My parents had just separated."

"Oh," Jane said. "I didn't know."

"Yeah, they're like this Coney Island power couple with their two bars. And with my mother doing all her Coney Islanders for Coney stuff. Only they're not." He nodded. "I think I wanted to prove to myself I could do something just for me. I wasn't allowed. I couldn't afford it. But I did it anyway. I can't explain, but it was like tricking myself into thinking things would get better, and that I was in control."

"Did they? Get better?"

"Yeah, actually. They did. In my head anyway. I guess that's why I haven't stopped yet."

Jane looked at his neck, saw his Adam's apple travel down his throat, and felt like she was struggling for air. He was too cute. Too easy. And way too close. She wanted, more than anything, to touch him. Just his hand, or his arm. Anything. Just to do it. To help her feel real and safe. Because something about the Thunderbolt all overgrown—strangled by nature and abandonment—gave her the creeps. And then she started thinking about the books in the attic, the fires on Coney, the millions of people crammed onto the beach, and the electrocution of Topsy and she felt, possibly for the first time, sort of scared of things.

Of Coney.

Of Leo.

Of herself.

She said, "Why'd you get the seahorse?"

"Oh, that one I just thought was kind of creepy and cool."

Jane took a moment then said, "I remembered where I knew it from when I got home the other night. It's in the book of mermaid pictures that my mother gave me when I was little. I dream about it sometimes."

"Cool." Leo sat back on his elbows, and his T-shirt—for

some rock band Jane didn't know, best she could tell—stretched tighter across his stomach. "What's the dream like?"

She spotted a lightning bug hovering over some tall weeds and tried to keep her gaze fuzzy so she could see it again the next time it glowed. "I'm suffocating and I see it and I grab onto it, thinking it's going to swim up to the surface with me, but then I realize it's fake and that it's not going to help me and only I can save myself."

"Pretty deep," Leo said with a smile.

"Yeah." She smiled back and saw the lightning bug again. "Doesn't take a genius to analyze that one."

They sat quietly for a while, and Jane felt like a spell had been put on them. She didn't want to break it, but then Leo did when he dug into his bag and said, "I brought these."

It was a pack of cigarettes.

"Do you smoke?" she asked, and he said, "On occasion. But in the spirit of the evening, I thought you might want one."

"Oh." She hadn't been expecting this. "I don't know."

"Okay." He put them down on top of the backpack. "I just figured the idea was sort of to, I don't know, retrace her footsteps?"

"Yes," she said. "That's the idea." Though she'd thought about it very little, had really just sprung into action. "At least I think that's the idea. But I don't think I want to smoke. I sort of can't believe she ever did."

"We'll pretend!" Leo took two cigarettes from the box and handed her one and then said, "Okay, imagine we've climbed up to the highest peak of the Thunderbolt."

"Okay," Jane said, then they both took fake drags and started laughing. Jane faked a cough and almost right away a beam of light fell on their feet.

A guard.

Or the police?

"We gotta go," Leo said, standing up and pulling Jane up and then shoving the blanket into his backpack as they ran for the gate. They were back on the boardwalk before the guard—the light—could catch up with them, and they just tore off into the night until they were breathless.

They slowed to a drag. A man in a black hoodie fell into step beside them, seemed to be eyeing them, and Leo said to Jane, "Hey," and stopped walking. He looked at her pointedly and said, very slowly, "Your shoelace is untied."

"Oh." Jane looked down to find both shoes in order. Then she understood Leo's hard gaze and bent to tie her shoe with a series of fake hand motions. When she stood back up Leo said, "Sorry. That guy."

"Is he gone?"

Leo nodded. "We should probably call it a night."

Jane nodded, and they walked quickly down off the boardwalk toward Preemie's. Leo stopped out front and said, "Which key next?"

Jane said, "Parachute. Since I have no idea what the other two are for."

"Well then, I would say that's an excellent choice." He

adjusted the strap of his backpack on his shoulder with his thumb and left his hand there, long fingers resting on the front of his own shoulder. "When?"

Jane could barely talk she was so winded—in her head, if not in her lungs—from their escape from the guard, the shoelace ruse, the sight of those lean fingers. "Tomorrow night?"

"I'm in."

She had the keys in her hand and looked at them. "What do you think 'Bath' means?"

"Don't know," he said. "Maybe just a bathroom they used to use?"

Jane smiled and shook her head. "Just doesn't seem right."

He shrugged and said, "We could ask my mom, but then she'd be onto us and no more sneaking out for me."

"Let's wait," Jane said. "I bet I can figure it out."

three

"ARE YOU SICK?" her father asked, poking his head into her room around dinnertime. He'd already dragged her out of bed once that day for lunch—Chinese food—but then she'd gone up to study and had started daydreaming about Leo, about being with him again, about maybe kissing him—about trailing a finger across that seahorse, that anchor, that lightning bolt—and had fallen asleep again.

"No." Jane sat up in bed. "Just didn't sleep well last night."

Again, not a lie.

"Well, we're going down to Brighton Beach for dinner. If you want to come, be downstairs in ten minutes. And get a little gussied."

They set out on foot down the boardwalk toward Brighton, which was the next beach down the boardwalk, where Russian sidewalk cafés with checkered tablecloths faced the ocean. Their table at a restaurant called Tatiana sat at the edge of a canopy that hung over the outdoor tables. All three of them sat facing out toward the stream of people passing on the boardwalk and, beyond them, the Atlantic—bright blue and calm.

The menu was almost entirely in Russian and Jane was having a hard time concentrating, but then her father asked the waiter a bunch of questions and ordered fish and sausages and stuffed pastries and cheese pies and pickled things and caviar and then he knocked back a few vodkas on the rocks. The clear liquid made him loose, chatty.

"So I reached out to some old colleagues," he said, after he'd stuffed himself. "One in particular. A big fan of my work. And a big fan of your mother's, too, for what it's worth. I think he had a crush on her."

Jane could barely find anything edible, had been washing down unchewed food with water.

Marcus said, "That's great, Dad. Good for you."

"But it gets better," their father said. "He was so interested in the idea of the Tsunami that he got on the phone over the weekend and got me a meeting with someone at Loki Equities. Apparently they're still in the market for their sort of flagship attraction."

The word—*Loki*—caught like something pickled in Jane's throat. "I thought you were showing the Tsunami to the city," she said. "Not Loki."

"Well, Loki seems to be where the action is, according to everyone I've talked to."

Jane said, "But I get the distinct impression that Loki isn't very popular around here. Their plan, I mean. The mall and all." She spoke with urgency. "You have to at least try the city. And there are other people you can try, too. Like the guy who owns the old Thunderbolt lot."

"Well, it sounds like you know more about it all than I do," her father said jovially. "But Loki is the biggest and seemingly really the only game in town for a project of this scale."

Jane stared at the clean white bread plate in front of her, watched the way it reflected shadows of the movements of the waitstaff. There were an uncountable number of light scratches on the plate's surface, and Jane felt like her heart probably looked that way up close, too. Because she wanted more than anything for her father to get the Tsunami built, and wanted equally badly for him not to.

Her father clinked the ice in his empty glass. "You said it yourself, honey, when we first got here, and it stuck with me. And then when you showed me that film."

"Said what?" She shook her head and studied the cherry in her drink, its sickeningly fake red color and crinkly skin.

"We got here and you said, 'That's it?'"

She didn't remember saying exactly that, or least not meaning it that way.

Marcus said, "The whole place really is a dump."

"I need to use the restroom," Jane said—though she really didn't, not urgently anyway—and she went inside and heard loud music and singing and saw, in a sort of banquet hall inside, lights and a standing-room-only crowd. She peeked through the door and then stepped into the darkened room and saw, onstage, a full-on cabaret-type show going on. Women in sparkly costumes were perched on trapeze-like swings, singing some pop song Jane didn't know—a big electronic, anthemic song about love and survival and hurt. The woman in the center was being lowered to the stage by her swing, and then huge wings came out of her back—made of a shimmery white material—and then she was being lifted back up into the air, swingless, her arms spread wide as if she was being crucified. In the audience, the women wore silky dresses and dangling earrings, had their hair professionally done in updos. It was a big night out for them, and it made Jane wonder, for the first time, whether she'd ever go to a prom, whether she cared.

When the song ended to applause and whistles from the crowd, Jane ducked out and used the restroom and returned to the table, where the conversation hadn't changed much.

"Well anyway," her father said, "it's just a meeting." His mind seemed to drift then, and when he said these next words, he seemed to be talking to someone who wasn't actually there. "I've got a good feeling, though. I really do."

Jane retreated to Birdie's Bavarian Bar when they got home—there were still many hours until two, until the Parachute Jump key—and started playing old records on the Victrola while she sorted through more stuff. In the bottom of a drawer of old papers she found a folder containing old newspaper clippings about the preemies of Dreamland. INCUBATOR BABIES IN PERIL! shouted one headline, and she studied the photo next to it, trying to deduce whether any of the babies pictured was Preemie. There was just no way to tell. Not when they were that small. That barely human, barely anybody.

The whole time, she was on the lookout for two things— a key that might open the padlock to the Claverack horse and a journal that might have belonged to her mother. When she saw the leather book hidden in the bottom of the Victrola cabinet, she could feel her heart beating. But she opened it and read a few lines and realized it wasn't her mother's journal, but Birdie's. Which was cool, sure, but also disappointing. It had been hidden, though, and Jane thought again about the Rite Aid mermaid costume and the underwater hiding game of her childhood. She would have to be on the lookout for a shipwreck or a submarine or . . . what else *was* there?

Most of what was left seemed to be, well, junk, but it was the sort of junk that had to be sifted through very carefully because every once in a while, mixed in with a pile of old, useless bills or receipts, there'd be a photo or a birth certificate or a baptismal gown or a program from a play her mother had been in as a child or the newspaper announcement of Preemie and Birdie's wedding. Her grandparents seemed normal in those moments of discovery, when the ordinariness of their lives loomed larger than the weird stuff. Jane liked it, though she didn't like that it made her wonder whether her mother had maybe overreacted. Leaving and staying away for so very long.

Leaving them.

Leaving her.

Putting on "Meet Me Tonight in Dreamland" before heading back up to the house, Jane lay down on Birdie's red sofa and thought back hard, to that day, that other sofa. She was getting better at this remembering thing, so thought she might try willing it into happening, willing a memory to life. The couch was blue, not red. The day was cold, not hot. They'd been shopping. Or something. Hadn't they? And there it was. . . .

I'm tugging at my mother, who is lying on the couch, with a hand to her forehead. "Come on," I'm saying. "Get up, Mommy."

We are having a dance party in the living room, dancing to some crazy loud and fast music—"Hey! Ho! Let's go!"—and I don't want to stop.

"In a minute, honey," she says, and she takes my hand and strokes it. "I don't feel so hot."

"Maybe you should take a little nap," I say, and she says, "Maybe I should." She smiles weakly and says, "Maybe I'll meet you tonight in Dreamland."

I lie down next to her and try to sleep, too—or at least I pretend to try to sleep—but then I sense that something has changed. Her body isn't as warm by my side. Her chest isn't rising and falling against my cheek.

"Mom?" I say finally, and I wait and wait and wait . . . for a reply that never comes.

She hadn't been upstairs long—just long enough to write about that last night in her journal—before the house phone started ringing. It took a while for it to register in her brain that that's what the sound was.

Not an alarm.

Not a bird.

Not a toy.

Once she had made her way downstairs, following the sound, she found her father standing in the kitchen. And so the two of them just stood there for a moment, dumbfounded, staring at the phone as if it were a wailing baby that had magically appeared.

"Should we answer it?" Jane asked finally, and her father, as if awakened from a zombie state, said, "Of course," then stepped over to the phone—a rotary one, the color of split pea soup, mounted on the wall. "Hello?"

He listened and then looked at Jane, held the phone out and said, "It's for you."

She stepped over and took the phone. "Hello?"

"You people sound like you've never used a phone before."

It was Leo.

"We just didn't know it worked." Jane exhaled. "I don't think there's been a bill."

"Same number as always. My mother still remembered it."

Her father was still hovering, so she covered the mouthpiece and said softly, "It's a friend from school."

As if that explained it all.

Leo said, "Hey, so I'm *really sorry* to have to do this, but something came up and I can't make it tonight."

"Oh." She looked pointedly at her father now, and he finally left the room.

Leo said, "Can you go tomorrow night instead?"

"Sure." It was no big deal. Something came up.

"It's just that Venus . . ." He trailed off. "Well, never mind. Tomorrow night for sure, though. Okay?"

"Okay." Jane managed through a lump of disappointment, and they rang off just as Marcus came home. He opened the freezer and held a bag of frozen peas to his face. His lip was bleeding.

"What happened to you?" Jane handed him a paper towel and he looked confused. She said, "Your lip."

He pulled the peas away to allow him to dab his lip and she saw his swollen eye.

"Dad!"

"Jane, don't."

She called out, "I think you better get in here."

Marcus put the peas back and sighed and sat at the kitchen table. Their father came in and said, "Let's have a look."

Marcus pulled the bag away again.

"Come on," their father said. "I'll walk you down to the hospital."

"It's not that bad, Dad. Really. It's just swollen."

Their father sat. "What happened?"

"It was dumb."

"How dumb?" their father said.

Marcus smiled and said, "I might have neighed."

"Why would you do that?" Jane snapped. "Why would you antagonize them?"

"I don't know, Jane. Maybe I'm sick of them acting like they own the place."

"It's just for one year!" she said. But for the first time, she doubted the truth of it. What if it wasn't just for one year?

Then maybe it wouldn't matter so much that Leo had canceled. It was just one night. Not out of 365, but out of *years*. One measly night she wouldn't even remember when she looked back on it all, on the early days on Coney.

four

THERE WERE NORMAL KIDS, of course. Hundreds upon hundreds of them. And Jane had met a lot of them. Sarahs and Jacintas and Kiras and Londas. A few Matts. A couple of Emmetts. She couldn't seem to keep any of them straight, though; couldn't seem to remember or connect. None of them seemed to know who she was—or who Preemie was—and none of them seemed to care. At first, she'd thought that would be nice. And she'd made some efforts to try to befriend some of them by the lockers and between classes. But she kept feeling drawn to Babette. To H.T. To the others. Even the ones who made her sort of uncomfortable, like Venus.

So when she walked into the girls' bathroom that morning and saw a slew of freaks reflected in the mirrors, she had to work hard to make sense of the scene. Gone was the backdrop of normalcy. Everyone in the mirror was skewed. Then she saw the sign above the funhouse mirrors—somehow layered over the normal ones—and it read ARE YOU NORMAL?

Smaller letters below the question read DEEP THOUGHTS FROM THE DREAMLAND SOCIAL CLUB.

Girls with long blond hair had been turned into boyish ghouls. Girls with cropped dreads had hair down to their knees or knees where their eyes should be. Jane could be either a dwarf or a giant, depending on where, in front of the mirror, she stood. There was laughing and gasping and a few people saying, "Ugh. Could you imagine?" And that's when Jane ducked out, decided she didn't have to go so badly after all.

In homeroom that same morning it became clear that word of Marcus's black eye had spread quickly, but not quite as quickly as word of *Harvey Claverack*'s black eye. Even Jane was caught off guard by the damage her brother had managed to inflict upon the geek, who was easily twice his size. Marcus's eye region had retreated to its normal size but turned a deep shade of lavender. Harvey's was a dark eggplant.

Ouch.

When she was sick of fielding questions about it for which she had no answers—and sick of pride and fear doing battle in her heart—she escaped into the basement halls and knocked on the door to the *Siren* offices.

"Oh, hi!" Legs said. "I was actually just coming to find you."

"Let me guess," she said. "You're doing a story about my brother's black eye."

"No." He smiled. "Though it's not the worst idea in the world. I wanted to show you something. You never came back to look through the archives, and I felt sort of bad that I brushed you off." He handed her a large black-and-white photo. "I think that might be your mother?"

Jane took the photo and studied it. In it, her mother wore an Empire-waisted dress in a bright red with black leggings underneath and black boots—like combat boots—on her feet. Three others—one a man with his arm around her mother's shoulder—stood side by side. "It is," she said. "What about the other people? Are there names?"

"No," Legs said. "Sorry."

And right then she recognized Beth in the photo. Younger, but definitely Beth.

Legs said, "You can keep it," and Jane said, "Thanks."

He was probably not the kind of guy who had ever canceled on Minnie. Jane was dreading having to look Leo in the eye and not show her hurt.

"Just don't tell anybody, okay?" Legs said. "Technically it's school property."

"Of course," Jane said.

The first-period bell rang and they both headed toward the door. Jane stopped to put the photo into her bag and saw, in a light pencil marking on the back, the letters D.S.C.

"So would you, like, maybe want to go rollerskating on

Friday?" Legs opened the door for her. "There's a benefit thing."

When she didn't answer right away but kept, instead, looking at those letters, so barely there it was a wonder she'd even spotted them, Legs stammered a bit and said, "A bunch of people from school will be there."

Sliding the photograph into a folder, Jane looked up. It was sweet of him to want to be friends, to include her in a group outing like that.

But *rollerskating*?

"Rollerskating isn't really my thing," she said, but then she felt such a rush of gratitude for him, for the photo, for his reaching out this way, she said, "But yeah, sure. Sounds fun."

Venus seemed to want something from Jane in biology lab that morning. A confession of some kind? An apology? But since Jane was going to give her neither, she ignored Venus's expectant looks and studied the instructions on the handout. They were doing a lab called "Invertebrate Diversity" and were going to be moving around the room to different stations, comparing general characteristics of a bunch of animals without backbones.

It turned out that Leo hadn't shown up for school, and Jane wondered what that meant about his backbone, or lack thereof. Fortunately, she found that it was much easier to bluff in front of Venus without him around to remind her of what she was trying to hide. And what, exactly, was she hiding? Her feelings for Leo? The night at the Thunderbolt? Their plans to meet again tonight? The fact that she had seen them, maybe, kissing?

It's just that Venus . . . he'd said on the phone.

It's just that Venus *what*?

"So I was hanging out with Leo last night," Venus said, and it felt like a kick in the gut. They'd just finished studying an earthworm—taking notes on whether it was symmetrical and had legs or eyes and how it moved—and had gone over to the snail station. Venus's tattoos seemed to be in full bloom that day—she even smelled like roses—and Jane wondered whether the bugs were drawn to her. "He said your moms were friends."

Jane nodded and studied the markings on the snail's shell, looking for patterns or anything of interest at all.

"It doesn't mean anything, you know." Venus wasn't taking many notes; just the bare minimum. "I just mean, it's not like that means you two are gonna be bestest friends or anything."

"Right." Jane struggled hard not to add, *Go play in traffic,* and said instead, "I know." She was sure now that their specimen had started to inch toward Venus.

Venus picked up the snail then, and Jane said, "I'm not sure you're supposed to—"

"Read the handout," Venus snapped, and Jane found the line that said "You are encouraged to handle the earthworms, crickets, and snails, but please be careful and don't handle them too roughly."

"He's out sick today." Venus coughed a fake cough. "I hope I didn't catch it."

Jane sat and stared at her lab sheet, not able to decipher her own notes and wondering: Did getting tattoos hurt more or less than conversations like this? Was there any way to measure physical pain against emotional pain? Did snails and earthworms and crickets know the difference? She wished for a note she could circulate—one about maybe treating her carefully, about not handling *her* too roughly. She'd give the first copy to Venus and the second one to Leo.

Babette barreled over at lunchtime and said, "Legs and Minnie broke up."

She was breathless: "I just saw her crying in the bathroom."

Practically bursting: "He wants to see other people."

"Other people?" Rita said with a swallow. "Like *who?*"

Jane studied the seam of her book bag; the speckled pattern on the cafeteria floor, like a bird's egg; the white skin showing through the openings of her Mary Jane–style shoes. Finally, when she could ignore the question no longer, she said, "I think he may have asked me out."

"I knew it!" Babette made a pouty sort of face. "That's so sweet. What did you say?"

Jane lost interest in her lunch entirely. "I said yes, but I didn't realize it was a date."

"So what if it's a date," Babette said. "That's awesome."

"I'm not sure it's a good idea," Jane said, and Babette said, "Jane. Come on."

"Come on, what?"

"You *know*." Babette wasn't actually tugging on Jane's arm but it felt like she was, with that look in her eyes.

"No." Jane was fuming, because she *did* know. "I don't."

Babette looked across the room to where Venus and one of Leo's friends were playing that game where you try to slap the other person's hands before they slap yours; a flat *thwack* cut through the din of the room as Venus nailed the guy hard.

"Fine," Babette said when she looked back at Jane. "It's your life. Waste it if you want."

"Are you guys going?" Jane said finally. "Rollerskating?"

"Yes, we're going. But you can't tell him you didn't know it was a date. You have to pretend."

"I can't."

"Oh, so you're going to tell him?" Babette put tiny hands on her hips. "You're going to say, 'Sorry I said yes, but I thought it was a group thing, and the thought of going on an actual date with you is so repulsive to me that I have to retract my yes.'"

"I never said I was repulsed!" Jane protested. "I'm not!"

"Still." Rita winced. "She has a point."

Jane was almost at the boardwalk with Babette at day's end when Mr. Simmons appeared and stopped her. "I'm still waiting for your postcard, Ms. Dryden." He rubbed his goatee. "I check my mail so often I'm starting to feel like an army wife."

"I'll catch up," Jane said to Babette, who had started to walk over toward the bench on the boardwalk where Rita and Marcus were sitting.

"I know," Jane said to her teacher. She would have made a postcard about the night at the old Thunderbolt site, her night with Leo, if he hadn't ruined it all the next day by canceling on her to be with Venus.

Mr. Simmons said, "You're losing points each day I don't have it."

"I know," Jane said again, and she was about to skulk away when she had a thought. "Mr. Simmons?"

He turned.

"What do you know about carousel horses?"

"Meaning . . . ?"

"Meaning, I don't know, how much money would a Claverack carousel horse be worth?"

"From what I know—anything from maybe ten grand to sixty grand? But here's the thing"—he paused and seemed to be choosing his words—"like any collectible of any real value, it's priceless to the right owner."

"But who *is* the right owner?" The answer to that question would solve everything.

Mr. Simmons shrugged and said, "The person who finds it priceless." He started to back away. "The postcard, Jane. Don't forget."

She turned and moved on to meet Marcus, Rita, and Babette but saw that Babette hadn't made it to the bench yet. She was frozen in place, watching from a distance, while Marcus and Rita sat side by side, laughing in the sun. They were watching H.T. and his friends dancing on the boardwalk to loud hip-hop music coming from a boom box. H.T. was doing some kind of fancy, spinning handstand. Marcus and Rita were sitting very, very close.

"Babette!" Jane called out—more loudly than was necessary during a gap in the music—and Rita looked up and elbowed Marcus, who quickly put space between them.

Babette turned to Jane, who caught up with her, and together they joined Marcus and Rita.

They all watched H.T.'s crew dance for a while more, and then Jane pulled out the photo of Birdie and the legless man, which was tucked into the front cover of one of her texts. What Mr. Simmons had said made her realize why she'd taken it from the house, why she'd been carrying it around. When H.T. stopped dancing, she walked over and said, "Hey."

"Hey." He looked at her expectantly.

"I was looking through some of my grandmother's old stuff and I found this picture." She looked at the picture again now and felt like this was probably a huge mistake. But there was no turning back. "It's her and a guy who also, well . . ." She suddenly couldn't find words.

H.T. snatched the photo out of her hand and looked at it, then said, "Oh, man, no way. Johnny Eck, the Half Boy. This guy's, like, my idol."

"Really?"

"Totally."

"Jane," Babette said, with a whine. "Come on. Let's go."

"You can have it," Jane said to H.T. "I mean, if you want it."

"For real?"

"Jane!" Babette said again.

"Yeah," Jane said to H.T.

"Awesome," he said. "Thanks." Then he turned to Babette and said, "And why are you in such a hurry, Little B?"

Jane thought it was cute he had a nickname for her.

Jane had done all her homework and made another search of the attic and her own room for her mother's journal—what a nagging thing that was, to know it existed and might still—but there were still hours to fill before she was meeting Leo. If he was even going to show up.

She'd found a VHS copy of an old movie called *Freaks* in the attic and decided to watch and see if maybe Birdie was in it. Heading downstairs with it she heard voices—plural—coming from her brother's room. He had a girl with him. Jane didn't even want to think about who it was and what would happen when Babette found out.

She fixed herself a snack in the kitchen and started the movie, which seemed like it had been made for shock value, with a thin plot about a circus sideshow. There were two pinheads and a torso boy and those same Siamese twins who had been in *Is It Human?* and, yes, there was a bird woman, but it wasn't Birdie. And what kind of crazy world was it when two women could get famous pretending to be part bird?

She almost turned it off a few times, it was so bad, but it was also strangely compelling, and then it was almost over and there was a banquet because a normal woman was marrying one of the freaks—some kind of miniature man—and they were at a table with big goblets and the freaks were stomping on the table, chanting, *"Gooble gobble. Gooble gobble. We accept her. We accept her. One of us, one of us."*

Pounding and pounding and stomping and stomping and then saying it again, over and over, in a strange sort of initiation ritual.

Gooble gobble. Gooble gobble.

It was creepy as all get-out and then, thankfully, it was over.

When her brother came downstairs with Rita trailing behind him, Jane was almost happy to see them.

Rita said to Jane, "Walk me to the door?"

Jane got up, followed Rita down the hall.

"Hey, do me a favor," Rita said, her hand already on the knob. "Don't tell Babette I was here."

Jane was studying her closely, looking at the way her hair—no longer pulled back in the ponytail she'd worn all day—seemed so unruly.

Rita said. "You know how she is."

"Yes," Jane said. "I do."

Marcus was whistling while looking for something to eat in the kitchen when Jane returned. She said, "I hope you know what you're doing," and he said, "Don't lose any sleep over it, sis."

"You know," she snapped. "You're sort of becoming a jerk."

"Why? Because I don't like Babette? Get real." He took

a Coke out of the fridge, snapped it open, and went up-stairs.

Jane sat down at the kitchen table, where a note from her father that she hadn't noticed earlier read *Loki meeting in city late afternoon. Order takeout.* A twenty-dollar bill peeked out from behind it. But Jane wasn't hungry, and anyway dinnertime had passed. She went to her bag and got out the photo Legs had given her, then looked at the clock on the wall.

It was late for a lot of people.

But not for people who ran clubs.

Walking down the boardwalk by the light of a crescent moon, Jane could almost feel its pull in the air around her. Something about the way she was moving in the world now made her feel like there were invisible tendons and connections everywhere. The gravitational pull of Coney, of Leo, of her mother's past, was right there in front of her, where she could touch it.

As she walked up the carpeted staircase to the Coral Room, she heard music—a deep, sultry, slow beat. Pushing through a set of doors at the top of the stairs, she slid into the room as inconspicuously as she could. At the far end of the room, in weird contrast to the seascape, a woman pranced around onstage wearing a polka-dot bra and some matching boy-shorts. She was dancing to old-timey piano music, making strange, pouting faces. During a drum break, she bent forward and blew a big kiss, jig-gling her breasts.

Jane slid into one of only two empty booths along the wall opposite the bar and hoped that no one noticed her until she figured out exactly what she was going to say if anyone other than Beth asked her what she was doing there.

But it was hard to think straight. A little card pyramid on the table announced that it was Burlesque Night, and Jane couldn't take her eyes off the woman onstage, her pale skin, her red lipstick, her increasingly scanty outfit. She'd just moved her bra straps off her shoulders while looking tantalizingly over her shoulder at the crowd. Then she turned and revealed breasts bare except for gold tassels hanging from her nipples, which she somehow managed to spin around. Looking back at the aquarium and finding some of those gold fish, Jane thought that yes, it was the same kind of shimmer, the same shade of gold.

She watched a white blowfish make slow progress across the bottom front edge of the tank. And when she looked up there was a new girl onstage. She was wearing a black bikini and dancing with two huge black wings made of feathers. The music was a classical song that Jane recognized from the deep boom of horns—"The Ride of the Valkyries."

BUM-BUM-BUM. Bum-be-bum. Bum-be-bum.

Flap. Flap. Jiggle. Jiggle.

BUM-BUM-BUM. Bum-be-bum. Bum-be-bum.

That's when Beth saw her and came over.

"Hey there," she said, sliding into the booth. "Everything okay?"

"Yeah," Jane said, wondering why it felt like a lie. Everything *was* okay, wasn't it? "I wanted to show you this."

She pulled the photo out of her bag and put it on the table in front of Beth. "It was in the archives at school."

"Wow," Beth said carefully, and then she held the photo closer to the small light sconce on the wall of the booth. Then, finally, she shook her head and put the photo down. "We were so young."

Jane picked it up and turned it over. "It says D.S.C. on the back. Do you know what that means?" It didn't matter that she already knew it had to be the Dreamland Social Club. She wanted to be *told*.

Beth's eyes got sad. "Oh, honey," she said, shaking her head again. She pushed the photo over so that it sat in front of Jane. "Here's what I *will* tell you." She pointed to the face of one of the boys in the photo and said, "That's one of your mother's ex-boyfriends."

"Really?" Jane studied the boy's face. "What was his name?"

"You're not going to like it." Beth tapped his face with her finger. "That's Freddy Claverack."

"You gonna walk right by?" the voice said. "You're a regular ole Looky Lou."

Jane's head snapped toward the voice, and she saw a man holding a microphone standing in front of the Shoot the Freak booth.

"Well, would you look at that?" He nodded at her. "She's got ears. Just not the nerve to shoot the Freak."

He had dark peach fuzz for hair and wore mirrored sunglasses that covered half his face. His neck pooled under his chin like a deflated inner tube, and his belly pushed out on a Mets T-shirt that barely met the top edge of his denim shorts. Turning away from Jane he said, to no one in particular, "Shoot the Freak in the freakin' head."

Jane looked up and down the boardwalk—saw no sign of anyone she knew, though it was a warm night so pretty bustling with people—and then she stepped up to the guy and studied the Shoot the Freak booth.

The target was standing among the field's scrap metal and trash, just standing there and waiting. The entire scene was splattered with paint, and paint guns rested on a ledge in front of Jane. She said, "How much?"

Peach Fuzz pointed to the sign that Jane really should have seen, hanging right behind him. Ten bucks for ten rounds sounded like a lot, and Jane thought maybe she'd just move on but suddenly she *really* wanted to shoot the Freak.

"I don't have all night," he said.

"Fine." She reached for her wallet and handed him the money.

Peach Fuzz loaded up a gun with paint pellets, then handed it to Jane. She stabilized her hands by propping her elbows up on the barrier between the boardwalk and the Freak's junk-metal obstacle course and found her target. He was moving slowly, swaying on his feet and holding a plastic shield. Jane aimed low and fired. Orange paint exploded on the Freak's leg.

He started to show a little more life as she fired again, and hit him again—imagining now that he was a Claverack. Harvey. Cliff. Freddy. It didn't matter. Right then something about the Freak's body movements—he took a few determined steps forward—made Jane think he was getting mad. But if he didn't want to get hit, he needed to move around more, show some hustle.

She popped him again, this time with a splatter of blue and this time imagining he was Leo, who'd canceled on her. Leo who was on course to break her heart.

Peach Fuzz was trying to attract a crowd. "Check, check, check it out. We've got a sharpshooter here." The last word sounded like *heeya*.

She let the rest of her rounds pop faster once she'd gotten the hang of the gun, and she hit the Freak each time. When the gun was emptied—and that last time, it was her mother, her mysterious, elusive, dead, fun mother whose image had flashed through her mind—she put it down and felt a rush of excitement at how well she'd done.

"Not bad," he said, and Jane said, "Thanks."

He gathered up some saliva in his mouth with a whipping sound and then spat on the boardwalk and shrugged.

High on catharsis, Jane blurted, "You should give out prizes or something."

"Yeah." He was counting a wad of bills. "I'll look into that."

five

SNEAKING OUT A SECOND TIME took some of the thrill out of it, but not much. This time there was the added edge of fear that Leo just wouldn't turn up—because maybe he really was sick?—or that she'd get delayed somehow and miss him. How long would she wait for him? How long would he wait for her?

She'd gone to sleep at 12:00 and set an alarm for 1:45 and saw evidence that her father had, in fact, finally come home within that window. So each floorboard seemed a little bit more squeaky, each lock on the front door seemed clickier. Because what if she actually got caught this time? What if Leo showed up and she didn't?

A *psst* whizzed by when she hit the sidewalk, and Leo stepped out from behind a lamppost in front of the abandoned lot next door. "You scared the crap out of me," Jane whisper-yelled, though there was a secret, calming thrill in feeling like she'd stepped into a scene in a noir film— all lampposts and shadows and lurking.

"Sorry," he whispered back, and then they took off, with him guiding her down the street with a hand on her elbow. "I realized I shouldn't let you walk by yourself. After the other night."

He had his backpack on again, and another tight band tee, and they headed straight for the fence around the abandoned tower. Quietly, they circled its perimeter, methodically trying the locks they found at the four gates— one per side—but had no luck at all.

"Well, it *has* been a long time," Leo said, and they took a break on a bench on the boardwalk. It was breezy and there was a cool edge to the air, a threat from fall.

"Are we giving up?" Jane asked, but Leo shook his head. Then he said, "Let's go back this way," and led her to a post at one corner of the fence. After looking up and down the boardwalk—they were the only two players in their noir scene—he cupped his hands down low and said, "Okay, step up and over, using the post."

"Seriously?"

"Seriously."

Jane had never climbed a fence or trespassed before, but she took one look at the moon—and saw the outline of the whole of it, lit by the crescent—and felt that gravitational pull again, this time like a tug in her Achilles' heel. And then there was her foot in Leo's cupped hands. And then there was her body going up, up, up. And then there were her hands grabbing fence, and then her belly was scraping wire, and then her feet were finding footing, and then moving down, down, down, and then with a jump backwards she was in.

In no time, Leo hooked his backpack over the fence to her, then scaled its rungs. Soon they were taking crunchy steps through tall grass toward the tower, which looked so much larger now, like it couldn't possibly be that same steel flower she'd first spied from the cab. Jane followed Leo right up to its base—the beams were so much thicker, wider, redder—where he stopped and unzipped his backpack and spread out his small blanket. He lay down, looking up, and patted the spot next to him.

"Best view in the world," he said, and Jane realized something. She said, "Why do I get the feeling you've done this all before?"

When he just smiled, she took her place beside him, looking up at the steel tower. From here, lit just so, it took on the shape of a roulette wheel in the sky, and that felt somehow fitting. She closed her eyes and imagined it spinning and spinning and spinning. Jumping off it had been a gamble, just like being here tonight. It was time to go for broke.

"I've been remembering things," she said quietly. "About my mom."

"What kind of things?"

"All these games we used to play when I was little."

Leo looked over at her and raised his eyebrows.

"We moved around so much so we didn't have a lot of toys, I guess." She looked up at the shadow moon as she spoke but felt Leo watching her. "So she'd always make up games using stuff we had around the apartment, like Trip to the Moon and Twenty Thousand Leagues Under the Sea. Like inspired by Luna Park."

When he said nothing, she just kept talking.

"Like she'd turn a box into a spaceship or pretend that green string was seaweed, or she'd dress up as an Eskimo or pretend to be the captain of a ship going to the moon." Jane put on a deep voice. "This is your captain. We are traveling through a storm. We are quite safe." She added, "That was from Trip to the Moon."

Leo spoke very slowly when he said, "That. Is. Awesome."

Jane had to keep talking to keep from crying. "One of my favorites was playing Elephant Hotel. One time she actually made a bed of peanuts for us to sleep on. I'd never seen so many peanuts."

Leo laughed.

"We had a game about living under a roller coaster, too. She must've been thinking of the Thunderbolt."

"How old were you when she died?" Leo asked tentatively, sadly.

"Six," Jane said. "So I don't remember a lot. Or didn't. Until lately. And I mean, I didn't even know she'd ever been to a mermaid camp or kept a journal or anything, really."

In the silence that followed, Jane felt a magnetic pull

between their hands, their bodies, and knew she wasn't making it up. "I just found out, from your mom, actually, that my mother actually dated one of the Claveracks."

"Oh, snap."

"Yeah," she said. "Exactly. I mean, how is that even possible? Nothing makes sense." She shook her head. "I really wish I could find that journal."

"It's been a really long time, Jane," he said, sort of sadly, and Jane said, "I know. But we used to play this game, hiding this little journal I kept when I was little. I feel like she must've hidden hers, too. And like maybe I could find it."

"Maybe," he said. But he didn't sound convinced, and Jane couldn't blame him. She wasn't entirely convinced either.

"So what was the deal anyway?" He pulled a blade of a grassy weed up out of the ground and played with it. "How come your mother never came back to visit or anything? My mom said she hasn't—hadn't—seen her in like twenty years."

"I don't know." *Should she know?* "I guess she never really got along with Preemie, and then she met my dad and they just started traveling and stuff and it sounds like Coney Island was pretty awful back then, too. But we were all going to come back together, apparently, when I was little. To meet my grandparents, probably even your mom, when I was six, but then she died and we never did."

"That's sort of wild to think about." Leo tossed his grass blade. "We could've met when we were six."

For a moment she imagined what that trip would have been like, what Coney would have been like all those years ago, what it would've been like to see this all as a kid, with her mom walking her down the boardwalk, holding her hand and playing tour guide, and not as who she was now, older, more alone, adrift. What it would've been like to meet some weird boy her age, with a weird accent, and what it would've been like to pretend to be interested in whatever he was interested in then, like comic books or guitars.

They sat quietly a while longer and finally she said, "Did you ever hear that story about the elephant that swam to Staten Island?"

"Sure!" Leo shook his head. "Poor bastard."

Jane knew it as a happy story, one of escape. "But he made it!"

"He did. But, I mean, it's Staten Island!"

Jane looked at him blankly.

"Never mind." He shook his head. "But anyway, they charged the elephant with vagrancy and put him in jail."

"Seriously?"

"Seriously. Then people from Luna went to get him and brought him back."

"Oh." Jane hadn't remembered reading that part. It made the story entirely different.

"I'm not really sure my mom would want us to be back here," she said finally, the thought having occurred to her right then for the first time. "I mean, she made such a point of leaving."

Leo shrugged. "I'm not sure it matters."

After another moment, he sat up and said, "All right. Time to climb."

"No," Jane said, looking at the thick base of the Jump.

"Yes," he said, and then he waited for her to come to his side. He put two fingers into his mouth and let out a piercing whistle.

"What are you doing?" Jane said, confused and a little panicked, and then she saw the lights coming their way. Two security guards. "Why did you do that?" she snapped, but Leo wasn't moving, wasn't running.

"It's cool," he said. "I know these guys."

"You sure about this, Leo?" one of the men said as they stopped in front of Leo and Jane and turned off their flashlights.

"I'm sure."

One of the guards went to the structure surrounding the base of the Jump and found a key on his waistband keychain and opened a door. He pushed it open—nothing but darkness in there—and stepped back, looked at his watch, and said, "I'm giving you fifteen minutes. Not a second more."

"Appreciate it," Leo said, shaking his hand and accepting the flashlight being offered. He nodded at Jane to follow him inside.

The ladder in the center of the room led them up to a hatch that opened with a good hard shove from Leo. Jane stood on the ground, waiting for him to abandon the ladder. It took a minute—he looked around a bit—but then he lifted his legs out, scurried around, then stuck his head back down and shined the flashlight in her face. "Come on up," he said.

"You didn't have to pay them, did you?" she asked.

"Nah," Leo said. "They both have unpaid bar tabs."

"Well, thanks," she said.

She climbed, the metal dusty and cold on her hands, and then took Leo's hand at the top and stepped up onto the roof of the base.

"You ready?" he said, and Jane nodded. She wasn't sure what the point of any of this was, the re-creating, but she felt good—different—doing it, being out on nights like this. Jane was not the kind of girl who would scale the Parachute Jump with a boy at two in the morning. Or at least she hadn't been until now.

So they climbed, on the inner side of the tower, and Jane tried to imagine that she wasn't climbing but instead was sitting in some kind of harness, being hauled to the top by cables. When she finally caught up with Leo, she said, "I think this is high enough."

He said, "Okay," and hung his elbows on a rung and Jane did the same, to give her hands a break, and they just perched there for a minute with the wind blowing and the ocean right there crashing and churning, and Leo said, "Your mother was one crazy chick."

"Her mother used to pretend she was half-bird, and her father called himself Preemie," Jane said.

Leo said, "Good point."

"The Anchor actually looks kind of nice from here," she said. It was true.

"Well, take a mental picture, since it'll probably be gone come spring."

"I don't understand," she said. "I mean, if they build new rides and stuff, won't that mean more people? People who would drink at the Anchor?"

"Loki owns the Anchor."

"I thought your dad owned—"

"My dad owns the bar. The business. But Loki owns the property."

Oh.

"And they keep jacking up my dad's rent. It's ridiculous. Probably illegal."

Oh, no.

Jane said, "But if more people spent money there, and it made more money, then the rent wouldn't be a big deal, right?"

"You're missing the point." Leo shook his head. "They'll knock the building down before they let the Anchor stay there. They're even making anonymous calls to the health department about violations that totally don't exist. Because that right there"—he nodded at the bar—"is where they want to put a big indoor water park or roller coaster or some bullshit, so they might not even renew my dad's lease."

"Oh, no." She said it out loud this time.

"Oh, no is right," he said. "They are seriously evil."

"My arms hurt," she said, because it was the only thought she was having that she felt she could share, and Leo said, "Mine, too," and so they went back the way they'd come—down the rungs and through the hatch, and down the ladder and out the door and then through the proper gate this time—with a thank-you for the guards—and then back out onto the boardwalk. And the whole time, all Jane could think was that she had to tell her father about Loki. About how awful a company it really was—*fake health code violations?*—and how he could not sell them the Tsunami.

"Two down, two to do," Leo said, and Jane pushed everything else aside but the keys and said, "I guess Wonder is next, since I still have no idea what 'Bath' means. But I still don't know if it's the Wonder Wheel or Wonderland."

"It sounds to me like a reconnaissance mission is in order."

"What do you mean?"

"I can't after school tomorrow—"

Jane had seen new signs for the Dreamland Social Club meeting. Was that why? Or was it Venus? Or both?

"But after school the next day, we'll scope out the 'Wonder' stuff."

Sneaking back in was as hard as sneaking out. Either way you were caught. But just knowing that Leo was watching from beside that lamppost made her feel stealthy and calm and confident. She wondered what he thought while he watched her, what parts of her, specifically, he kept his eyes on, and whether he wondered those kinds of things, too, about her, when she was the one doing the looking. Then inside she wondered whether she'd ever find out what the deal was with him and Venus, and then up in her room she wondered whether he'd ever touch her or kiss her or want to. With Leo in her life, there were endless things to wonder about—not just the keys.

CHAPTER

six

IT WAS A NIAGARA OF CONDOMS when Jane opened her locker before Pre-Calc. Hundreds upon hundreds of XXLs in square packets cascaded into the hall and formed a river of jagged rapids on the floor. She slammed the door shut, disappeared into the girls' bathroom, and started to cry. The temptation to scratch something awful into the stall's thick pink paint was enormous, but Jane wasn't sure what she'd even write.

She hadn't been in there more than ten minutes before she heard a voice.

"Jane. It's Principal Jackson. Collect yourself and come to my office."

She took some toilet paper and blew her nose, then came out of the stall and went to the mirrors. She wiped the tears off her cheeks, took a deep breath, and headed out.

Harvey Claverack was already in Jackson's office. Cliff was there, too. "I'm telling you," Harvey said, "I didn't do it!"

Cliff said, "Me neither."

"And I'm telling you that I don't believe you." Principal Jackson was twirling back and forth on her rotating desk chair. "You've been orchestrating a campaign of intimidation based on this nonsense about your grandfather and that dumb carousel horse and I want it to stop."

"I have no idea what you're talking about," Harvey said, and the principal snapped, "I know what goes on in my school, Harvey." Which was a surprise to Jane. Why did the principal even know or care? And how?

Principal Jackson opened a desk drawer and pulled out the naked baby doll that Jane had dumped in the trash.

"But it wasn't us," Cliff said.

"This is your first and only warning," the principal said. "One more misstep and you're both suspended. Now apologize to Jane and go."

"Sorry, Jane," Harvey said, in a sort of fake singsong.

"Yeah," Cliff said. "Sorry."

The whole scene was pathetic. It wasn't like they meant it. Though their denials had been rather convincing, even Jane had to admit.

"Now go!" Principal Jackson pointed to the door. "All of you!"

"I want to meet with your father or your grandfather," Jane said to Harvey's and Cliff's backs in the hallway, and they both turned. "I want to talk to someone else. Someone other than the two of you."

"And why should we let you do that?" Cliff said.

"Because I have the horse."

"Fine," Harvey said. "Come over after dinner. My grandfather's always home, and my dad gets home from work at like seven."

"Fine," she said.

And that was that.

Jane watched Leo closely all day, hoping that he'd validate what she felt, which was that last night had changed things between them. The way they'd sat so close and talked for so long, the easy way they had with each other, the charge she was sure had been in the air. It had to mean something. And nothing having to do with Loki or the Anchor could ever change that. It took the better part of the day before she got any indication that maybe he had felt it, too.

"Hey," he said to her on the way out of the cafeteria after lunch. He had a funny look in his eye, and she feared he was going to say something about the condoms, about her "date" with Legs. How had she gotten herself into such a mess?

"I can't stop thinking about you." He ran a hand through his hair, a mess of unwashed black strands. "About you and your mom, I mean. Those games. I swear I dreamed about the Elephant Hotel last night."

The next bell rang and he said, "Tomorrow afternoon." He was backing away. "The Wonder stuff."

She had to consciously act calm when she nodded and said, "Yes. Definitely."

"Hot date?" someone said, and Jane turned to find Legs towering over her.

"No," she said.

"Well, I should hope not," he said, and then he added, "So Friday. I'll pick you up around seven?"

"I could just meet you there," Jane said.

"A gentleman such as myself could never allow it." He headed off down the hall, and the bulletin board he'd been standing in front of revealed a new poster. It said

dreamland social club
TODAY, ROOM 222
Put yourself in the picture.

▪   ▪   ▪

The flush came before the stall door swung open, but Jane saw it only in the mirror's reflection. She didn't see anyone coming out of the stall and got spooked, so she whirled around, looked down, and saw Minnie Polinksy. She was wiping her cheeks and her eyes were bloodshot. She'd been crying.

She looked up at Jane, took her hands away from her face with one more swipe of tears, and sighed loudly. She went down to the far end of the sink counter and pulled a small stool out from underneath. She climbed up, turned on the water, looked at herself in the mirror, and breathed hard, then looked over at Jane's reflection.

Jane didn't have anything to say to her and Minnie didn't seem to want to say anything either, but Jane's feet wouldn't move. She thought maybe she should tell Minnie that it wasn't really a date. She hated that it seemed like she was in some way contributing to the breaking of Minnie's tiny heart when Jane's own heart wasn't really into it. Jane would have stomped on anybody's heart for Leo; not even Venus shooting daggers at her would make one bit of difference. But not for Legs.

Minnie turned off her water and reached for a paper towel. She said, "He wants to be normal, you know."

Jane just waited.

"It's the only reason he wants to be with you and not me." Paper towels looked like bath towels in Minnie's small hands. "He thinks being with you will make him more normal."

Jane's feet still hadn't heeded her command to move when Minnie stepped back off the stool and walked out. Looking in the mirror just then, Jane suddenly felt newly determined to go rollerskating with Legs. Not to help him be normal—how could anyone possibly help anyone be that? least of all her?—but to prove that Legs had the right to go out with whomever he wanted . . . and so did she.

This time when Jane walked past Room 222, she definitely saw Leo inside. So he *was* a member of the Dreamland Social Club. He had put himself in the picture.

This time, she had half a mind to just open the door and walk in and sit down and see if anyone cared. Minnie was there, though, which was reason enough to stay out. In fact, there were now more reasons to stay away than to go in. Many, many more.

Still, she needed to ask Babette for a homework assignment she'd missed when she'd been with Principal Jackson and the Claveracks. So she walked back up to the door and knocked. The voices inside went silent, and Jane just waited. Babette opened the door and said, "Well, hello, Jane."

Debbie stood up from a desk at the front of the room and H.T., who'd been sitting atop that desk with his back to the door, spun himself around, a wide white smile on his face. Leo looked up from where he was sitting next to Venus, their heads bent together over some sort of book or album. Minnie just stared and Legs did the same, though with a softer look in his eyes than his ex's.

"Well, hello, Babette," Jane mimicked. "Can I get our homework assignment from Pre-Calc?"

Babette looked back over her shoulder into the room; Jane watched a few of the others make and then drop eye contact with Babette, who turned back to Jane and said, "Can I swing by your house in like an hour?"

"Sure," Jane said, and then Babette all but closed the door in her face.

CHAPTER

seven

AT HOME, MUSIC MADE OF STRINGS and swells emanated from the heating vents in the kitchen. Jane went out into the yard, opened the metal doors to the basement, and called out, "Dad?"

"Yup!"

Once downstairs, Jane saw an old record spinning on the Victrola.

"This Victrola's in great shape." Her father turned down the volume. "And you'll never believe this thing." He pointed to a weird-looking cylinder and horn on the table. "Hang on."

He lifted the needle on the Victrola and went back to the cylindrical contraption and started to crank a handle on it. A woman's high-pitched, garbled voice came from the horn, singing, *"I'll be your little honey, I will promise that,/ Said Nellie as she rolled her dreamy eyes,/It's a shame to take the money,/Said the bird on Nellie's hat . . ."*

"Crazy, right?" he said.

Jane thought, *Yup, officially.*

"So how did the meeting go?" she asked, but her father was now singing along, cranking with intensity: *"Then to Nellie Willie whispered as they fondly kissed,/I'll bet that you were never kissed like that."*

"Good! I think!" her father said, and Jane deduced that he was drunk. He sang the rest of the song with the lady on the weird funnel record—*"Well, he don't know Nellie like I do,/Said the saucy little bird on Nellie's hat"*—and then he plopped down on an old couch, out of breath.

"There was a picket line." He waved a hand. "I hadn't been expecting that. Some woman stopped me and went on and on and on about Loki and said that I was making a deal with the devil."

"That's what I wanted to talk to you about, Dad."

But he wasn't listening. "You'd think I was single-handedly responsible for Loki owning the property the Anchor and Wonderland are on, like it's my fault they might lose their leases. I told her that's life. If you can't afford to stay somewhere, then you can't afford to stay. It's nobody's fault. It's the way of the world."

Jane felt the thrum of dread. "What did she look like?"

"I don't know. Crazy. That's what she looked. Pretty. Like super-sophisticated. But crazy."

Yes, probably Beth.

"But it's true that Loki is raising everyone's rents like crazy," Jane said. "Shutting people down. You don't care?"

Her father took his glasses off and said, "A horror made of cardboard, plastic, and appalling colors; a construction of hardened chewing gum and idiotic folklore taken straight out of comic books written for obese Americans."

"Dad," Jane whined. "What are you talking about?"

"You were too little to remember. No, wait." He paused to think. "You weren't even born yet. But when I worked on Euro Disney, the French people hated what was happening. They called the park 'a horror made of cardboard.' And worse. And there were protests from labor unions and problems with the housing requirements needed to support the massive staff the park needed to function."

"What's your point?" Jane asked, though she already sort of knew.

"You can't please all of the people all of the time," he said, and he started gathering up his documents. "Now I need to go run through my presentation a few times, honey. I'm sorry you're upset about this, but it's really nothing new."

"It's new to me," she said weakly.

"I know." He nodded. "And it's complicated stuff. Especially if you know the people involved. But there's really no right thing in a situation like this."

"Doesn't mean there isn't a wrong thing," she said. Then, "What do you think Mom would make of all this? The Tsunami? The redevelopment?"

"I don't know." He rubbed his eyes. "I only know that

she loved this place and hated it, and she was justified in both of those things. Maybe the development will get rid of some of the hate for the rest of us who are still here."

"I don't hate it the way it is." It felt like a lie. But a white one.

"But you don't love it either. You love its past and you love its potential, but only if it turns out to be what you want it to be."

"What's so wrong with that?"

"Nothing, except that it's not really love. Love has to exist in the present tense, flaws and all. And anyway, it's not the way the world really works."

Jane didn't have the energy to argue, wasn't sure he was wrong. "I'm going to see a man about a horse," she said. "After dinner."

"Are you sure that's a good idea?" His eyebrows went up. "I could come with you."

"I'll be okay. I just want to decide if we should give it to them or to someone else."

He said, "I can't imagine anyone else would want the thing."

"They're called museums, Dad."

"You think it's worth something?" He seemed genuinely intrigued.

"One of my teachers says it might be worth up to sixty thousand dollars. But that it's priceless."

"Nothing is priceless."

"Do you really mean that?"

"No, I don't suppose I do." He started to fiddle with another record. "You, my dear, are priceless."

Jane rolled her eyes and looked at her watch. "I've got a friend coming over." She got up. "Try not to appear shocked when you discover that she is a goth dwarf."

"Look around," her father said. "She'll fit right in."

Babette wound up the mermaid doll. "So do you think he's cute, at least?"

"It's broken," Jane said, and thought again about telling Babette all about the keys the doll had hidden but wasn't sure she wanted anyone but Leo to know about them. Not yet. She said, "Do I think *who* is cute?"

They'd already discussed and done the homework assignment Jane had missed. Her postcard for Mr. Simmons would have to wait a little longer.

Babette put the mermaid down on the bed. *"The guy you're going on a date with."*

Jane really did think Legs was cute—*for a giant*—which she knew was wrong. So she said, "It's not a date."

Was he cute or wasn't he?

Babette started to whistle "By the Beautiful Sea," then stopped when Marcus peeked his head into the room. "Oh," he said. "Sorry. Didn't know you had company." He closed the door.

Through a tiny pout, Babette said, "Okay, is your brother gay or something? Because I'm throwing all sorts of mad vibes at him and they're all just getting deflected big-time."

"No," Jane said. "Not gay."

Babette leaned in. "He doesn't have some crazy long-distance relationship with some hot Brit chick, does he?"

Jane shook her head. "Nothing like that."

There was no nice way of saying that her brother was into Rubber Rita. Didn't Babette see it? Wasn't it obvious by now?

"Well then, you've got to help me out." Babette started scribbling in her notebook. "Tell him how cool I am. And, I don't know. I mean, can you give me any insider tips? Stuff he likes? *Anything.*"

"I don't know, Babette. He's my *brother.*"

"Fine, don't help." Babette crossed her tiny arms.

"Don't get mad." Jane just wanted to smooth things over. "People have to grow on him."

They were quiet for a minute, then Babette climbed up onto the bed, sighed, and said, "You know, Legs is really, really sweet. Way sweeter than Leo. And available, too. You should give him a chance."

"Thanks," Jane said, once more fighting the urge to tell her about the keys to Coney Island and the fact that she and Leo were meeting up for secret outings. But Babette wouldn't understand—or wouldn't even believe her. And besides, if Babette could keep the goings-on of the Dreamland Social Club a secret, Jane could have her secrets, too. "I'll keep that in mind."

Babette looked at her watch. "I should probably go home and watch my parents pretend they like each other."

Jane said, "You can tell me about it if you want."

"Snore," Babette said. "It's so boring. I keep waiting for them to tell me they're getting divorced."

"They might not," Jane said.

"I actually want them to," Babette said. "I just don't know which one I'd hate living with more."

Babette gathered up all of her notebooks and textbooks and papers and shoved them back into her exploding book bag.

It was only after Jane had escorted her to the front door and gone back upstairs that she realized Babette had left a piece of paper behind.

Across the top, it said *Dreamland Social Club Membership Questionnaire*, in curvy handwriting that looked a lot like Jane's mom's. The print was fuzzy and blurred, like it was possible the original document had just been photocopied and photocopied for some twenty years.

Below that were a series of questions:

What's your earliest memory?
What sound makes you happy?
What was the last dream you had that you remember?
Name one thing you want to do before you die.
Why is a raven like a writing desk?
What's the best thing about being you?

So the raven question meant her mother had also read of Alice's adventures. No surprise. But had that last question been one that Jane's mother had actually asked her at some point, maybe more than once? Is that why she'd so often wondered it of others? Jane had no idea, nor did she have any clue as to how she would answer any of the questions if anyone asked her. But it didn't matter.

No one would.

She was the lone member of the Jane Dryden Social Club and its motto was "You *don't* know who you are."

And no one else really does either.

Except for Leo. Wasn't Leo maybe starting to come close?

The Claveracks lived one block away in one of those row houses with bars on the windows on the second floor. In this case she wondered whether the bars were there to protect the outside world from the house's inhabitants instead of vice versa. She took a deep breath, found the bell, and pushed the button. The ho-hum *ding-dong* struck her as almost too ordinary for a house inhabited by Claveracks, but maybe she had built them up too much in her mind. Geeks were people, too.

A shockingly old man opened the door, took one look at Jane with an eye that had to be lifted out of a wrinkle pool resting on his cheekbone, and said, "You again?"

He turned and shuffled down the carpeted hall and yelled out, "Freddy! It's that gal of yours!"

The door was about to close on Jane, so she put a foot on the threshold and then waited. A man around her dad's age—and this one looked like the guy in the picture—came to the door. He had a large oblong head and a salt-and-pepper ponytail and wore work boots, jeans, and T-shirt that said BADA BING! next to a silhouette of a naked woman. He reopened the door fully and said, "Can I help you?"

"I think you knew my mother," she said—though it seemed suddenly very hard to believe they'd ever dated—and he took a look at her, rubbed his eyes like he'd just woken up, and said, "Tiny?"

The old man's voice from another room said, "And what kind of name is that anyway? She's not that small!"

"I heard you were here," Freddy said. "In the old house."

Jane just nodded, not sure anymore why, exactly, she had thought this would be a good idea. Until she remembered the photo. "I just wanted to ask you a few questions," she said.

"About what?" he said. "Your asshole grandfather?"

"No." She bristled. "About a photograph."

"And I'm right here!" the old man said. "So no funny business." He was sitting at the table in the adjoining dining room playing solitaire. "My own son," he grumbled. "With that prick's daughter."

"Shut it, Dad," Freddy said, then he turned to Jane. "He thinks you're her."

Jane nodded and pulled out the photo. "I was hoping you could tell me what this photograph is. You're in it and it says D.S.C. on the back. What does that mean?"

He took the photo and breathed out hard, and it smelled suddenly like stale cigarettes in the room. "Even if I remembered, why would I tell you?"

"Because I'm Tiny's daughter." She pointed at the photo. "You have your arm around her."

"Here's the thing, kid." He reached for a pack of cigarettes and slipped one out. "If I want to, you know, honor your mother's memory or whatever, I shouldn't tell you."

It wasn't the sort of opening she'd been looking for, but it was an opening. Wasn't it? "It's the Dreamland Social Club," she said. "Isn't it?"

He just lit his cigarette, then exhaled and looked at her. He wasn't going to say anymore.

"What about her journal?" Jane tried. "Do you remember anything about that?"

He waved his cigarette dismissively. "Just that she carried it everywhere and was always scribbling."

"Do you know where she may have hidden it?"

He shook his head, then reached back and ran a hand down the length of his ponytail. "Didn't know she hid it nowhere."

Jane's gaze fell to the photo again, to his arm around her mother. "So you were, like, girlfriend and boyfriend?"

"For a millisecond," he said. "As long as it took to get a rise out of our fathers. But your mother always knew she was leaving and I always knew I was staying. She thought she was too good for me anyway." Something occurred to him then, and he seemed suddenly agitated. "The boys said you wanted to talk about the horse." He stubbed out his cigarette, only half smoked.

"That, too," Jane said. "I heard you're going to sell it to the city if I give it to you?"

"The city can bite me," Grandpa Claverack muttered.

"He's got some private buyer in Europe," Freddy said.

"You tell your father," Grandpa Claverack said slowly, "that when I can get to that key I'm going to waltz right into his living room and take what's mine."

Jane turned to him. "You know where the key is?"

"Of course I know where it is." He was counting cards in groups of three at the table. "I just can't get to it is all."

"Where is it?" Jane asked.

"At the bottom of the damn ocean!" Grandpa Claverack shouted.

"It's not at the bottom of the ocean, Dad." Freddy shook his head and turned to Jane. "He's been saying this for years. He says Preemie said to 'go fish' whenever he asked for it."

Grandpa looked at Jane and squinted. "You said yourself it's the only place worth hiding anything."

There must be a shipwreck or a submarine around here somewhere. . . .

"Why did Preemie keep the horse?" she said, hoping to capture some more from this moment of clarity. "Did he ever say why he even wanted it?"

"To spite me!" Grandpa Claverack hissed, but Jane just felt certain there had to be more.

eight

N HOMEROOM, BABETTE MARCHED OVER and produced a newspaper from her bag. "Loki's trying to buy a weenie."

"What?" Jane couldn't parse the words.

"A weenie. It's carny talk for a big flashy ride." Babette pushed the newspaper toward Jane, who picked it up. "They're going to present an official plan to the city next month, and it's supposedly going to include a weenie."

Jane studied the article and confirmed that her father had not been named as the potential designer. "That could be a good thing, right?"

The article said the whole purpose of a weenie was to draw big crowds.

"A weenie, sure." Babette said. "A Loki weenie, not so

much. Because a Loki weenie is going to shut down the Anchor and Wonderland, since that's the land they own."

"This spring," Jane said aloud, because suddenly it all started to feel real and spring didn't seem so far away. It'd be a miracle if she could keep the Tsunami a secret that long. "But the city has to approve the Loki plan first, right? This winter? And they might not?"

"Finally!" Babette patted her on the back. "She gets it!"

"This is bad," Jane said. But if the city just didn't give Loki the go-ahead, she'd be saved. Then the city could buy the Tsunami and everyone would be happy.

Rita said, "You're going to have to tell him sooner or later."

"You're one to talk," Jane snapped.

Babette looked back and forth between them. "Him who? Tell him what?"

"Exploitation," Mr. Simmons said. "I want to talk a little bit about exploitation in Coney history. So, for starters, what does it mean?"

"To take advantage of someone," someone called out.

"Yes," Mr. Simmons said, then he wrote on the board, *an act that exploits or victimizes someone; treats them unfairly.* "Can anyone name some examples of groups of people who have been exploited, historically, right here on Coney Island?"

Leo raised a hand and was called on. "At Dreamland, they shipped people in from Africa and brought Pygmies here against their will."

Mr. Simmons turned and scrawled SAVAGES in big letters across the board. "What else?"

Babette raised her hand and, when called upon, said, "Little people."

MIDGETS! Mr. Simmons wrote. Then: DWARFS!

"Who else?" Mr. Simmons said.

Jane raised her hand and contributed, "Premature babies."

PREEMIES! Mr. Simmons wrote, then he put down his chalk. "Savages! Midgets! Dwarfs! Preemies! Freaks! No one was safe. If people were willing to pay a couple of cents to look at you, the businessmen on Coney historically provided these human amusements without punishment or judgment."

"But Mr. Simmons," Legs said, "wasn't it true that normal people were exploited here on Coney, too? Just like freaks."

"And the student becomes the teacher." Mr. Simmons smiled. "What do you mean, Mr. Malstead? Enlighten us."

"Well, at the Blowhole Theater at Steeplechase, it didn't matter who you were."

"Excellent point," Mr. Simmons said. "And that, dear students, brings me to your next assignment."

Groans filled the room. *Here we go,* Jane thought.

"I want you to imagine that some evil circus sideshow person has come to your home and captured you with the intent of putting you on display for profit, for all the world to see and gawk at. I want you to come up with your stage name and draw up a sort of banner advertising your talents. Or, if you're not feeling artistic, I want you to write the script that the barker would use to introduce you and to try to lure people into your tent. 'Step right up and behold the ninth wonder of the world,' that kind of thing."

"But Mr. Simmons?" It was one of the Kiras or Stephanies whom Jane could never keep straight. "What if there's nothing weird about us to even exploit?"

Mr. Simmons smiled and said, "I am confident that if you all think hard enough, take a look in the mirror and inside your soul, you'll come up with something."

"Pretty deep, Mr. Simmons," Leo said, and everyone laughed.

At day's end, Jane stopped in the hall and watched Leo for a moment before he saw her coming. There seemed to be a new urgency about him. He was at her locker—waiting, eager, tapping his foot and fidgeting. Something had shifted. She had no idea what it might be but feared, in that second, that he knew.

About her dad.

Loki.

Everything.

He spotted her in the middle of another of his yawns and turned the yawn into a smile, relaxing his whole body along with his mouth. "I'm dragging this week," he said, when she reached him.

She smiled, relieved. "Me too."

They walked down to the Wonder Wheel and got on a swinging car after a few cars got loaded up with members of a tour group wearing badges Jane couldn't quite read.

The wheel spun them up high and around, and Leo opened up his backpack and took out two cans of Budweiser, dangling from the plastic loops of what was once a six-pack. Jane couldn't help but wonder what had become of the other four beers, but she took the one offered her.

Retracing her steps. Wasn't that the idea?

Leo took the can back briefly and snapped it open for her, then handed it back, opened his own beer. He looked at her across the car—they were on opposite benches—and then slid over to sit beside her and said, "Cheers."

They banged cans with a dull clank, like a dampened bell, and then sipped. It was cold—was his backpack a cooler bag? had he swiped them frozen from the Anchor?—and tasted bitter, but good. And it turned out Jane was thirsty. She drank more. She felt sort of loose and good as she studied his knees in his jeans. They were skinny but squarer than her own.

"I think it's safe to say"—Leo stretched his legs out, his knees disappearing into his jeans like quicksand—"that this is the best part of my day so far."

"Mine too," Jane said, looking out at the sea and thinking about the first time she rode the Wonder Wheel with Marcus, how much had already changed, and wondering whether Leo was going to explain about his day or not, but not entirely caring.

"What do you think that says about us?" Leo said with a smile, looking over at her.

She laughed. "No idea."

"So what's up with you, anyway?" He sat up straight. "Like, what do you do? Like, are you going to join the school paper or the basketball team or anything?"

"Do I look like I play basketball?" She looked down at her clothes, her general way of being.

"No." He shook his head. "I don't know what you look like, exactly."

"Thanks," she said. "Thanks a lot."

"I don't mean anything." He nudged her with an elbow. "I just mean I've never met anyone quite like you before."

"Quite so boring, you mean?"

"Who said anything about boring?"

"Well, I don't think it's a reach to say that I'm the least interesting member of my family."

"Meh," he said. "Being born a few weeks early doesn't make you that interesting. Neither does pretending to be part bird."

"It doesn't?"

Leo laughed. "Okay, you got me on the bird bit. But I don't know. You seem like you have, I don't know, an interesting point of view. I mean, just having lived so many different places."

"If you say so," Jane said.

"I heard you gave H.T. some old photo of his idol."

"I hadn't known it was his idol."

"He won't shut up about it."

The car swung then, and they both almost dropped their beers. Then they sat there swinging and swinging and swinging. Finally Jane said, "I don't think this was the Wonder key."

"Why not?"

"I don't know. Just too hard to sneak onto at night, don't you think? And then to operate? It feels different than the others. And your mom said they used to sneak *beers* onto the Wonder Wheel, not that *they* snuck on."

The ride was over; the beers were empty and the cans put back in the backpack. Leo said, "Next stop, Wonderland."

A water-gun game was open for business when they walked by the games section and they looked at each other, shrugged, and stepped up. Leo paid for the both of them, and the guy barking the booth shouted out to try to scare up some other customers, but none came. "Can't run the game without three," he said. "That's the rule."

Jane looked around for any takers, but the place was pretty empty. Leo slapped down a few more bills by a different gun and said, "How about we pretend."

"Fine," the guy said. He flicked a switch and announced the beginning of the race and then suddenly, Jane's water gun was alive in her hands. She focused the spray of water on the clown in front of her and then studied its features: the exaggerated arch of the eyebrows, the candy-color red of the stretchy lips, the big ears and red dot on the nose. She realized that in her mind, images of this kind of water-gun clown and of her grandfather had sort of morphed into one another so that her vision of her grandfather was one of a clown.

The balloon over Leo's clown head burst, and he put his gun down. Jane put her own gun, no longer working, down too.

"What's it going to be?" Leo said to her. "Inbred panda bear or inbred crocodile?"

"Panda bear," Jane said, and Leo said, "You heard the lady" to the guy working the booth, who handed over a small white toy.

"Why was the baby bear so spoiled?" Leo asked as they walked away. She could only shrug.

"Because his mother panda'd to his every need."

Jane groaned and Leo smiled and said, "Admit it. You've heard worse." He took the panda out of Jane's hands and studied it. "There's this old dude downtown. Like near Wall Street. He's like sixty and unemployed and he dresses up as this sad panda to try to make money. It's one of the saddest things I've seen, really. Almost sadder than that orphan film."

"Does it work?" Jane asked. "Do people give money to a sad panda?"

"I guess," Leo said. "Sometimes." He handed the panda back and, somehow, it looked even sadder now.

"People really liked your grandfather," Leo said out of nowhere as they stopped in front of one of the kiddie rides. "I just mean, don't let the whole Claverack thing skew your perspective. And my mom said your grandmother was really great. Kooky, but great."

A mishmash of trucks and fire engines and cars were going round and round. In one fire truck, a little girl's face went from delight to horror in a matter of seconds when she lost sight of her mother, who was standing outside the gate surrounding the ride, waving and calling out, "I'm over here, Sadie. Over here!"

Over and over.

But it was no use and, finally, the operator stopped the ride and the mom went and got her crying Sadie out of the fire truck. The relief on the little girl's face was so immediate, so primal, that it made Jane swell up with empathy, not for Sadie but for her own six-year-old self. A self that had no way of comprehending the magnitude of that loss. All these years later, Jane was still struggling to understand, still silently screaming *Mommy*.

Over and over.

They walked the perimeter of the park then, checking the padlocks, but the key didn't open anything. Jane couldn't hide her disappointment.

"Listen," Leo said. "It *has* to be one of the old gates here. It's the only thing that makes sense. So let's just figure the locks are long gone and leave it at that."

"Not very satisfying," Jane said with a frown.

"Well then, when we've figured out the last one we'll ask my mom and see if she knows for sure. Deal?"

Jane considered this plan, then nodded. "Deal."

"And anyway, I have an idea," Leo said when they were about to leave the park. "Someplace we can go. Tonight. Even if it's not technically the Wonder key. It'll be great."

"Okay," Jane said. "Where?"

"You'll find out soon enough." He turned his back to the boardwalk, where Venus was hanging out with a few of her friends. "Let's go back this way for a second." He walked deeper into the park, toward the Polar Express.

"Everything okay?" Jane said.

"Yeah," Leo said. "Fine."

They walked home past the Claverack Carousel building, and Jane stopped and watched the horses do their strange frozen gallop. The music was slowing down—the ride, too—and Jane looked at Leo and said, "Do you mind?"

They bought tickets and climbed atop two horses set side by side, then waited for the ride to start again. Jane studied the horse she'd chosen and tried to look for some kind of sign that the one in her living room had been sculpted or painted by the same craftsman. But as she studied the thick paint on its mane and the slightly dulled sheen of the saddle, she could only conclude that the one in the living room was a more spectacular specimen, probably because it hadn't been ridden in years. Studying the center of the carousel now, the drum that spun it around, she saw paintings of deserts and cacti and Western sunsets and then scenes of cupids and cherubs with arrows poised in tiny angel's bows. The whole thing needed a facelift, yes, but you could tell that it would be amazing when it was fixed up.

The music started and the horses began to vibrate with power, and then they were moving and their horses were out of sync, Jane's going up as Leo's went down. This made conversation sort of tricky, especially with the loud tinkle of some kind of ragtime-piano tune. But Jane didn't mind. It was enough to just be there, to be next to Leo, though it was true she was hoping to intuit what to do about the horse.

"Check it out," Leo said. "The brass ring."

Jane saw it dangling overhead and then it was gone. "What is it?"

"You grab it, you win a prize."

It was coming back and she stood—feet in stirrups— but couldn't reach it.

"Close but no cigar," Leo said.

As Jane sat down she saw her brother whiz by. And then the room was a blur of lightbulbs—a fast-moving kaleidoscope of color—and there he was again, playing some video game by the far wall, and there was the blur of Rita beside him. And then again, and the blur of his arm around her waist.

"Here it comes again," Leo said, but Jane just said, "You try."

Leo didn't grab the brass ring that time, but by the time they'd gotten around to it again, he'd climbed up so that his feet were perched on his horse's saddle. Jane had been sure he was going to fall, with his one arm hooked around the horse pole, but then his fingers touched the ring and he pulled it and a bell started dinging and he smiled, victorious. Jane said, "Bravo."

But when the ride finally stopped, the crotchety old operator came over to take the ring and said, "Standing on the horse disqualifies you."

"But how else are you supposed to reach it?" Leo asked.

The old man shrugged and walked off. Jane and Leo turned to go, but then Jane said, "Hang on a second" and followed the old man. He was taking tickets from a few people who'd climbed aboard and taken seats in a sort of sleigh chair by the ride's center. "Did you, by any chance, know Preemie Porcelli?"

"Only well enough to know I didn't want to know him."

"Do you know why he took the horse?"

"Why does anybody around here do anything?"

They turned to go, but then Jane turned back. "You didn't happen to know his daughter, did you? Clementine? People called her Tiny?"

"Sorry," he said. "No."

But wow, it had felt good to just ask.

Her father was coming out the front door of the house with a big black trash bag—full to the top. "What are you doing?" she asked.

"We've got to start getting rid of some junk." He shrugged. "I had some spare time."

Jane approached the bag, looked inside, and saw the poster for *Is It Human?* and the two-headed squirrel. "I told you I would do it," she said through gritted teeth.

"I know, but I thought I'd help."

"You think this is helping?" Her fingers tightened into

fists around the straps of her backpack. "Throwing out my grandmother's stuff?"

"Calm down, Jane."

She let go of her backpack and grabbed the trash bag and started dragging it back into the house. She used two hands to lift it off the ground and carry it up the stairs and into her room. When she came downstairs to make sure there weren't any other bags about to meet the same fate, her father was sitting at the kitchen table with his Tsunami sketches. He'd worked on some close-up renderings of different parts of the coaster and had typed up some specs about speed and duration of the ride. "I didn't mean to upset you," he said.

"I know." She got herself a glass of water from the tap.

"I'm sorry this is all so hard on you." He took off his glasses and rubbed his eyes. "I guess I didn't think it through. What coming here would dig up."

"It's okay," Jane said. "I mean it's *good*. It's just that . . . well, I'm leading the dig. I mean, if that's okay."

"Of course," he said. "Dig away."

CHAPTER

nine

T HE FLOORBOARDS WHINED. The stairs whistled "Dixie." The noir scene replayed itself as Leo stepped out from behind the lamppost, and then they walked and talked until Leo shushed her as they slid down an alleyway behind Wonderland, backs to the wall. He held a finger to his lips to emphasize the point. Jane got it.

Quiet.

He poked his head around the corner of the building and pulled it back.

A metal clang, and then the sound of something being dragged was followed by a slow, scraping hiss.

Leo indicated with a nod of his head that they were

about to move, and then he took her hand—a shock of warmth, strength—and led her just a few steps around the corner and through a door. The man dragging the trash bags to the nearby Dumpster didn't see or hear.

"Quick," he whispered when they were inside. "Over here."

They ducked behind something after climbing over a low wall, and Jane saw they were on a bumper-car course. She'd walked past it a few times in the last few weeks, had heard the pounding techno beats and the hum of the electric cars. But now the room was dark, the cars uncharged. She waited and breathed and waited and breathed and felt a sort of tingle lingering on her hand where Leo had held it until just a second or two before.

Jane heard the sound of the door closing, and then the sound of a key in a lock. She had to fight the irrational need to pull her key from her pocket and try the same door.

Leo said, "Okay," and stood up. "Coast is clear."

"What are we doing here?" Jane said, dearly hoping Leo didn't want to ride bumper cars.

"You'll see." He headed for the stairs. "Come on."

When they had reached the black tar roof and sat down on Leo's small blanket, Jane said, "Are you going to explain?"

She wasn't complaining about the view—she could see the Wonder Wheel, the Parachute Jump, the Cyclone, the projects, pretty much everything there was to see on Coney—but she'd hoped for more.

"This"—Leo slapped the roof with his palm—"is where the entrance to Luna Park used to be. I still think of it as the heart of Coney Island."

But why bring her here? It's not like he knew about her name, her namesake. Unless maybe his mother knew and had told him?

He said, "Which means that the Elephant Hotel was here, too, even before that." He pulled a bag of peanuts out of his backpack and Jane felt a rush of love—yes, love—for him. "I know it's not enough to make a bed, but . . ."

He opened it, offered nuts to her.

"I actually don't like peanuts," she said, and he laughed and said, "More for me."

She stuck a hand in the bag, pulled out a peanut, and sniffed it. "But I appreciate the gesture all the same."

Leo cracked open a nut, popped it into his mouth. "You used to be able to look out of its eyes, they said, and see the ocean." He produced a small map from his backpack and shined his flashlight on it. "So the way I see it, the entrance to Luna would have been there." He pointed to his left and then turned around to face the long roof behind them. "And the Helter Skelter would have been over there." He pointed. "And the Shoot the Chutes just beyond it and then the lagoon. . . . And right there would've been Trip to the Moon."

Jane felt herself drift away from his words, into her mind's eye, imagining that Electric Eden, those spires and minarets, the herky-jerky motion of the vessel that would take people to meet the singing Selenites on the moon.

Leo stopped talking, sat, and lay back. Jane did, too. After a quiet moment thinking about all those crazy games, and the mermaids and turtles she'd met on her way to the North Pole, she said, "I'm sort of sad that the Bath key is the only one left."

"Have you tried it out anywhere?"

"Just every bathroom door I've come across anywhere the last few days." Jane was looking at a cluster of faint stars, trying to decide if they were a constellation she should recognize. "Ever since your mom mentioned the journal, I've been wondering if it would say stuff about the keys."

Leo sat up. "Well, you know what they say."

"What do they say?" Jane sat up, really wanting to know.

"You'll find it as soon as you stop looking for it."

"What's that even referring to?" Jane shook her head. "Find *what*?"

Leo laughed. "I don't know. Love, probably. A million bucks. Whatever you're looking for."

Her face got warm, just hearing him say the word *love*. "I really can't believe this is where Luna Park was." She looked around at the roof, scattered with old bottles and cans; it was hard to see it as the hallowed ground she'd imagined. "It's sort of depressing."

Leo ate another peanut. "I read this essay once about how being on Coney Island is like looking at a double-exposed photograph, how past and present are both always there."

Jane nodded. "I feel like my life is like that lately."

His voice was quiet, calm. "I don't know. But it seems like maybe that's a good thing, right?"

Jane nodded again, couldn't find words, heard Leo's saw song in her head. "How'd you learn to play the saw?"

Leo tilted his head at the question. "I saw this old dude playing a saw on the boardwalk once. I asked him if he'd teach me and he said, 'The saw finds you; the saw teaches you.'"

Jane furrowed her brow.

Leo said, "I thought it sounded crazy, too, but then I saw a saw in the basement at the bar like a day later and I took it home and started experimenting and that was it. I was hooked."

"I'd like to be hooked on something," she said, and for a second she thought she might actually say it:

Actually I am.

I'm hooked on you.

But then Leo said, "You, my dear, are hooked on Coney." He tapped her sneakers and said, "You've got sand in your shoes."

"Sand in my shoes?"

"It's an expression." Leo looked around and nodded approvingly and said, "I think Luna was my favorite."

Just hearing him say that other L word, *Luna*, made Jane wish she went by that name, had the courage to tell him it was hers.

She said, "Mine too."

There was a charge in the air then, like the buzz of a

phantom carnival ride, and Jane felt pretty sure Leo was going to kiss her. Then he said, "I heard you're going out with Legs Malstead this weekend," and the charge dissipated.

Jane said, "It's not a date," and Leo said, "He thinks it is."

"Are you and Venus going?" she dared.

"I'm going," he said, then quickly added, "Wait. What do you mean *me and Venus*?"

"Yeah," she said. "You're together, right?"

"No," he said, and he shook his head. "She wants us to be, but, well, no."

Relief was like a crashing wave followed by a series of gentle ripples.

"So when you canceled the other night . . ." Jane sort of wished she could shut up, but her mouth wouldn't listen. "She said she hung out with you that night."

"She wanted to talk." He smiled. "Actually, she wants to do more than talk. That's the problem. And I don't know, I just don't think you should ever have to talk. In quotes. It just shouldn't be that hard, you know?"

He looked her right in the eyes then and she said, "I think I do." Then she looked away and just nodded in the dark and wished things were different.

Then Leo said, "Legs is cool" and nodded, too—solemnly, slowly.

"It's not a date," Jane said again.

That night she sat down with the Dreamland Social Club questionnaire in the dimly lit living room, on Preemie's dusty old couch. She didn't overthink it. She just started filling it out with the first answers that came to mind, whether they were right or not.

What's your earliest memory?

Dancing. In my mother's arms.

What sound makes you happy?

Leo's saw. How it sounds like my mother humming.

What was the last dream you had that you remember?

Driving through the countryside toward a burning Ferris wheel.

Name one thing you want to do before you die.

Fall in love with someone who loves me back.

Why is a raven like a writing desk?

There is no answer.

What's the best thing about being you?

She paused there and thought about writing again, *There is no answer.*

But she didn't.

She looked around the room, at that Claverack horse—which looked sort of possessed in the golden glow of the table lamp on the end table—and at the pewter Siamese squirrel and the poster for *Is It Human?* back on the wall, and she wondered whether this was it. Whether all of this was the best thing. *The whole carny thing*, but not just that, being here.

She picked up Birdie's diary then, and started to read. It started years before Birdie had gotten married, years before she'd met Preemie, and she only wrote in it every few months, if that. Then Jane found an entry that read *"I met someone today. Frank, his name is. He was one of those preemie babies in Dreamland. He saw me riding a carousel horse in Steeplechase and said that when he did he realized it was time to settle down and get married. I asked him how the horse felt about that, whether it had a good dowry, and he laughed and said that he'd build a stable to last a lifetime for that horse if I'd just go on one date with him. What a character. I guess I like characters."*

The next entry wasn't for another bunch of months. *"We're getting married,"* read a clearly dashed-off entry. *"I got cast in a picture. More soon . . ."*

There was a card shoved into the pages of the journal right there, and Jane picked it up and studied it. It had a picture of a bird on the front, and on the inside, someone had written, *"Birdie, I told you I'd always love you . . . and the horse you rode in on.—Frankie"*

So was that it? Was *that* the horse she'd been riding at Steeplechase the day they'd first met? Was Preemie—it was almost laughable to think about—a sentimental softie? And at the outset none of this had really had anything to do with Claverack at all?

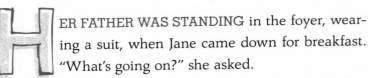ER FATHER WAS STANDING in the foyer, wearing a suit, when Jane came down for breakfast. "What's going on?" she asked.

"Loki's sending a car. They want to talk again today, and they don't want me to have to deal with picket lines. I don't even know where the meeting's going to be."

"Dad," Jane said pleadingly, "please, please, please don't sell them your design."

"Love," he said, fixing his tie in the foyer mirror, "I know you have your concerns, but I don't think you understand. I mean, to build a roller coaster on Coney Island. The most famous amusement park to have ever existed. Do you understand how huge that would be for me? For us?

It would be the biggest possible comeback that I could have ever imagined. And I need that badly. A comeback."

She felt like she was going to cry, and could only nod.

A horn tooted, and her father looked through the small window next to the front door. "That's my car," he said, and she just nodded again and managed a small "Good luck."

The funhouse mirrors were long gone, but in school that morning Jane still felt like her eyes were drawn into large droops and like her whole stomach bent and curved to the side. She felt too tall one second, too short the next. Too skinny, too fat. Too stocky, too lanky. Too normal, too weird. Too quiet, too loud. Too sad, too happy. Too everything, too nothing.

What was normal anyway?

Deep thoughts from the Dreamland Social Club.

Was that all they did as a club? Stunts like that? If so, it seemed sort of silly, but also sort of, well, challenging. How had they pulled it off? And who'd come up with the idea? Had it been Babette? Or Leo? Maybe even her mom? And what would they do next, and when?

Looking in the real mirror and trying to focus in on the actuality—of her face, her body, her edges—brought her back to the reality of her situation. Her father was meeting with Loki again. She would have to tell Leo. There was no way around it. She had to tell him before anyone else did so that she could explain. About how badly her dad needed this. And, by association, how badly she needed it. The Anchor was just a bar. They could move it, open up a block or two away. Everyone could be happy.

Right?

"Where's Leo?" she said when she hadn't seen him all morning and didn't see him at lunch.

"Some Loki protest or something," Babette said. "His mother pulled him out of school to go with him. His dad was going, too. Something about the weenie."

"Shoot me," Jane said, and Babette said, "What's gotten into you?"

"My dad," Jane said. Because she couldn't see the point of hiding it anymore. "My dad is the weenie."

In Mr. Simmons's class it was time to share the sideshow banners/barkers assignment, and Jane thought that meant it was time to suddenly come down with a violent forty-five-minute flu, but when Babette volunteered to go first, she decided to stay put.

Mr. Simmons nodded at Babette—"Okay, you're up"— and just like that, she stood up on top of her desk and said, "Step right up and witness the ultimate in doom and gloom! You'll be glad you aren't her! She's challenged in both stature and outlook and has dealt with this cruel world's gaze the only way she knows how, by trying to shrink into shadows of darkness and hide. She is the Goth Dwarf of Coney Island and has only recently come out of hiding. Do you dare to tower over her tiny, ill-proportioned limbs? Can you stop yourself from gasping in horror as you stare?" She looked at Mr. Simmons and said, "I was hoping for a bigger finish, but that's all I have."

"I like it," Mr. Simmons said. "But I hardly think of you as someone who is trying to shrink into the shadows, Babette." She shrugged agreement and said, "It's theater, Mr. Simmons."

"Indeed it is." He faced the room. "Who's next?"

No one volunteered, and so Mr. Simmons called on the Stephanie or Kira who'd questioned her potential exploitation. She huffed, then got up and went to the front of the class with a rolled-up piece of paper in her hand. "Step right up," she said in a perky voice, "and witness one of the rarest specimens on earth. You will look at her and wonder how it is that she could be this way!"

Mr. Simmons was stifling a laugh.

"For she looks *exactly the same* on the left as she does on the right. She is like a mirror image, split down the middle. She is Symmetrical Girl! Come have a look!"

"Thank you, Kira," Mr. Simmons said. Then, almost under his breath, "You tried."

And then he called on Jane. She knew he would. So she was ready. She went to the front of the class with a page she'd ripped out of her notebook and cut a certain way and cleared her throat. "Step right up and witness one of the most spectacular examples of genetics gone haywire the world has ever seen! Her grandfather was a preemie, one of the tiniest souls to ever survive to walk the planet, and her grandmother part-bird. Her mother, if you can believe it, was a mermaid! Imagine, if you will, the foul gene pool and what monster it might spawn for its next generation." She started to unroll her paper, the center of it cut out in a square, and said. "Rest your eyes upon the hideous, dreaded face of ABSOLUTELY NORMAL GIRL." At that she held up her paper frame and stuck her face through it.

Mr. Simmons laughed, and Jane just looked at him and shrugged.

"A mermaid?" he said, eyebrows raised.

"Long story," she answered, and went to her seat.

A DISCO BALL HAD EXPLODED into a billion tiny pieces that floated in the air. Or at least that's what it looked like. The building that housed Lola Staar's Dreamland Roller Rink was an old landmark that had been shuttered up every time Jane had passed it before, and she felt happy that it had become protected property before Loki had come to town. It was elaborate and grand—if run-down and generally in disrepair—but Jane loved it for its oldness, for its history. It had once been a famous restaurant. She'd seen pictures of it in its heyday.

Legs hesitated by the line to get in. "Is this okay?"

She said, "Better than okay."

"Oh, good."

Legs nodded happily, and Jane made a mental note to be careful about what she said. She was pretty sure she would fall head over heels for the roller rink—makeshift and dingy as it was—and she needed to be sure Legs didn't think it was he who was making her swoon. More than anything she wanted to get inside so she could find Leo, so they could talk.

She had never seen a giant rollerskate before and was surprised by Legs's grace, though not surprised he'd had to bring his own special-order skates. The motion of skating came back to her faster than she'd imagined it would, and she felt steady enough making lazy circles with him, but he was a better skater—*faster*—and he soon took off to take a few laps of his own. She slid off the rink and turned to watch the flow. Compared to Legs, all the other skaters looked like little people. Debbie was there, H.T. and some of his crew, Babette, Rita—and Marcus. She dearly hoped her brother didn't know she was on a date with a giant. Even though she really wasn't.

She still hadn't seen Leo.

Legs swung by and waved her back out, and they were just settling into the rhythm of a new song when she saw him reach out to take her hand. Right then someone blew between them superfast—saying, "Watch out, slowpokes"—and skated off. It was Venus, her dark dreads flying out behind her.

Two seconds later a laughing Leo whizzed between them. "Sorry, lovebirds."

Jane's face burned as she watched him chase after Venus with such confidence that she couldn't believe he was on skates. Then he shouted, "You can run but you can't hide!" when he lost his prey in the crowd. He turned and skated backwards for a minute, looking right at Jane. "We need to talk," she almost said, but then she didn't. Leo didn't like "talk."

"I've got to go to the bathroom," she said to Legs, and she broke off toward the edge of the rink. Right then, something tugged on her leg and Jane looked down. Babette said, "Is something going on between your brother and Rita?"

Jane looked over at her brother—too fast, too guiltily—and Babette said, "I feel sick," and skated away. Jane skated over to Rita and said, "She knows."

"Crap." Rita looked at Marcus, who just shrugged.

Jane skated back to the edge of the rink and made her way to the girls' bathroom, where she found Babette by the sink, wiping tears from her eyes. Black mascara lines dragged down her cheeks.

Rita came in behind Jane, and Babette said, "How could you?"

"I didn't do anything wrong." Rita smacked her gum.

Babette said, "Spare me. You're a backstabbing slut."

Color drained from Rita's face. "If that's what you think, then screw you."

She skated out of the room, leaving Jane with Babette.

Babette glared. "You should've told me."

Jane said, "I don't *know* anything."

"I saw a hot-pink hair band in the bathroom at your house."

Jane took a second to find the lie: "It's mine."

Babette skated toward the door. "I think your nose just got bigger."

Leo was coming out of the boys' restroom when Jane came out of the girls'. They rolled together down the hall toward the rink, where they stopped by the rails. He looked down at his hands on the rail in front of him, shook his head, then looked up. "So when were you going to tell me?" He only looked at her for a second before he looked away.

She looked over to try to read the expression on his face as a sort of landslide of nausea started to create a crater in her gut. A new song started then, and its bass line was way too loud.

"When there was something definite to tell." Jane's heart started thumping too fast, to the bass line.

When he turned back he had to shout above the music: "When was that going to be? When your father turned up at the Anchor with a wrecking ball?"

"Please don't be like that." She was watching H.T. circle the rink; he looked like he was dancing on skates. "I only just found out it was going to have any effect on the Anchor at all, and then you weren't even in school for me to talk to."

"What are you even doing here?" he said.

"What do you mean?"

"This is a benefit for Coney Islanders for Coney. And clearly, you are not one of those."

"I didn't know. I swear." She thought she might be having a heart attack, wished someone would *turn the music down*. She thought maybe she could say something to fix things, to make things right, but then Leo shook his head and said, "I guess I'll see you around, Jane," and all she could think to say was, "What about the Bath key?"

Leo looked, for a moment, more sad than mad but said, "I guess you're on your own," and turned to skate away, then turned back. "You know, I know you're not your dad. It's not even about that, what he's doing. It's that you didn't tell me."

The bass line, finally, died.

Legs suggested a walk out onto Steeplechase Pier after skating, and Jane said yes just to get away from everyone else, to get some air.

They stopped short of the end of the pier and sat on a bench that ran along the pier's left side. There was a green garbage can across the way from them, chained to the pier with a rusty chain link. Jane imagined it was to stop people from throwing it off the edge, then tried to imagine the kind of person who would do such a thing and think it was fun.

Something about the can—and it wasn't a can, really, because you could see right through it—seemed odd, and then it hit her. It was empty; they were all empty, all six trash cans on the pier. Having seen her share of overflowing cans for weeks, she took it as a sign of things to come, of the coming quiet of winter.

Legs said, "I'm really glad we did this," and Jane wanted to cry.

So when he leaned in to kiss her, she turned away and said, "I had fun. But I really have to head home."

"Oh." Legs seemed surprised. "I thought we'd get something to eat."

"I can't," she said, feeling a bit like Cinderella, all tragic and mysterious. "But I'm really glad we're friends."

"Friends." Legs looked shaky and Jane felt that way, too.

"Yes." She looked away.

He exhaled loudly and said, "A lot of that going around."

"What does *that* mean?" she said.

"Oh, nothing." He waved a hand. But Jane figured it out. He'd told Minnie he wanted to be friends. Leo had told Venus that, too.

"Come on," Legs said. "I'll walk you."

"Actually, I might just sit here a minute. But thanks."

"You sure?"

"I'm sure."

She watched Legs walk back toward the rink, where a few police cars had arrived, their lights blinking blue and red in the night. The music had stopped and a sad female voice came through a microphone. "I'm sorry, folks. No permit. Party's over."

She turned to face the water and, a few minutes later,

Marcus was there beside her. "Everything okay? That giant told me you were out here."

Not even looking at him, she said, "The cat's out of the bag."

"Which particular cat?"

"The Tsunami. The fact that Dad is selling it to Loki."

"It's not that big a deal," he said, and Jane said, "It is to me."

Marcus leaned his elbows on the pier's rail. "I've been remembering, too, you know. Some games."

"Yeah?" Jane looked at him now.

"Remember the game about the flood? I think she called it Flood City?"

Jane could suddenly see herself curled up in an armchair, pretending it was a boat. Trying to pull her brother and mother aboard. There had been a Johnstown Flood attraction at Dreamland at some point. Over two thousand people had died when the dam failed in that Pennsylvania town.

"And remember the fire game?" Marcus said. "When she'd tell us the building was burning and to grab what we could and meet her by the front door or on the balcony, depending on where we were living."

Jane nodded. The games hadn't seemed so at the time, but they were scary. Weren't they? And why had she remembered the fun games, but not these?

"Sometimes I wonder." He lifted his elbows, put his hands in his jeans pockets. "I wonder if maybe she was preparing us or something. For the bad stuff."

"Well, it didn't work," Jane said. "I wasn't prepared."

"Maybe you were and you just don't know it yet."

He turned to leave and said, "You coming?"

"I'll catch up."

She looked down into the dark, churning water, lit only by the slight glow of the boardwalk lamps and the glow of nearby buildings. If the moon hadn't been out, she probably wouldn't have seen much at all, and she wouldn't even have minded. She knew the ocean was there—steady, faithful—and that was all that mattered.

Once she saw that Marcus was long gone, she looked out into a black void of sea and air and said, "Who *are* you?"

When her voice, so small in that big space, got carried away and it was obvious no one was around to hear or care, she called out, louder this time, "Why did you have to leave?"

It felt wonderful, cathartic, because maybe someone—someone out there or up there—would listen and send her some clues. To where the journal was—if it even still existed. To what the Dreamland Social Club was all about. To what "Bath" meant.

It was cold out; Jane was underdressed. Fall had arrived without her noticing. But before turning to go home again, she gathered up her voice once more with all the power she could find.

"Who am I?" she screamed, and then she listened to the ocean's roar for an answer.

_T_he beach is the last place I want to be today—the coldest day in years according to giddy weathermen—but Babette insisted. She takes a dip with the Polar Bear Club every year on New Year's Day, and she wants an audience. She spent about half a second last night trying to convince me to put on a swimsuit and join the fun today; the look on my face must have been pretty clear. It said, Shouldn't you be listening to sad music and scribbling depressing poems? Shouldn't a goth have a little less fun?

"Fine, then," she said. "Be that way."

"Fine," I said. "I will."

"But you'll come watch?" she asked.

And so here I am.

I can't feel the tips of my fingers or my nose or my toes, but I stand on the beach and hold Babette's towel for her as she wades into the water—not very far on account of her stature—and then dips her head under, resurfaces, and tips back into a float. While keeping one watchful eye on Babette as she attempts a backstroke, I watch old men with sagging bellies and Speedos, and women with crinkly thighs in square-cut one-piece suits—even hipsters with shirts that say things like Kenya Dig It? They all shriek and splash, and the whole scene looks almost black-and-white on account of the grayness of the day—like an old photo.

Some things are never really gone.

There are old people, young people, fat people, thin people, sane people, crazy people, every kind there is. I watch a few small girls running into the water—their smiles too white; their swimsuits too new, too bright—and their parents watch them with pride so powerful you can sense it through their fancy sunglasses.

Those are my girls, they're thinking. Fearless.

One thing I've never been.

An old, wet man whose butt cheeks are showing walks past them and says, "Go back to Westchester."

I don't know exactly what he means, but then again, I do. They're rich. They're Looky Lous. They don't really belong here.

Babette comes back to shore looking even smaller, like the cold water has actually shrunk her, and I have a fleeting thought about my friend's vulnerability in the world. I've never thought about it before, the fact that grown men could drop-kick her. Would she be at the front and center of a photo of the new Dreamland Social Club? Will I ever be invited to sit by her side?

Something lands on my head then—a towel—and Leo screams, "Last one in's a rotten egg."

I pull the towel off my head and watch him run into the surf. Seeing him without his shirt on is jarring, and not only because it's the first time I can see his back. There is a whole seascape there with a shark at the center that has its jaws opened wide and almost appears to be three-dimensional, like if I touched his skin it would bite me. I feel sort of dizzy, watching the bones of his shoulder blades—like bird wings—as he splashes around, and then more dizzy still when he turns around, his chest facing the shore. The skin there, so far at least, is ink-free, and looks so very white. He shouts, "Come on, you slackers!"

Someone in the crowd shouts, "Look at these idiots!" but I wonder, who are the idiots here, exactly? The people in the water or the Looky Lous on the shore?

We have called a truce, Leo and I. There have been no more late-night meet-ups—no more tours of forgotten Coney with my mother's keys as our map—nor have there been any more fights. Once a week or so we find ourselves leaving school at the same time, though we never actually plan it, and then walking down toward Brighton Beach for a knish at Mrs. Stalz's, like his mom said she and my mom used to do. If it's not snowing and I've remembered my hat and gloves, we take them back up to the boardwalk, sit on a bench, and eat the steaming-hot potato pockets while seagulls and pigeons appear as if from nowhere to inspect us and our deep-fried treats. There are more birds than I can count, and when we get up to leave, they follow us. Their caws sound like heckles, like they're berating me for eating the whole knish and not even leaving them a crumb, or maybe berating me for not telling Leo how I really feel. We don't talk about the fact that Loki's plans were vetoed by the city just after Thanksgiving, or that my dad's coaster most likely won't be built, or that a new plan is being presented in the spring, or that all of this is the reason why we've called a truce, why I've been given a social reprieve, why school has become manageable.

We chase after birds sometimes, making fun of their lazy ways, how it seems like pigeons would rather run a marathon than actually fly.

"I was just in!" Babette shouts, and Leo looks at me and yells, "What's your excuse?"

I shrug and hope he never tattoos his chest. My excuse is simply that I am Jane. I understand why the birds would rather run than fly.

I am trying to coax a memory to light—a memory of a bathtub, a dark room, a lightbulb dangling on a wire but hidden so as to only project a tiny bit of light. A memory of bath toys that look silver-and-black and of my mother, splashing the water around me and laughing in the near-dark.

Legs arrives then, holding a thermos. "Want some?"

I take it from him and sip hot chocolate. Because Legs has actually become my friend. And even though I'm sure he still wants us to be more than that, he never says anything about it and neither do I. He doesn't care that my father designed a coaster for Loki, thinks maybe a big slick coaster would be really cool for Coney. Even if I'm not sure anymore, it's nice to not be judged.

Down the beach a ways, I spot Rita—squeezed into a black string bikini and wearing a hot-pink bathing cap. I marvel that it can contain all that hair. I can tell that one of the women she is with is her mother and figure the other is her grandmother. They all three take hands and then walk straight out into the surf, exclaiming things in Spanish that I don't understand. Watching them, I feel a pang of envy, like a jellyfish has somehow pulsed its way into my heart and stung me there. Rita and Babette have a truce of sorts, too. Rita pretends nothing is going on with Marcus and Babette pretends she believes that. Or maybe she really does.

H.T. has arrived, too, and he says, "You'll notice that most of those idiots are like y'all." He's bouncing on his legs, trying to keep warm. "White."

He's right.

"Why is that?" I ask, because I sense an opening where openings rarely exist.

He pulls his hat down to better cover his ears and breathes icy fog into his hands. "You tell me."

"Seriously," I say. "Why aren't you out there?"

"'Cause it's COLD!" he says, and we all laugh.

Legs says, "This is ridiculous. I can't take it." He turns to go. "You coming?"

I take one last look at the ocean, with the winter sun glaring off it in a shocking white burst, making me squint.

Tomorrow, things will go back to sleepy and only the pigeons and seagulls will miss the crowds. Winter will settle over Coney again like an invisible igloo. The streets will be cleaner, the nights quieter, and there will be no girls with pigtails and oversize sunglasses, no smart-alecky T-shirts, no families from Westchester, wherever that is. I will go back to poking around the attic for keys and journals and contemplating the Bath key and hiding my heart away in a shipwreck or submarine. I will go back to puzzling over the increasingly cryptic Dreamland Social Club fliers—"You really don't know, do you?"; "Are you daft?"—and wait to see what they do next.

I will hum the Dreamland song and hear Leo's sad, sad saw song in my head and hope that the tsunami of spring will never come.

Part Three

GABBA GABBA HEY

CHAPTER

THE FIRST DAY OF SPRING, a Friday, actually felt like the first day of spring. Even Jane had been in a light and breezy mood—and had dared to wonder why she'd ever dreaded the onset of the new season—until she walked into the cafeteria at lunchtime only to have her red skirt blown chin-high by a cool blast of air.

The room was full and staring and laughing as Jane froze—*Idiot! She froze!*—and tried to hold her skirt down against the wind and then, finally, stepped aside. A small ramp had been placed over the steps down into the room, with a fan blowing up through a grate. She was thinking *Claveracks!* when she saw these words written in thin black paint on the ramp's wooden top step:

IT'S WHAT'S UNDERNEATH THAT REALLY MATTERS.
Deep thoughts from the Dreamland Social Club.

Everyone in the room was still laughing.

She stormed out, blushing, as another unsuspecting person walked in and had her skirt blown up and the laughter roared louder. It was only when she went into the girls' room and locked herself in a stall that she remembered the Blowhole Theater at Steeplechase Park. Which made her feel slightly better—she had not been the intended target but just one of many unsuspecting ones— but at the end of the day, she snapped when she saw the fliers all over that said:

dreamland social club
EMERGENCY MEETING TODAY, ROOM 222

Which was familiar enough, but they all had a new slogan:

Your Mother Wears Combat Boots.

She ripped down the closest flier she could find and stormed up the stairs and knocked on the door to 222. Babette opened the door, and Jane was thinking of that armless, legless girl in the white dress in the old photo and feeling just that vulnerable, when she said, "What's the deal with this club and its deep thoughts, anyway? And *You know who you are? Your mother wears combat boots?* Why be so exclusive? So vague? I mean, what if *I* wanted to join?"

She stepped into the room, and a chorus of voices let out a rhythmic *"Gooble gobble. Gooble gobble."*

Legs was there. And Minnie. Leo. Venus. Rita. And Debbie, too. Pounding out a beat on the desks with their hands.

"Gooble gobble. We accept her. We accept her. One of us, one of us."

For a second Jane wanted to scream, wanted to play her part—was that what she was *supposed* to do?—and shout out "FREAKS!" because that's what the normal woman in the movie had done, but then something dawned on her. Her mother never would have started a club so exclusive; there was no way. The signs weren't meant to exclude but to tease those who might want to be included. So when the chanting and pounding stopped, she said, "It's the opposite of exclusive, isn't it?"

"Yes, you idiot." Babette closed the door. "And we've been *waiting*. All freaking fall and winter. I mean your mother founded the damn club."

Jane was elated and incensed. "But you never said anything or asked me to join or anything. None of you."

Not that Venus or Minnie would have, but still . . . Leo could have. Or Legs!

"That was the whole idea," Legs said. "The whole way your mother set it up. No recruiting. No asking your friends. No *talking about it*, even. Ever."

All of which would explain why Beth wouldn't talk about it. Freddy Claverack, too.

Leo said, "New members have to turn up on their own

and they have to be let in, whoever they are. So it never becomes cliquish."

Babette pulled out a beat-up notebook, opened to the front pages, and read: *"I hereby found the Dreamland Social Club as a haven for the wayward and curious, for those interested in the strange in the normal, the normal in the strange, the old in the new, the new in the old.*

"Anyone who walks through the door must be accepted with the following refrain: 'Gooble gobble. Gooble gobble. We accept her. We accept her. One of us, one of us'—preferably recited in the style of the scene in the film Freaks—*even if the person is technically not a her, but a him.*

"Or generally despised.

"Or too popular for his or her own good.

"The Dreamland Social Club is, therefore, a safe haven for outsiders and outcasts of all kinds. Even those who appear to be insiders."

Jane went closer to Babette and saw that the club's mission statement had been written in her mother's own hand. "So that day when I knocked on the door . . ."

Babette said, "We thought you'd caught on."

"So I could've become a member back then?"

"All you had to do was walk in. And my God. *The clues!*" Babette shook her head. "I left the questionnaire at your house."

"You did?" Venus protested.

"And I gave you that old photo," Legs said.

"Against the rules," Minnie said, but Legs just shrugged.

"And I started rewriting the posters just for you," he said. "To try to get you to come in."

"My mother wore combat boots," Jane said. "Are you daft?"

"Exactly," Legs said. "Actually, Leo came up with those two."

"Did the trick!" Leo said. Jane wasn't sure, but he seemed happy she was there. His *gooble gobbles* had seemed especially spirited.

"I didn't know!" she said to them all.

"Obviously!" Babette said.

Jane studied the flier. "So what's the emergency?"

"The *emergency*," Babette said, turning to the group, "is that we're all set for Electric Bathing, but we've got no ideas for the Mermaid Parade."

H.T. came in then and sat down, then spotted Jane and said, "Gooble gobble. Gooble gobble." He flashed a smile. "Finally."

But Jane's brain was like a record that had skipped, back at the words *Electric Bathing*.

Stuck on four letters in particular.

Bath.

She hadn't actually thought all that much about the key over the winter, but now that a possible clue had presented itself, she felt a phantom itch.

"*Come on*, Babette," Venus whined. "It's *March*. It's *Friday* and I want to go home. We'll think of something."

"Seriously," Minnie said. "There's plenty of time."

They had both said their own gooble gobbles. But did it really mean Jane had been accepted?

"That's what we *always* say, and then we were totally

scrambling last year." Babette furrowed her brow and said, "I know! Let's meet Sunday at the Anchor, just for a little bit. It's opening day. The boardwalk. Fresh air. Maybe we'll be inspired."

Everyone grumbled agreement, and a noon meet time was decided upon.

"What's Electric Bathing?" Jane asked as she and Babette walked home. "It sounds sort of familiar but—"

"Every year, last day of school," Babette cut in, "since your mother's year, we rig up a light on a pole in the water, and there are ropes that lead you out and then we wade in and swim by the light of a forty-watt bulb. They used to do it back in the thirties or something."

And just like that . . .

I'm in the bathtub and the lights are out except for a flashlight that my mother is holding up high over me. Through the skylight in the ceiling I think I can see stars and even part of the moon, and my mother is saying, "Gosh, ain't electricity grand?"

"Earth to Jane," Babette said. "Come in, Jane."

"Sorry," she said. There hadn't been much more to the memory anyway. "Any keys involved?"

"Keys?" Babette said. "Like to what?"

"I don't know. Never mind." Jane tripped on one of the boardwalk's uneven planks but recovered quickly; one of her middle toes panged. "So that's all you do? Weird Coney-related stunts?"

"Yeah, pretty much." They stopped by a bench and sat. "But don't blame me, your mother started it."

Jane looked out at the empty beach and wondered how Sunday's crowds would compare. It wasn't warm enough to swim yet but it was a mild March so far, more lamb than lion. She said, "What kinds of things have people done before?"

"Well, last year we tried to build a Helter Skelter slide from the gym windows." Babette played with one of her seven looped earrings for a second. "With one of those inflatable slide things, but decorated to look cooler. But the whole thing was a disaster."

"What did the first club do?" Jane asked. "Is there a list in there?"

"Oh," Babette said, "yeah, that's pretty much all this book is, notes about stunts." She started to flip through the official Dreamland Social Club notebook.

"Do you mind?" Jane held out her hands, and Babette handed the book over. Jane turned back to the beginning and to the pages that came right after the club's statement of purpose, the rules of membership. When she found the list of stunts from the club's first year she said, "It says here that they made a papier-mâché version of the beast in *The Beast from 20,000 Fathoms* and put it on the roof of the school."

"Turn the page," Babette said. "There's a picture."

Jane turned and found the photo taped into the book and studied it. "I saw that movie," Jane said. "My brother has it."

They hadn't talked about Marcus in any real way in a

long time, not since they'd both accepted that Jane knew more about her brother and Rita than Babette really wanted to know. Jane regretted even mentioning him.

"Any good?" Babette asked. She'd become a professional at this nonchalance thing over the winter.

"Not really," Jane said. "No."

Babette looked at her watch. "I better go." She stood. "So I'll see you Sunday at the meeting?"

"That's really it?" Jane held out the book and Babette took it. "I'm a member?"

"That's really it."

They both shook their heads.

"Here," Babette said, handing the book back. "Why don't you take it home? There are some old questionnaires in there, in the envelope in the back."

"My mom's?"

Babette just nodded.

Jane sat with the book in her room when she got home and started to flip through the opening pages, where more rules were laid out.

"In addition to not speaking about the existence or activities of the club when not at an official meeting, members are asked to refrain from claiming membership in yearbooks or on résumés and the like. The founder of the club will claim credit for its foundation in one publication of record, The Coney Island High Tide, *solely to put the club in the history books."*

It all seemed sort of dopey to Jane, in a way, but it was also thrilling to glimpse these insights into her mother's world. It wasn't her journal, no, but it was sort of close. She turned to the envelope taped to the book's inside back cover and saw a note written on the envelope:

The official Dreamland Social Club Membership Questionnaire is NOT mandatory for membership, but if members are inclined to answer a few random probing questions so that future generations might glimpse the inclinations and personas of some former members, so be it:

She flipped through the stack until she saw the one with *Clementine* written in the top slot for "Name (first only)."

What's your earliest memory?
> *Waking up to the noise of my parents' crazy parties.*

What sound makes you happy?
> *Silence.*

What was the last dream you had that you remember?
> *I dreamed I was the singer of a band that had a sort of B-movie dragon as the drummer.*

Name one thing you want to do before you die.
> *See the world. Or at least part of it.*

Why is a raven like a writing desk?
> *Because you cannot ride either one of them like a bicycle.*

What's the best thing about being you?
> *I have a lot of secrets and an active imagination. Seriously good daydreamer.*

Setting the page down, Jane lay back on her bed. She'd been hoping for more insight, but there were some clues, weren't there? That the girl her mother had been had been pretty similar to the woman she'd become, or at least the woman Jane remembered. She'd wanted to travel before she died, and the fact that she had accomplished that struck Jane as a good thing, a happy thought. But what did it mean if one of the best things about being you was that you were a serious daydreamer? It meant you were good at escaping, which meant that you had a life worth escaping from, which was sort of sad. Then again, all those games—Elephant Hotel, the house under the roller coaster—that was a kind of daydreaming, a kind of reverie, too, and a good kind.

Secrets.

That word again.

Going to her desk, where the mermaid doll sat with its secret keys stuffed back inside where they'd spent the winter, Jane pulled them back out again.

Thunder. Jump. Wonder.

Those had all been sorted out—for the most part, anyway. The Wonder key still nagged, but not as much as the Bath key. And when her fingers found it, she felt a new determination to try to figure out what it was. Electric Bathing wasn't a clue, wasn't the answer. Still, it was out there. So she took the key off the ring and put it on her keychain with her house keys so that it would be with her when the answer presented itself.

two

HER FATHER CAME HOME that Saturday afternoon with a garment bag and wanted to model his new suit. Jane couldn't think of the last time her father had bought a suit and admitted it looked good on him, though possibly just because it was new. "What's the occasion?" she asked, feeling playful. "Hot date?"

"With Loki," he said. "And the city council."

"Oh," she said, and she instantly, viscerally—like in the buzz of her fingertips and the quiver in her throat—remembered why she'd dreaded spring to begin with. "What's going on?" she asked and felt wobbly—as if she were on skates. As if winter had been a smooth glide on a frozen lake but now cracks were forming on the surface.

"Big presentation of Loki's new plan Thursday night at

the Aquarium." He was straightening his jacket. "Loki is opening it to the public on a first-come, first-served basis and footing the bill for a dinner buffet. To try to win people over, I guess."

"And the new plan is a lot better?" Jane asked, pushing down the sick feeling in her gut. She'd sort of assumed the new plan would take longer, even though they'd been saying spring all along.

He nodded. "Which tie do you like?" He held up two, and Jane pointed to the one with gray and blue stripes on a diagonal.

"How is it different from the old plan?" she asked.

"I'm not sure. I just know the Tsunami made the cut." He looked in the mirror. "Speaking of which, I need to get this mop trimmed." He ran a hand through his hair, then disappeared upstairs.

Jane sat in the living room for a moment, absorbing this new information. The presentation was happening. She knew about it. But did Leo? Did anyone? Had the news been made public already? Because she did not want to make the same mistakes she'd made in the fall. She wanted to be open. Honest. Wasn't that the way forward?

She went upstairs and knocked on her father's door. "Have they announced the event yet?" she asked when he opened.

"I don't know," he said. "But I think so. Or it will be. Maybe tomorrow. What's on your mind?"

She sat in a chair in the corner. "I don't know. There's someone I might need to tell about it, just to be sure he doesn't hear it somewhere else and realize that I knew. It's complicated."

"Sounds it." He was hanging up the suit, brushing off a few bits of fuzz.

"Dad?" There was more on her mind than she'd actually realized at the start of the conversation. "If they veto Loki again—and I know it's a big if—do you think the *city* might be interested in the Tsunami?"

He turned to her. "I'm not sure it works that way, honey. And the city seems to have just stalled its own plans anyway. Something about a change in leadership, I think."

He was emptying his shopping bag and said, "Oh, I almost forgot." He handed her a postcard—"This was in the mailbox when I came in"—and she studied the image on the front—a black-and-white shot of a million people on the beach. She didn't have to turn it over to know it was from Mr. Simmons, but she did anyway. It said, "Are we having fun yet?"

After dinner that night, Jane went to the window in her room and looked out at the Parachute Jump, lit red in the night. Tomorrow all the boardwalk stores and clam shacks and pizzerias and bars would open for the season, and the crowds would be endless and annoying.

Crowds were good, she knew.

Good for Coney. It depended on them.

But she was going to miss the quiet, the knishes, the truce. She was going to miss the way Coney felt more like a secret than the playground of the world.

Crossing the hall to Marcus's room when she couldn't shake a restless feeling, she poked in her head. "I'm going to go for a walk. You want to come?"

So they went up toward the boardwalk together, with light jackets on, and just walked and walked until they hit Brighton—where Russian women in fancy dresses were talking and smoking in groups in front of Tatiana. The sounds of the cabaret—electronic drums and poppy female vocals—floated out into the air.

And then they turned around and walked back and cut down the side of Wonderland, where a barker stood outside the sideshow building with a megaphone. "Free show tonight!" he said to no one, then he spotted Jane and Marcus. "Hey, you two," he said. "Free show. Come in. You don't have anything better to do. It's our dress rehearsal for tomorrow."

Marcus looked at Jane and shrugged, and she said, "I don't know."

"Jane," he said, "we go to school at a sideshow practically every day. And I mean, look at your friends. You, of all people, shouldn't be squeamish about this."

She still couldn't believe the mystery of the Dreamland Social Club had been solved. If it weren't a secret society she'd be telling the whole world—or at least Marcus—about her new-member status.

"Fine," she said, and they ducked into the dimly lit theater and climbed to the middle of a set of small bleachers facing a stage. Jane had, she only realized now, been consciously avoiding the sideshow ever since they'd arrived on Coney. It had seemed sort of scary to her when she'd first laid eyes on that mural on the building. But now, well, now she wasn't sure. Marcus was right. Maybe something about being a member of the Dreamland Social Club— a club inspired by a group of freaks—made her sort of calm about geeks and sword swallowers and fire-eaters. They were just people. People with tricks, sure, but still just people.

The sideshow performers didn't seem that enthused about working for a crowd of two, but Marcus and Jane did their best to clap loudly after a man lifted the bowling ball with a chain attached to his tongue, and after another man put a power drill up his nose. And when that same performer—the Human Blockhead—asked for a volunteer, Marcus said, "Go on," and elbowed Jane. "It's your destiny."

"You're making fun of me."

He sunk down in his chair.

"Fine." She stood. "Whatever."

So she went down to the stage—no one but Marcus was there anyway, so what did it matter if she looked dumb?— and then the Human Blockhead explained what he wanted her to do, and she thought she was going to throw up right there on the stage. But when he put the sword down his throat and tapped his chest—the signal they'd agreed upon—Jane climbed up the small step stool that had been put in front of her and took hold of the sword and very, very slowly pulled it up and out. And when she did, she felt strangely victorious.

When the Human Blockhead told her to take a bow, she did.

"Bravo," Marcus called from the bleachers, and he stood up and clapped, lazily, three times.

They walked past the Anchor on the way home and Jane saw Leo inside. "I'm just going to go say hi," she said to Marcus, who just said, "Okey-dokey," and walked off.

She went into the bar and sat next to Leo, who looked up from his crossword puzzle, startled. He said, "Spring has sprung, and so have you."

She crinkled her nose. "What does that mean?"

"I don't know." He sipped his Coke, studying her. "You seem different."

"I do?"

"Yeah," he said. "You do. A little gooble gobble magic, maybe?"

"Don't be stupid." She was looking at the crossword clues, trying to think of a three-letter word for "Paris to Berlin dir," whatever that meant.

"I'm just saying." Leo tapped his paper with his pencil. "It must be a relief. To have finally figured it out." He tilted his head. "You seem, sort of—I don't know—happy? No, not that. Sassy?"

"Sassy?" She shook her head. "Me? No way."

"See, right there." He pointed at her. "That was some sass."

"It was not!"

He just shrugged. "Look at this." He pointed at 18 down's clue, "Anchor's job."

"To sink?" Jane was looking for the right boxes.

"Ha," Leo said. "But no, five letters." He pushed the paper aside. "I sort of hate crosswords."

"Me, too."

"Where you coming from or going to? You want a Coke?"

"No, I'm good. Coming from sideshow. Going home."

"Really?"

"Yeah." She stretched the fingers on her hand. "I pulled a sword out of the Human Blockhead's mouth."

He made a clicking sound and pointed at her quickly, like taking a shot. "Sass, I'm telling you."

"I'm leaving," she said, rotating on her stool, though she had no intention of going anywhere.

"No," he said, grabbing her arm. "Stay a few minutes. It's a big night. Sort of like Christmas Eve."

"I feel it," she said, looking around at the couple leaning into the jukebox picking songs, and at the guy by the outside tables who was trying to sell DVDs to the people there, and at Leo's father, who was polishing up the old cash register. "Something in the air."

What she couldn't bring herself to say was that there was something else in the air, bouncy molecules of dread ricocheting around with all the excitement. He just couldn't feel them. She simply didn't have the heart to spoil the mood with the word *Loki*, not when he seemed so happy.

"We have this tradition," Leo said. "My dad and me."

"You're not going to trim a tree, are you?"

"No, but every year since I can remember, he closes the bar a little early on the night before opening day and we watch *The Beast from 20,000 Fathoms*. Ever see it?"

Jane nodded and said, "It's pretty bad."

"But that's the beauty of it!" he said with an elbow nudge. "I was obsessed when I was little. Now it's just for old times' sake. Or something. I don't even know. I thought it was cool your mom made the beast once, though."

Jane nodded. "Yeah. Me, too." She was studying the words around the "anchor's job" clue and the word popped out. Not a boat anchor but a news anchor. "Recap," she said, pointing.

"Huh?" Leo said, then he thought for a second and said, "Oh," and wrote it in. "Yeah, definitely hate crosswords."

His dad called out, "Drink up, folks, we're closing early!" and was met by a few lazy groans.

three

THE STORE FOR LEASE BANNER hanging on the Anchor rippled in the wind like a flag. Just down the boardwalk, similar signs—PROPERTY FOR LEASE—wrapped around the gate to Wonderland. Jane and the rest of the Dreamland Social Club stood outside and watched as people walked by, then stopped, midsentence, when they noticed what was going on.

What the feck?

The signs had appeared overnight, as if by magic. Jane knew for certain they had not been there last night.

But there was no mistaking their origins.

Jane looked at the serpent bolt of the logo and swore she heard a hiss. This was all very wrong.

Leo had gone inside to talk to his dad and now came back to report. He said, "They're trying to mothball the boardwalk."

"*Mothball?*" Jane crinkled her nose. It didn't make sense.

"It means that Loki's pissed their first plan got vetoed, and now they're going to shut down the Anchor and Wonderland even if they can't replace them. Just to prove a point."

Jane shook her head. Still didn't get it.

Babette rolled her turquoise eyes and said, "The point being that they can just let the land sit there. *Gathering moths*. Unless the new plan they're presenting on Thursday gets approved."

"Oh!"

So the news of the presentation *was* out. And Loki had obviously timed this power play for maximum impact. Jane's father had neglected to mention the mothballing, to warn her. Had he known this was going to happen?

Leo shook his head. "My dad said that's it. The jig is up. Six weeks and he's shut down. And Wonderland only has two, so they might not even bother opening up again next weekend."

The park was open now. You could hear a few of the rides whirring and tinkling.

"Let me get this straight," Legs said. "This is supposed to force the city to approve the new plan?"

Leo said, "Yes."

"Do you think it will work?" Rita asked. Rita, like Coney, just *looked* better, happier, now that winter was over with. Her skin seemed to thrive on a particular kind of sun.

"No idea," Leo said, and then they watched a few more people stop and point at the STORE FOR LEASE signs.

Moving over to the plastic tables in front of the bar, they took seats, and Leo's dad came out to say hi and to clean their table.

"We're really sorry, Mr. LaRocca," Babette said, and everyone muttered their regrets, too.

"Crazy days," he said, and then his sinewy arms ran a cloth around—he was wearing a shirt this time—and rearranged some condiments. Jane tried to glimpse Leo's future in his father's form, tried to imagine what he might look like in a bunch of years, what kind of man he might become. She still wasn't sure she agreed with what her father had said about how loving someone's potential wasn't really love. She was sure, though, that she loved Leo just as he was right then, even if he didn't feel the same way.

Finally, Mr. LaRocca took the ashtray away and said, "I'll send over some sodas."

"I'll help." Leo sprung up out of his chair.

H.T. took the seat next to Jane. He had his legs on but was wearing shorts, so the metal joints glinted in the sun. She watched the people around them do double takes and gawk and elbow friends and found herself staring at one woman who was staring intently at H.T.

Look at me, she thought, trying to will the woman to turn her head. *I dare you.*

And when she did, Jane just stared at *her,* like *she* was

the freak, until finally, the woman looked away, whispered something to her friend.

"I wonder what they'll do with that," Babette said.

She pointed over to the neon sign at Wonderland, and Jane wondered whether Alice and the Mad Hatter and their fluorescent blue teapot would suffer the same fate as the Hell Gate demon and the Claverack horse, locked away in some old man's dusty old house. It didn't seem right.

Mothballing.

A funny word.

Preemie had been doing his own variation of it for years.

Leo's dad was back with sodas, and then Leo reappeared with a clipboard. He said, "Petition to save the Anchor."

Babette signed the hastily drawn-up document. So did Rita. And Minnie and Venus and H.T. But when the clipboard came around to the other side of the table, to where Jane was sitting, she hesitated.

Leo said, "What do you say, Looky Lou?"

It was the first time he'd called her that in months, and she felt like it meant something, she just wasn't sure what.

She studied the statement at the top of the petition, scrawled in Leo's handwriting: *We, the undersigned, object to the amusement park and mall planned by Loki Equities and want a fair renegotiation of leases for establishments including the Anchor.* She looked up and said, "I don't think I can."

"Figures." Leo slid the clipboard away.

"What's that supposed to mean?" Jane snapped.

"I'm just not surprised is all."

"Well, you shouldn't be," she said. Maybe he was right about the sass. "We knew this was coming."

"Yeah, I guess *we* did." He shook his head.

"And it wouldn't look good for me to have my name on that if my father's project goes ahead. It's that simple. So what's your problem?"

"My *problem* is that I'm wasting time talking to you when I could be getting signatures." He pushed the clipboard toward Legs. "What about you, Legs?"

Legs looked at Jane, then back at Leo and said, "Sorry, man."

Leo said, "Whatever."

The woman who'd been staring at H.T. got up and gave him one last stare and he smiled at her—big, white, happy teeth—and said, "Have a nice day."

She hurried away, and H.T. turned to Jane. "I saw you giving her the evil eye. What was that about?"

Jane shrugged. "I just think it's rude."

"It's normal."

"Still."

Debbie slid into a seat then and said, "Sorry I'm late." She'd bleached her facial hair over the winter and it was an improvement, yes, but it was still a lot of hair.

Babette had brought a bunch of old photos so that they could try to get inspiration from the kinds of things people had done in the past—like dress up as sushi or make a procession for King Nemo or craft huge monsters from the deep. Hundreds of thousands of people came to the parade, apparently. It was a big deal. No one at the table, however, seemed particularly inspired.

"Well, whatever we do," Babette said with some annoyance, "I think it should have music. I want people to hear *and* see us."

"Well, sign me up for music," Leo said. "I'm going to try to get some signatures."

Jane watched him walk away, to a table where a few tourist types had just sat down, and she thought of the sound of his saw playing the Dreamland song. How sad it had been.

"What about some kind of funeral procession?" she said.

Babette looked like she'd just smelled day-old fish. "A funeral for who?"

Jane was looking up at the STORE FOR LEASE sign that would be the Anchor's death knell. "I don't know," she said. "For Coney Island?"

But that wasn't *quite* right.

"No, wait!" She sat forward in her chair. "It's for a mermaid. It's a mermaid funeral."

She could picture the scene then instantly—more vividly than she could picture even her own mother's funeral, which had been reduced to a series of flashes: *Muddy ground. Hugs from strangers. Big cars. White lilies tossed onto a black coffin.*

"We'll make a big funeral bier and someone will dress

up as a mermaid and we'll all push it down the parade route." She was getting excited. "And the music can be like a dirge or some kind of old sad sea shanty or something, and we'll all wear black."

"I don't know," Babette said, but her eyes seemed to light up.

Jane said wryly, "You're already in costume."

Venus said, "It's not much of a stretch for you either. Some of your clothes are so old they *should* be dead." Jane had been visiting vintage and secondhand shops all winter, assembling a wardrobe sort of inspired by Birdie's old clothes. Today she was wearing a blue-and-white gingham dress with short cap sleeves and a mildy frilly old-fashioned collar.

"Not nice," Babette said.

"I'm kidding," Venus said, then added brightly, "Gooble gobble!"

"A mermaid funeral," Babette said again—trying it on for size—and Rita said, "It's pretty good."

Legs agreed, as did H.T. and Debbie.

Venus and Minnie just shrugged, but for some reason Jane didn't even care anymore. It wasn't like Leo had picked Jane over Venus. It wasn't as though she'd done anything with Legs but become his friend. And she was a member of the D.S.C. now, so they were just going to have to get over it.

"I can make the mermaid tail and fin out of some of my grandmother's old costumes," she said in an attempt to cinch the deal.

"Nobody has any better ideas?" Minnie said, sort of desperately, and everyone shook their heads. When Leo walked by their table, Babette said, "Feel like writing a funeral dirge?"

"Always," he said, and then he approached another group.

Petition to save the Anchor.

Petition to save the Anchor.

The phrase lodged itself securely on a loop in Jane's head.

Jane and Legs—the only two people who were famished—headed over to Nathan's after the group split up to find that hundreds of other people were also craving hot dogs on opening day. Jane would have been happy to redirect to pizza or anything, really, but Legs was determined to get a hot dog—or four, as the case may be—and so they waited and waited and waited and pushed and shoved and finally ordered five dogs and three orders of fries. When Legs announced the order, it became obvious to Jane that everyone on line was staring at him.

At them.

People had, she realized, probably been doing it the whole time, and every other time they'd been out together—as friends, just friends—but Jane hadn't actually noticed. Now that she had—now that she and H.T. had talked about it, the staring—she couldn't *not* notice. She didn't like it.

Legs acted like he didn't notice—trying to make light conversation about the weather—but Jane could tell he did, and that he sensed the change in her. They finally sat down with hot dogs at a table outside and he said, "Does it bother you?"

"What?"

"You know." He looked off to his right, and Jane followed his gaze and saw a bunch of guys in baseball caps avert their eyes and then laugh. "The staring."

She suddenly wasn't interested in her hot dog. "It's weird," she said. "I never noticed it before today for some reason."

Leo walked by them then, though he didn't see them, and neither of them called out to him as he stopped people on the street to get signatures.

"You know, it's funny." Legs was already on his second dog; Jane was still spreading mustard on hers, squeezing it out of the small, soft paper cup she'd filled at the condiment pumps. "For a while there I thought you were going to end up with Leo."

Jane stared at her dog, covered in off-white kraut and golden-brown mustard. It suddenly looked like horribly fake food, like it would be wrong to eat it. Someone named Nathan got rich because of *this*? "Why would you think that?" she said steadily.

"Just a sense I got, and I mean, there's some history, right?"

"Right," Jane said. "Our mothers were friends."

As if that explained it all.

"I heard that. And I thought you were going to go for him, but then I guess the whole Tsunami thing happened." Legs chewed a bit, moved onto his third dog. "People stare at him, too, but it's different."

"How is it different?" Jane was pretty sure she already knew.

Legs swallowed, and Jane watched his Adam's apple— like the size of a baseball—travel down his neck. "They look at me because they're grateful they're not me. They look at him because they want to *be* him."

Jane said, "I bet there are people out there who'd want to be you."

"Name one good reason why anyone would want to be seven and a half feet tall." Before she could say anything he added, "And the reason can't be basketball."

She was stumped for a second, but then she said, "I think some of the, you know, little people. Minnie. Babette. I think they sometimes wish they were you."

"They wish they were taller," he said. "Not *this* tall."

"Well, there are good things about it, right? I mean, you can always see if you go to a concert."

Legs let out a loud "Ha" before continuing. "I have to stand in the very last row or at the back edge of a crowd or I piss people off."

She felt her own pout.

"You're sweet." Legs started to gather his trash. "And it's not the worst thing in the world, no. But it's not that great either."

"Dude," someone said as Legs stood up. "You play basketball?"

"No," Jane snapped. "He doesn't."

She was angry—had been angry the whole time, she realized—and finally felt the need to ask Legs, "Why didn't you sign the petition?"

"I didn't think you wanted me to."

"What did *you* want to do?" Her whole body seemed to tighten.

"I don't think it's a big deal either way." Legs threw his trash into a large bin. "It's not like a stupid petition is going to change anything."

He was right. But Jane wanted to smack him anyway.

Peach Fuzz had a new Mets shirt but the same tire belly and the same old lines. "Check-check-check it out," he said into the mike. "Shoot the Freak in the freakin' head."

Jane had half a mind to slap down ten bucks and let rip. She'd pretend the Freak was Leo again and she'd nail him.

He deserved it.

Not for trying to save his father's bar or trying to stop Loki from building a shopping mall, but for just not getting it. Not getting that none of it—Loki, the Anchor, the Tsunami, nothing—had anything to do with them, not really. For not getting that they had had something that was worth pursuing that fall and that they owed it to themselves to follow through and see what it really was.

The more time that had passed, the more knishes they'd shared during their truce, the more sure Jane had become that he'd wanted to kiss her that night on the roof of the bumper car building, when they'd gone to Luna Park and the Elephant Hotel in their minds.

The more time that had passed the surer she was that she was the one who'd screwed it up, by not realizing she'd agreed to a date with Legs, by not telling Leo about the Tsunami sooner.

But he hadn't helped.

She watched as a few shooters splattered orange and green paint on the trash can the Freak had ducked behind and then found herself, once more, staring at the Mad Hatter and his teapot. She was suddenly very, very thirsty, like there was a webby moths' nest in her throat. And when she walked by the carousel house and saw the sign that said that the ride had been removed, to be restored, and would be back next year, she knew what she had to do.

four

I THINK WE SHOULD GIVE THE HORSE BACK," she said at dinner that night. The three of them were eating sausage-and-pepper sandwiches made with sausages Marcus had cooked out back on the grill, and from her seat at the table Jane could see the horse, frozen in its gallop to nowhere. She was surer than ever of what was right.

"What?" Marcus said, chewing. "No way. Why?"

"I thought you said you didn't care." Jane took another bite.

Marcus wiped his mouth and put his sandwich down. "I thought you said Birdie was on it the first time Preemie met her."

"She was?" their dad said, and Jane nodded, then turned

to Marcus. "I repeat," she said. "I thought you didn't care."

"Children," their father said. He had already devoured his own sandwich and was picking at a salad Jane had made.

"Harvey gave me a black eye," Marcus said, then he popped the last bit of his bread into his mouth.

"You *neighed* at him," Jane said between bites.

"Have they been bothering you again, Jane?" her father asked. "Is that what's going on?"

"No, actually." They'd stopped—right after she talked to their father and grandfather. She almost hadn't realized it at the time. "But I've been thinking." She glanced into the living room again. "It just doesn't belong here."

"But it was *beloved* by your *beloved* grandparents," Marcus said with a hand to his heart for drama.

"Yeah," Jane said. "And they're gone."

"Keep talking," her father said.

Jane wiped her own mouth and hands with a napkin. "Well, I mean it had sentimental value to them but now they're not here anymore, and it has sentimental value to me but I'm not sure the value I have trumps the value that Grandpa Claverack has."

"But he's going to sell it," her brother said.

"And that's his prerogative."

"But that means it has *no* sentimental value to him, so none is less than whatever you have," Marcus said.

"Yeah, but I don't know. Maybe he'll be sentimental once he has it. Maybe he'll get it and then realize he doesn't even want to sell it. Anyway, it's just dumb for us to keep it." She was about to say, "We're mothballing," but instead she just looked at her father and said, "We have no good reason to keep it is all."

"This seems like an unexpected change of opinion."

"I don't know," Jane said. "Maybe I'm just sick of looking at it there, sick of thinking about it. Call it, I don't know"—a cool breeze tickled the kitchen curtains—"Call it spring cleaning. You said we had to clean out the house, Dad, and we haven't even really started."

"Well, now that you've brought it up"—he put his plate in the sink, then came back to the table—"I think we should talk about what my job means for us, for the house. Because if all goes well this week with the presentation, the Tsunami will be built. Which means I'd want to be here. I'd need to be here. I just wanted to see how you felt about that."

Marcus said, "Whatever you want, Dad."

"Well, that's easy for you to say," he replied. "You're going away to college."

Marcus had just that week started obsessively checking the mailbox hanging on the porch. Letters of acceptance—and Jane was sure they'd mostly be acceptances—were due to start arriving any day.

Their father said, "Jane, what about you?"

"When is the house officially mine and Marcus's?" she asked, surprising herself. But all the talk of real estate this year made her realize that stuff like this was important.

They hadn't actually spoken in months about the fact that the fate of the house was really up to Jane and her brother, not their dad.

He rubbed his eyes and then looked at her. "The easiest thing would be to stay here until you're both eighteen and entitled to proceeds. And then sell it and divide the money down the middle. Earlier than that and the money will go into a trust."

"You want to stay until I'm eighteen?" Jane asked. In July she was going to be seventeen. That meant staying another year and a half or more. It meant *graduating*.

Her father shrugged. "Well, it depends on what happens with this vote."

"I think I'm okay with that," she said, though she wished this moment could have ended up being more joyful. The idea of spending more than one year somewhere—*anywhere*—was enough to make her want to cry with happiness, but things with Leo were complicated enough now that fleeing had its appeal, too. But it was better to be here on the wrong side of things than to be right but be gone. Wasn't it?

Her father went to look for an ax, claiming he thought he'd seen one in the back of a closet on the second-floor hall. They were going to try to bust the horse free. Jane went into the living room and approached the horse and petted it the same way Leo had the night he'd come over. She wanted to ask her father whether he had known about the FOR LEASE signs, about the closings of the Anchor and Wonderland, but she almost didn't want to know the answer. "I was thinking," she said when he came in with the ax, "about the Tsunami."

"What about it?" He knelt and surveyed the radiator, the chain.

"I was just thinking about how when they built this other roller coaster, the Thunderbolt, they ran the beams and stuff through the hotel that was in the way, so that they didn't have to close it down."

He rubbed his eyes. "Honey, I know it's your friend's father's place, but you don't know the whole story."

"Well then, tell me." She turned away from the horse.

"Okay," he said. "Apparently, your friend's father owes *thousands of dollars* in back rent because one day he just decided to stop paying."

"That's ridiculous," Jane said, but her father just kept talking.

"They've been cited for violations of a few safety and fire regulations, which they've done nothing to fix, *and* they have a ton of open health code violations. There are rats, mice, roaches, you name it."

"Loki made those up. Leo told me."

"There's video of the rats, honey. I'm sorry to have to be the one to tell you," he said. "But it's really easy to romanticize a place like that if you get to thinking that way. It's just not all it's cracked up to be. It's just not worth saving."

"What *is*, then?" Jane grew suddenly angry, remembering the trash bags on the porch. "What does someone like you think is worth saving?"

Her father got up, almost sadly, and walked out of the room, and then he came back with a small wooden box in his hands. He put it down on the coffee table and opened it and pulled out a bunch of items: a ticket stub "from my first date with your mother," a program from a play "from my second date with your mother," a penny that had been stretched long like a funhouse mirror "from my third date with your mother." He didn't stop until the box was emptied of letters and trinkets and notes, leaving only a few pieces of jewelry and a photo.

"My favorite picture of her," he said, and he handed it over. Jane saw her mom sitting on a beach chair, a bandanna on her head, drinking a cocktail out of a pineapple with a straw.

"I was saving *this* for you," he said. "Her wedding band. For when you were older."

Jane thought she was going to cry when he held out the ring toward her and said, "I guess I might as well give it to you now, though this isn't exactly the scene I was picturing."

"No," she said, pushing it back. "When I'm older, whenever you think is right."

He was still looking at the trinkets and tickets.

"I'm sorry, Dad," Jane said, and he sighed.

"I don't want you to be sorry, honey. I want to be able to talk about stuff like this and disagree and have that be all right. And sometimes I want you to trust that I'm right."

"But you're not right about this." She shook her head. "You can't be."

"Well, I guess you'll have to find out for yourself, then." He started to put his mementos away. "In the meantime, come with me on Thursday, will you? To the presentation? So you can see the whole of the plan and judge for yourself. I have four tickets for VIP seating. Marcus is coming. And you can bring a friend."

Jane nodded. "Sure, Dad. Of course."

"Okay," he said when Marcus came into the room. "Here goes nothing." He lifted the lock and chain so that it rested on a block of wood he'd found and then pulled it as far away from the horse as it would go. "You'd better stand back," he said to Jane, and she stroked the horse's mane before she did.

"Should I pre-dial 911 right now?" Marcus asked from the couch.

The ax missed the chain entirely on their father's first try. He swung again, and this time the sound was hot and hard but still, the chain remained strong.

After a few more useless hacks, he put the ax down and rested his hands on his hips. "Tell them if they want it they have to come get it."

It had been a long time since Jane had climbed the stairs to the attic, pulled the tiny metal beads of the bare bulb's pull-string, breathed in all that dusty air. It was less dusty than it had been when they'd first arrived so many months ago, but it still felt heavy, old.

Mothy.

She studied the demon from Hell Gate up close for the first time, felt the chipping paint and the smooth lines of the curvature of its lips. She tried to imagine what it had been like to ride through Hell Gate, tried to understand the desire to pay hard-earned money in order to take a boat ride through a simulated hell, to confront its fiery circles, to look Satan in the eye. It seemed that people who lived all those years ago had had a hard enough time just dealing with the realities of their own world—epidemics, wars, outhouses. Did they really have to make it any worse? Any scarier? What was this fascination with the morbid and terrifying and weird? And why didn't people have it anymore?

Or did they?

Looking around the room, Jane saw a few other things she was going to have to part with, whether her family ending up staying or not. Those "swinging" and "stationary" signs, for example. The invitation to Trump's Demolition Party.

Those she wouldn't miss.

But those films!

She'd grown so fond of those orphans, those diving horses, the old footage of Luna Park. They weren't old family movies, no, but they'd started to feel that way. Apart from *Is It Human?* they were all she had.

But still . . .

She found a pen and paper and started to make a list

of things she thought the Coney Island Museum might want. After she wrote down "Old Film: *Orphans in the Surf*," she decided to watch it again, maybe for the last time, and it didn't seem quite so horribly sad this time around. The shock of it was gone, and in its place was sadness, sure, but not nearly as much of it. When it ended, she returned to her list and wrote down, "Old film reel: *'King' & 'Queen' the Great Diving Horses*."

She had neglected to turn off the projector, and after she added a few more items to her list, new words appeared on the attic wall.

Baby Class at Lunch.

A new film started playing, tacked onto the same reel as *Orphans*.

It was impossible to tell for sure if it was the same toddlers. This time there were more of them, sitting on a staircase and eating sandwiches from brown bags. They were chewing and smiling and laughing and making funny faces, and even the herky-jerky grain of the film couldn't change that fact.

They seemed . . . happy.

In the quiet of the attic, Jane let out a laugh.

Baby Class at Lunch?

The title seemed ludicrous.

Hilarious, even.

And the laugh turned into a giggle as she watched these orphans chew and mug for the camera. She couldn't stop.

That's *what they'd called it?*

Baby Class at Lunch?

Because if they'd called the first one *Baby Class at the Beach* instead, she would have been spared an awful lot of heartache.

When the film was done, just a minute after it started, Jane took the reel off the projector and put it in a box with the others. It was time.

five

_____

ALL RIGHT, PUT YOUR BOOKS AWAY." Mr. Simmons turned to the board and started to draw a big building. It had columns on the front and peaked roofs, and above the doorway, where an inscription might appear cut into marble, he wrote TOWN HALL.

"Since you're all aware that Loki Equities is trying to force 'the future of Coney Island' to arrive"—he put the chalk down and brushed his hands together—"I thought we'd take today to talk about some of this past weekend's events in our own mock town hall meeting."

He looked out at the room, stroked his goatee. "Anyone want to get us started and jump right in?"

Leo stood. "My father's bar is getting shut down. It's not fair."

Somebody in class, maybe an Emmett, said, "Nobody's making him sell it! Just don't take the money!"

"They don't *own the land*." Leo turned to speak directly to the guy. "They rent the space, and Loki is forcing them out by not negotiating a new lease."

"The Anchor's a dump," another person, possibly a Stephanie, said.

Leo said, "Sure, it's run-down and stuff, but it's old. And it's run-down because it caters to thousands and thousands of people. It's a Coney Island institution."

Meanwhile, Mr. Simmons was writing years on the board: 1949, 1964, 1985.

Then after that he wrote, *History repeats*.

"Today, my dear students, you are taking part in an age-old Coney tradition. Namely, fighting about what Coney means, what Coney's future should be. We can, and should, look to the past as a series of cautionary tales, because each time"—he pointed at each year with the piece of chalk in his hand, making a click each time—"Coney was going to be redeveloped . . . and each time . . . what happened?"

"Nothing," Legs said.

"Exactly," Mr. Simmons said. "What, if anything, is different this time?" He put the chalk down on the ledge beneath the blackboard.

"It's hard to say," Babette said. "Something is different every time. This time it's Loki."

Mr. Simmons said, "Well put. Loki does seem to be serious. And of course the city has a few acres of its own to develop. Though politics seems to have brought all that to a screeching halt."

Jane had sort of hoped her father had been misinformed about that.

"The long and short of it," Mr. Simmons said, "is that I might be—*any of us* might be—rolling in our graves by the time any of this actually happens."

"Mr. Simmons?" Leo said. "Why don't you ask Jane for any insider information she might have? In case you haven't heard, her father designed Loki's weenie."

Something about the look in Leo's eyes when he turned to her made her blood boil, and she said, "The only inside information I have is that your father hasn't paid his rent in months and that there are rats in the bar."

"You're joking, right?" Leo rolled his eyes.

"Now, now," Mr. Simmons said, patting the air in front of him with his palms to say calm down. "I am curious, though, Jane. What do you think of Loki?"

She said, "I was thinking of reserving judgment until after I actually see the new plan."

"I suppose that's sensible enough," Mr. Simmons said, and Leo snorted.

He took his petition up to the front of the room after class ended. Mr. Simmons signed without batting an eye. Was she the only one who saw how complicated all this was?

"Yikes," Babette said, appearing by her side in the hall.

"Yeah."

And then there was Leo, right in her face.

"I just don't get you. At all." He looked visibly shaken for the first time since she'd known him; even his seahorse seemed agitated, blurry. "It just seems sometimes you do one thing, then do something else that's like the total opposite."

"What are you even talking about?" Jane said.

Legs walked past them then and Leo looked up at him and nodded briefly, and it felt like some sort of weird exchange of male sympathy, like they both felt they were better off not even dealing with crazy girls like Jane.

"Forget it, Jane." Leo looked back at her, seemed to shake something off. "But I mean, what side are you on anyway?"

It wasn't about sides.

There *weren't* sides, unless there could be like a million of them.

Nothing about it was black and white, this or that.

"You know what?" Jane said to Leo, and Babette drifted away with an apologetic raise of the eyebrows. "I don't get *you* either. I don't get how you can be so smart about so many things and have such ridiculous tunnel vision about this. About the bar. And I mean, have you even *looked around* lately? Taken a good look? Coney is a *dump*, and Loki's the only person—or company or whatever—who's really trying to do anything about it."

He threw his hands up into the air. "There aren't any rats!"

"And your father hasn't stopped paying his rent?"

"That's just a flat-out lie."

"Are you sure?"

He was winding the dial on his combination lock. "Your father's obviously been fed some crazy propaganda. And I mean, seriously"—he pulled his lock open, then opened the locker door—"your dad isn't the first person I'd trust right about now."

"It was just a question."

"Whatever, Jane." He started putting away books, taking out others. "Why don't you go back to looking for journals and solving mysteries about keys and teasing Legs and holding carousel horses hostage and whatever else it is you do."

Jane didn't like being whatever-ed and liked what came after it even less and, stunned, let herself drift into the flow of kids in the hall and bumped right into Legs, who'd obviously decided to hover. *Had* she been teasing him? Just by being friends?

He said, "Hey, do you have any tickets to the presentation?"

She nodded and saw, on the bulletin board, a flier that hadn't been there that morning.

dreamland social club
TODAY. UNFINISHED BUSINESS.

"Can I have one?" Legs said. "I'm covering it for the paper and I want to make sure I get in."

"Sure," Jane said.

A meeting?

Today?

Babette need to chill. Out.

"Thanks," he said, then nodded toward Leo's locker. "I hope he apologized." Legs shook his head. "The guy has lost all perspective."

"He's just upset," she said, not wanting to make things worse. "I mean, it's his father's bar."

"You know what, Jane?"

"What?" she snapped. She closed her locker and Legs looked like he was going to say something really urgent, and then he just huffed and said, "Never mind."

She had been planning on finding the Claveracks that day, to tell them about her decision about the horse. But when she saw them picking on a dowdy freshman between classes, she just couldn't bring herself to do it. And really, it didn't have anything to do with them—with Harvey and Cliff. It was their grandfather she should be talking to. He was the one who'd made the damn thing. He was the one who cared, if anyone did.

Did anyone really care as much as she did?

About anything?

She went to the meeting of the Dreamland Social Club after school, hoping that the spirit of the club would make everything better. But the mood was icy, at best. Nothing like it was the first time she'd walked in, just last week, and even then, there'd been Minnie's and Venus's cool stares to contend with.

"Let's get down to it so we can get out of here," Babette said, obviously sensing the tension.

"We need people to take the lead on the funeral bier," Babette said. "We either need to build something with wheels or we need to find some kind of wagon or cart that we can decorate, because holding something or carrying it that whole time will be too much."

"I have some ideas," H.T. said, so Babette wrote his name down, and then Legs said, "Me, too," so she wrote again.

"Music." Babette looked over at Leo, who said, "I'll scare up a dirge band the likes of which you've never heard."

"Excellent," Babette said, and then she added, "And we need to pick a mermaid."

There was a moment of silence before she said, "I nominate Jane."

Venus snapped, "Why her?"

"Yeah," Minnie said. "Why her?"

"Well, look at the rest of us," Babette said. "We're not exactly mermaid material."

"*I'm* mermaid material." Rita puffed up her breasts.

Venus snorted. "When's the last time anybody saw a Puerto Rican mermaid?"

"Same time they saw a mermaid with tattoos," Rita snapped.

"I'm starting to question the rules of membership in this club," Leo said from the back of the room, and Jane's face burned. "Me, too," she said. "Because the whole idea was that it wasn't going to become a clique and it is. None of you would really know what to do if someone really different, someone who challenged you, walked through that door."

"You know what?" Leo said. "I told my mother I wouldn't be late."

And he left.

And then Venus followed, saying to Jane, "You really want to be a dead fish, go ahead."

Minnie left, too, saying, "I wouldn't want to just lie there the whole time anyway."

Rita left, then Legs, and Babette said, "Then it's decided."

"You've got to be kidding me," Jane said, and Babette said, "Unless anyone objects on the record?"

H.T. said, "This seems like a decision for the women-folk."

"Then Jane it is." Babette wrote something down, seeming pleased. She declared the meeting adjourned.

"You should have asked me first," Jane said to Babette after H.T. skated away.

"Are you saying you don't want to do it?"

"No," Jane admitted. "Not exactly. It's just, I don't know. My mother went to mermaid camp once. With Leo's mom. And she had this thing about mermaids, so it all makes me sort of sad."

"I'm sorry, sweetie." Babette patted her leg. "But think of it this way. It's your chance to take back the mermaid. And make it not sad anymore."

"I guess," Jane said, though it all sounded sort of dumb. "But it's a *funeral*."

"Well, it was your idea."

"I know. I just didn't think it through."

Babette took a small card out of her backpack and handed it to Jane. "Leo gave this to me," she said, "but he probably meant it for you."

It read Mermaid Auditions @ The Coral Room, 4:00 p.m., and it had that day's date on it.

"You're joking, right?" she said.

"Not to audition," Babette said with an eye roll. "To watch. To be inspired."

"Oh, what's the point?" Jane said, but she was still studying the card.

Babette looked at her watch. "If you hurry, you can get there in time."

Jane took off toward the Coral Room as fast as her legs would carry her. Leo would probably be there. She didn't care. Or maybe that was the whole reason she was going. She wasn't sure. She thought maybe she wanted to apologize for saying the stuff about the rats and the rent in front of everybody. But she'd been provoked. Shouldn't he have to apologize, too?

The club was packed, mostly with women in bikinis, so Jane shrunk her shoulders and slid through until she was right up behind the people sitting at the bar, right near the tanks. In front of her a pair of twin girls swiveled on bar stools—"Mom is up first," one of them said, and their small bodies seemed to vibrate with anticipation. Jane felt that way, too.

Buzzing.

Buzzed.

She looked around for Leo but couldn't see past the people nearest her and, really, she didn't feel like dealing with him right then anyway.

When the first mermaid drifted down into the tank—the fish darted away in a sudden bolt—the crowd let out a collective gasp and she was there, a beautiful brunette who was waving and smiling, which had to be hard, in a pink and red polka-dot bikini. Was smiling underwater something they taught you how to do at mermaid camp? Had all of these women who were auditioning been to camp? Or did Beth run her own? Was Jane too old to go?

Between mermaids, she studied the glass, looking for that starfish she'd seen, and finally found it stuck to the side of the treasure chest of jewels. For a second she thought the journal had to be in there, but then she remembered: the club hadn't even been around then. Jane knew that sea stars could grow new limbs when they were hurt and, as she watched mermaid after mermaid take their quick turn in the tank, she wondered if maybe she was starting to regenerate missing parts in her own way, too.

It was sort of heartbreaking how un-mermaidy some of the women were—they were old and misshapen or had straggly hair or wrinkled bellies—but they all got their turn, and sometimes there were surprises. Like right at the end when the skinny old woman with the long white ponytail got in the tank in her black one-piece suit and let her hair loose and swam like she was putting on a mermaid show for real, waving and pretending to be having tea with a blowfish that seemed drawn to the sheen of her floating white hair. Jane would have hired her in a heartbeat.

Jane walked over to say hi to Beth, who cleared the room with the announcement that she would be calling three or four women tomorrow, and wished she wasn't a little bit scared of her, but she was. She was scared of how good that hug had felt, scared that Beth was—besides Jane's father—the one living breathing tie that existed to her mother's past, scared that if Beth knew about her father and the Tsunami—she must!—she'd never want to talk to Jane again.

"Did you just come to watch?" Beth asked, pulling her into a hug.

"I did," Jane said. "It was fun."

"Leo was just here." She looked around, as if he still might be in the room.

"Oh," Jane shook her head. "We're not—" How to explain? "I just mean, I'm not looking for him. I don't think—"

"Sit," Beth said, and she pointed toward a booth; they moved over to sit.

"Here's the thing." Beth straightened a tent card for Burlesque Night on the table. "Leo *worships* his father. So the idea that his father might not have done everything he could have to save this sinking ship, well, that's not so easy for him to accept right now."

So it was true about the rent, the rats. Jane stole a glance at the tank, where some fish had decided to come out of hiding. "But why is he so mad at me?"

"You're the messenger," Beth said. "Never a good role."

"So what do I do?"

"You wait. Or you move on. Or both." She took Jane's hand and said, "Your father is quite a roller coaster designer, by the way."

"I'm really sorry," Jane said, and Beth said, "Oh, honey. Don't be. It's not about one roller coaster or one amusement park or bar. It's about how to go about things is all. How to do things so that people feel they're being heard. That's all Coney Islanders for Coney is really about."

"So you don't hold it against me?" Jane said, almost crying with relief.

"Of course not."

Jane reached into her bag and took out her keychain and isolated the one labeled "Bath." She held it out and a smile crept across Beth's face.

"Do you know what it means?" Jane's heart thumped wildly.

Beth sat back in her chair. "I know this is going to seem terribly cruel of me. But your mother had a thing about secrets and keeping them."

Jane wasn't sure she understood what was happening. "Do you mean that you know what it is and you're not going to tell me?"

Beth seemed to be considering what to do one more time. "I'm sorry, honey," she said finally, and then she fake-zippered her mouth shut.

"Please," Jane said. "You *have* to."

Beth unzipped her lips and said, "As your mother would have said, where's the fun in that?"

CHAPTER
six

JANE HAD NEVER PLAYED HOOKY BEFORE, but when she woke up Tuesday morning, head throbbing, she told her dad she felt sick and wanted to stay home. He had better things to worry about and so said only, "I'll call it in."

She crawled back into bed, and soon the house was quiet and then it turned out she couldn't sleep. She had the "Bath" key on her night table and she kept turning it over in her hands, as if it might suddenly develop a mouth and tell her what it opened.

Eventually, she pulled on some clothes and went out into the yard and down to Birdie's Bavarian Bar and started to pull out costumes while also setting aside a few things that would go on her museum list.

Looking at the bird getups, it occurred to her that maybe cutting them up and using them to make a mermaid costume wasn't the best idea. To help her decide, she put one of them on. She picked a green one—the same color as the mermaid doll's fin—and then she found the matching headpiece, a feathery plume—and stood in front of the old mirror. She looked ridiculous. And so it was decided that she'd set aside one costume to save for the family—maybe for a Halloween party somewhere down the line—and then another for the museum, just in case they'd want that sort of thing. That left her three costumes to work with. Green. Orange. And yellow. Perfect.

It was possible the whole mermaid funeral would never happen, of course. But if it did she wanted to be ready. She wanted to prove to anyone who ever doubted it that she could be a mermaid.

And a damn good one.

So she put on some old records and found some scissors and pins and grabbed the mermaid doll from her room for inspiration and got to work. Eventually, she moved the operation out to the yard when it was clear that the sequins and glitter could not be contained. Soon the small lawn—which was actually beginning to turn green—sparkled in the sun.

Marcus stepped out into the yard after school and slumped into a metal chair that was covered with a layer of green seeds that had fallen off a tree behind the bait-and-tackle shop. Jane had quickly bagged up a lot of the dead vines and leaves in order to have more room to work in and had uncovered, in the process, a white swan, a birdbath, and a two-headed gnome. Marcus rested his hand on the gnome head closest to his chair, as if it were a pet dog.

"So what's the deal with the Dreamland Social Club?" he said after he watched her work for a while.

"How should I know?" She was cutting a fin, this one out of the green sparkling costume. She'd already made most of the bodice and only prayed it would fit when she actually tried it on.

"I thought you belonged," he said.

"I don't know why you'd think that," she said, and it felt sort of wrong, since her mother was his mother, too, and she wanted him to know, but it was also sort of fun.

"Whatever," he said. "It's not like I really care."

After a pause during which Jane's scissors could be heard splicing fabric, he said, "I got my first letter."

Jane stopped cutting and looked up, eyebrows questioning.

"NYU," he said. "I'm in."

"That's awesome," she said. "Congratulations."

"I was thinking of living on campus."

Jane nodded and went back to cutting. "You should."

Marcus said, "You're happy we might be staying, aren't you?"

"I guess," she said.

He took a tree seed off the arm of the chair and split it and tried to get it to helicopter though the air, with moderate success. "I see it," he said. "The thing with Leo."

"What do you see?"

"Hard to say," he said. "But something."

"Well, it's not that," she said, wanting to move on. "Or it's not *just* that. Not that that is ever even going to happen. I'm sick of moving. It's getting boring. It's nice to feel like I have roots here. Somewhere. Anywhere."

"I'll tell you one thing, though." He patted the gnome's head. "If you're staying, you can't go on like this. With all this old crap around."

"I was thinking of giving some of it to the museum," she said. "I started a list."

He looked up at the back of the house. "Maybe you can just airlift the whole place over."

"So you don't mind?"

"You know me." Marcus shrugged. "Not the sentimental type."

She really did have to talk to Grandpa Claverack about the horse, but she had been letting herself be easily side-tracked, since she was sort of dreading having to see Freddy and his ponytail again. But it was the right thing to do to tell the old man he could have it, to maybe even show him the entry in Birdie's journal that explained it all, or at least explained some of it. Just thinking of Birdie's journal awakened that old itch.

And my God, the doodling.

"Okay, so here's question, Mr. Unsentimental. If, totally hypothetically, you found Mom's diary"—Jane lifted the fin-shaped fabric—"would you read it?"

"You found Mom's diary?" he asked.

"No," she said. "It really is hypothetical. I think it's probably gone."

Marcus tilted his head. "I would probably read it. But just out of curiosity. And probably only once."

Jane looked up now. "And then you'd what, *throw it out*?"

"It would depend, I guess. On if it was any good, if it said anything meaningful. But I've read some diaries in my day, and most of them suck."

"Whose diaries have you read?"

"Doesn't matter." He looked at his watch and got up. "I guess what I'm saying is, I'd have pretty low expectations. And I certainly wouldn't expect it to solve the great mystery of life."

On another day maybe she would have argued with him, would have said he was wrong. But maybe he had a point. There were things worth keeping and things worth letting go of, and figuring out which was which wasn't that easy. Do you save an old journal if it's boring? Do you save an old bar if it's got rats?

Her fin was ready to be attached to the tail bit that she'd laid out on the table, so she pinned it in a few places, then slipped on the whole sequined concoction. Her entire lower half sparkled in the sun.

"It's cool," Marcus said before heading back into the house. "But the fin needs to be, I don't know, firmer?"

A bell tinkled overhead when, a few minutes later, she pushed open the door of the bait-and-tackle shop next door in search of some stiff wire. There was no one at the cash register, but a male voice in some back room called out, "Right with ya!"

She started to cruise the aisles, looking for something that might help her fin stay finlike. She passed stacks of crab and lobster traps and endless spools of fishing line. There were rubber worms and tackle boxes and hooks as far as the eye could see. A refrigerator-freezer in the back right corner held boxes labeled FROZEN SEA BAIT. There were knives and scales and lamps and batteries and fishing rods and rod bags and a million other items Jane had never seen before. Overwhelmed, she wondered whether maybe she'd do better at a regular hardware store or a 99-cent store. Just because she was trying to make a mermaid didn't mean a shop for fishermen would have the right stuff.

"Can I help you?"

Jane turned and saw an old man standing at the end of the aisle. He wore black pants tucked into big rubber boots and had white hair and wore a black-and-gold sailor's cap. He was smoking a pipe, and the woody aroma suddenly filled the room.

"I'm not sure," Jane said, thinking maybe she'd just back away down the aisle and out the door.

"You're that gal who lives next door," he said.

Jane nodded, then realized she shouldn't have. What if he was a psycho? Now he knew where she lived.

"Preemie's grandkid, right?" He puffed his pipe.

"Right." It was too late to deny it.

"I miss that idiot." He shook his head. "Couldn't fish to save his life but acted like he was Hemingway." He looked Jane over. "How about you? What are you trying to catch?"

"Oh, it's nothing like that." She eyed a box of rubber worms and decided to charge ahead. She was here. She might as well see if he had anything that would work. "You know the Mermaid Parade?"

He raised his brows at her, like she was an idiot.

"I'm making a costume for a mermaid funeral." It probably sounded dumb, but she kept going. "And I just need some wire to help the fin stay fin-shaped."

"A mermaid funeral." He puffed and was momentarily blurred by white smoke. "Sounds sort of kooky."

"It is."

He shrugged and said, "Well, I guess we better have a look around."

As he started to poke through bins and weave through the aisles of his tiny store, Jane thought to ask, "Did you know my mother?"

He stopped his poking and said, "I did. But only when she was a girl, you know. It broke Preemie's heart when she died." He looked up at her. "Yours, too, I'd imagine."

"Was he an asshole?"

He raised his eyebrows. "The mouth on you!"

"It's what everyone calls him."

"He wasn't an asshole." Back to poking with a shake of the head. "He was mostly just having fun, but he didn't know that his fun was sometimes at the expense of others. Like his daughter's. But I liked him enough." He held up a spool. "This should do the trick."

Jane studied the wire he handed her and thought that yes, it would. She trailed him to the register and he said, "Oh, and don't let me forget the key."

"The key?"

"Your grandfather's key. No use my hanging onto it now that you're here."

"Oh, a spare key to the house, you mean?" Jane was absentmindedly fingering some rubber worms.

"No, my dear, the horse."

No one answered the door at the Claveracks, but Jane was pretty sure she heard a TV inside, so she knocked louder.

Then louder.

Then louder.

"What is that infernal knocking?" Grandpa Claverack said when he whipped the door open.

Jane held up the key.

"Well, if you had a key, why'd you knock?" he said, and then he turned to shuffle away.

"No, Mr. Claverack." She'd almost said "Grandpa." "You don't understand. It's the key to the horse."

He turned.

"Your horse." She pointed across the street in the direction of Preemie's house and the bait-and-tackle shop.

"When he told you to 'go fish,' it didn't mean the key was in the ocean. It was in the—"

"What are you talking about?"

"I'm Preemie's granddaughter," she backtracked. "I thought you should do the honors." She turned the key in the air to make it clear. "Unlock the horse. So you can take it."

"Oh," he said. "Well, why didn't you just say so?"

It took longer to get the old man down the block between their houses than Jane would have thought possible. Halfway there, she thought she should run home and see if her father or Marcus was there, so they could help her carry the old carousel maker the rest of the way, but she was afraid, too, of leaving him—a wisp—on the street by himself. Not in this breezy weather.

Her father poked his head out onto the porch while Jane was helping Claverack up the stairs. "What's going on?" he said.

"I've got the key." Jane held it up. "This is Mr. Claverack."

In the living room, the horse was reflecting sunlight from the window. Its coat seemed shinier, its mane more alive. Even the horse's eyes seemed to have more life in them, like they sparked with recognition of their creator.

"There she is," Claverack said. "Still a beaut after all these years."

He stepped up to the horse then and ran a shaky hand

down its hide, then down its mane. "They just don't make 'em like this anymore."

Jane and her father stood back a bit, letting him have his moment. But when his fingers found the chain around the horse's tail, Jane stepped forward. "The lock's right there," she said. "And we'll figure out how to get the horse to your house, or to your buyer."

"You do it," he said. "Knees don't bend as well as they used to."

Jane looked at her father, who shrugged, and then she went to the lock, inserted the key, and opened it. Gingerly, she took the thick chain and unwound it so that it was no longer holding the horse. The heavy links slumped by the radiator in a pile.

"That bastard really said I could have it?"

He looked at Jane, and she could see something missing in his eyes. They looked a lot like the horse's eyes right then, without memories or proper focus.

Jane said, "He did."

"Well, what am I supposed to do with it?" he said. "It won't fit through the front door of my place."

"Your son said you had a buyer."

"Not me, no," he said. "He's the one with the buyer." He studied her again. "I just wanted to see her again. She should be in a museum, don't you think?" He sighed and said again, "They just don't make them like this anymore."

"Actually," Jane said, "I *do* think it should be in a museum."

"Well then, get on the horn."

"But what about your son, and the European buyer?"

Claverack rested a hand on the horse's nose and seemed to look right into its empty eyes and see something that Jane couldn't. When he looked back at her, he said, "They'll live."

CHAPTER

seven

THINGS WERE SUDDENLY very grim on Coney the next morning. Word spread quickly through homeroom that a six-year-old girl had been hit by a stray bullet from a robbery in the building next to hers the night before and was dead. That very same night, a famous competitive eater—he'd won the hot-dog-eating contest at Nathan's a number of times—had been killed in a hit-and-run accident on Surf Avenue at the age of 103. And while it shouldn't have inspired nearly as much grief as the other two tragedies, the announcement that Wonderland was going to be dismantled and packed up on Saturday seemed to be the thing that pushed everyone over the edge. Even Mr. Simmons seemed incapable of talking about it without getting visibly upset. "It's been here forever," he kept saying, which everyone knew wasn't exactly true, but apparently it felt that way.

In class he dimmed the lights and pulled a movie screen down from above the blackboard and said, "No field trip today, but I managed to get my hands on a few more Edison films with a Coney connection. He filmed some re-enactments of the Boer War, which was also one of the larger spectacles ever staged at Dreamland." He seemed to lose his train of thought for a second and just said, "Let's watch."

He stood by the projector set up in the room's center aisle, and its tube of light shot through the room to the screen. The words, white on black, said "BATTLE OF MAFEKING, April 28, 1900, Thomas A. Edison."

It was even harder to see what was going on here than it had been with Topsy. There were two groups of people in a field—one line in the distance and another in the foreground with their backs to the camera—and there were frequent bursts of smoke, presumably made by gunfire, and then one group appeared to charge forward and the other retreated but not fast enough, and they clashed. Some men rode by in the foreground on horses.

Immediately following that reel came *Capture of a Boer Battery*, in which a bunch of people stood in a field firing into the distance. Then a group of men on horseback charged at them from the distance and captured some of them, and then you could see that the men on horses were wearing kilts. They were taking the Boer peasants prisoner.

After that came one called *Boers Bringing in British Prisoners*—Edison sure was fascinated by the Boer Wars—which was basically just a bunch of people walking through a field together, with some horses. The man at the back took off his cap and waved it, as if to signify victory.

"Exploitation," Mr. Simmons said, after the last film was over and he asked Babette to get the lights. "We talked about exploitation, meaning to treat poorly or take advantage of, earlier, but there is a second definition, which is merely the act of making some area of land or water more profitable or productive or useful. There isn't, in those cases, any wrongdoing or ill intent.

"People have been trying to exploit land and water the whole world over as long as humans have been roaming the planet." He was pacing the aisles. "To raise more, better crops, for example. To find oil to fuel our cities. To provide seaside amusements and services on beaches much like our own. So Coney has exploited and also *been* exploited. And, as we all know, it is still happening now."

He seemed distracted, unfocused, like he'd sort of forgotten what he had been planning on teaching. "Uh, Mr. Simmons," Leo said. "Why bore us to death with the Boer War?"

"Africa," Mr. Simmons said, "in the nineteenth century was the victim of an unabashed landgrab by the more wealthy, industrialized nations of Europe. France, Germany, Italy, and even Belgium carved up Africa arbitrarily. And the Boers, understandably, didn't like it. It was their land. But then again, they—the Boers—were Dutch settlers. They'd just gotten there first." He looked mean-ingfully at Leo, and Leo said, "Is this a call to arms, Mr. Simmons?"

"Something like that," Mr. Simmons said. Then he sat and his desk and said, "You can all use the rest of the pe-riod to read or catch up. Whatever you want."

Jane got her book out and pretended to read but was mostly looking over at Leo, who was doing a very good job of not making eye contact with her and who kept touching his seahorse, like the creature itself had an unscratchable itch.

All day she looked around for fliers announcing a meeting of the Dreamland Social Club—surely Babette couldn't stand for things to stay the way they were for long—but none appeared. Jane half feared they never would again—that she had destroyed her mother's legacy and that her moment as a mermaid would never come to pass.

When she found Cliff Claverack waiting by her locker near day's end, she thought she might have to disappear into the girls' room for a good cry. But when he saw her, he waved sort of timidly, so she decided to approach.

"I heard about what you did yesterday," he said, and his voice actually sounded nice, normal. "Showing my gramps the horse."

"Yeah, and?"

He stared at the floor, fidgeted. "And, I don't know, it made my gramps happy."

"Is this your way of saying thank you?" Jane asked.

"Don't push your luck, Preemie." He actually tousled her hair, like she was a child, and then he walked off, leaving her awash in relief. When Cliff Claverack made your day, it was obviously a pretty bad day.

Fueled by that interaction, she went down to the museum after school with her list and handed it over to the man at the desk. He'd looked bored by her mere presence, then taken aback when he said, "You have a Claverack horse?"

"I do."

"Give me a minute, will you? Have a look around."

In other words, buzz off for a second.

He picked up the phone, dialed a number.

Jane could hear his side of the conversation only in muffled tones as she strolled around the museum. She hadn't been there since her first day of school, and that seemed somehow wrong; then again, she had practically been living in a Coney Island Museum the whole time. Still, when she came upon a large bell and saw that it was a bell that had been on a pier at Dreamland, she could not resist the urge to ring it, not with anything loud but with a few taps of her fingernails. Just enough to hear a tiny ding. She also couldn't resist the urge to take out her keychain and see if the Bath key opened any of the museum's bathhouse lockers. But it was entirely the wrong kind of key.

The guy came into the room just as she moved away from the lockers. "And you said you want to donate it, right? You don't expect any payment?"

Jane nodded, then he said, "Back in a second."

Jane walked over to look at the contents of a big glass case by the far window and found the same photo of the Dreamland Social Club that she'd seen in Preemie's old book. It appeared to be an original print—with scalloped edges and a wrinkle in it—and Jane's eyes fell again upon the girl in the white dress. She noticed a sort of gash in the print right near her nose and it brought back a memory she really would have preferred to forget.

We're walking down a cobblestone street and my mother has a bag full of food like carrots and baguettes and there is a lady walking toward us and I can tell that something funny is going on. On her face. As she gets closer, I see that she kind of sort of doesn't have a nose, and that there are two metal spikes coming out of what should be her nostrils, and I have no idea what any of it can mean. "Mom?" I say, and I feel her squeeze my hand so tight that I think she may break my fingers.

"Lovely day after all!" she says to the woman as she passes, and it's all I can do to not scream, SHE DOESN'T HAVE A NOSE! YOU'RE TALKING TO A WOMAN WITH NO NOSE!

The woman's voice is totally normal when she says, "Yes, a nice surprise!"

And then she's gone and my mother drops my hand and I say, "She didn't have a nose, Mom."

She stops at the corner and looks at me, sort of disappointed, and says, "Did you happen to notice that her eyes were the most remarkable green?"

■ ■ ■

Looking out the window of the museum toward the water, Jane squinted and imagined she was looking out of the eyes of the Elephant Hotel, and she thought there were worse things in life than being funny-looking and maybe worse things in life than not having a nose or not having any limbs at all. Like not being loved. Not being able to feel. Not having anything to lose or give away.

The museum guy came back into the room and stopped at Jane's side. "We'll take it all," he said, just like she knew he would. "We'll send a truck."

At home all the furniture in the living room—even the horse—was covered with sheets and tarps, and Jane had this sinking feeling that something had gone wrong, that the whole thing—inheriting the house—had been a mistake and they had to move out. But then she smelled paint and saw her father up on a ladder with a roller at the far end of the room.

"Whatcha doing, Dad?"

He turned and pulled a face.

"Okay," she said. "You're painting."

"Thought the place could use a little touch-up," he said. He'd chosen a pale orange color, which Jane thought strange.

"Orange?" she said.

He kept on rolling, and it was actually sort of peachy and lovely. "It's called Clementine Dreams," he said. "I took it as a sign."

Jane went upstairs to change into old clothes and then went back down and picked up a second roller. "You were right," she said. "About the Anchor."

"I'm sorry, honey." He was pouring more paint into the tray.

"No." She shook her head and got her roller wet. "It's okay."

She turned and rolled a tall stripe onto the wall. "So the guy at the museum said they'll take the horse, and a bunch of Preemie's stuff, too."

"Well done," her father said. "Really. I mean it."

Marcus came through the front door then with an open letter in his hand. "Columbia," he said. "In." He looked around the room and said, "Is that peach?"

"It's Clementine Dreams," Jane said, and he took up the third roller.

This time when the house phone rang, Jane's dad didn't move an inch. He said, "I think that's probably for you."

Jane perched her roller on the tray and approached the phone warily, wondering what Leo could possibly have to say to her now, why he could possibly think that calling their house was a good idea.

She picked up and said, "Hello?"

"Can you meet me?" he said. "Like now?"

"I don't know." She twirled the phone's cord in her fingers. "It's been sort of a crazy afternoon here."

"Here too," he said. "Please. It's important."

"Okay," she said. "Where?"

"I'm at the bar," he said. "I'm alone."

"I don't understand." It was the thick of happy hour.

"Just knock on the gate when you get here," he said. "I'll explain."

Health department notices glued onto the gate to the Anchor announced it had been shut down. There were some numbers and letters and codes listing violations, but Jane already knew what they'd be. She rapped on the gate and it shook and rattled, and then she heard a sort of cranking sound as it started to lift, rolling into itself.

"Can you fit?" Leo said when it was about two feet off the boardwalk. Jane lay down and rolled into the Anchor under the gate. Leo helped her up, then cranked the gate back down and shut.

He said, "Can I get you a drink?"

He had a beer bottle in his hand and Jane said, "I'll have one of those." She felt very grown-up here with him, in a bar. Alone. She'd put on jeans and a sort of tank top that had been Birdie's but looked new, never worn. It was sort of low-cut and, for once, Jane liked that.

Leo went behind the bar and slid open a bin refrigerator, then took the bottle cap off and slid the bottle on a coaster onto the bar in front of Jane. She took a sip and waited for him to say something, but he didn't. "What are we doing here?" she asked finally.

"He fessed up about not paying the rent, and about the rats, too."

Jane just waited.

"And did you know you can get shut down for 'excessive fruit flies'?"

Jane shook her head. He wasn't drunk, she didn't think. But there was something sort of off-seeming about Leo. He shook his head and looked around the bar. "I think this might be the Anchor's last hurrah. You and me right now."

"I'm really sorry." She wiped condensation off her beer, then wiped her wet finger on her jeans.

Leo said, "It's okay. I'm the one who owes you an apology. You can't help those who don't help themselves. Isn't that what they say? I mean, he could've done something, you know? Cleaned up?"

Jane just nodded in agreement, and Leo came around and sat on the stool next to her. "I've been thinking a lot about this place lately, and I figured out why I'm so messed up about it all." He sighed. "This was my Trip to the Moon, this place. My Elephant Hotel."

He shook his head. "I used to build forts behind the bar and pretend we were under attack by some evil foreign navy. I used to pretend I had records of my own, songs I'd written, in the jukebox. I used to build igloos out of the toilet paper supplies in the storeroom." He paused and seemed sadder for a flash. "I was here on nine-eleven, even though I didn't really understand what was going on."

He hung his head now and said, "I'm sure it sounds awful, but I grew up here. At the bar. It's the one place I remember my parents together and happy."

"It doesn't sound awful," she said. "It sounds fun."

"I used to think a lot about growing up and being old enough to tend bar and take over from my dad, you know. I guess that ship has sailed. I've never even gotten drunk here. It just seems"—he laughed—"*wrong* that I never will."

She was so happy that they were talking again—and like this—that she had to fight the urge to smile, to dance.

"We could get drunk now," she said. "We can build a fort out of toilet paper. Whatever you want."

They stocked the jukebox with songs, and almost every time one started Leo would say, "Oh my God, I almost forgot about this song" or "I love this song" or "I hate this song," but Jane didn't really recognize any of them, didn't care. She remembered dancing—that had been her earliest memory—so there must have been music, but she couldn't remember any songs beyond "Meet Me Tonight in Dreamland," just a feeling. Some of these songs sparked that feeling again. Others, not so much. And then the song that started with "Hey! Ho! Let's go!" came on and Jane felt a sort of explosion in her brain. *This* was a song she knew. Even though she didn't know it by name.

They danced in the bar and *on* the bar and had a few more beers and went to the storeroom, but there wasn't much in the way of toilet paper, and then they sat up on the bar, facing the wall behind it—feet perched on fridges of beer—and looked at all the old postcards and signs on the wall.

"I just can't believe this wall is going to be gone," Leo

said as they read from old postcards and bar tabs and IOUs, studying pictures of people who'd been to the Anchor—celebrities, the mayor, but also just a woman who'd gone into labor while walking past and tourists who'd gone home to faraway lands with tall enough tales that they'd sent postcards from Peru, Amsterdam, Berlin.

"This is one of my favorites." Leo pulled a postcard off the wall and read from it. "Everyone has a holy place, a refuge, where their heart is purer, their mind clearer, where they feel close to God or love or truth or whatever it is they happen to worship."

"I like it," Jane said. She'd just spotted a stack of postcards advertising the Anchor itself, next to the cash register. "What is it?"

"It's from some book about a bar, I think."

Jane studied the attribution on the card—J. R. Moehringer—and read the quote again.

"That's what this place is for me," Leo said. "Not just the bar. But Coney. And this wall is a sort of monument."

"You should talk to the museum," Jane said, still high on the fact that the museum was going to have its very own Preemie collection. "Maybe they'll move it."

"Move the wall?"

She shrugged. "They're coming to get the Claverack horse on Thursday."

"They are?"

She nodded. "Or they could re-create the wall. Just move the stuff."

"I don't know," Leo said. "I don't really see the point if the rest of the place is gone."

Jane didn't want the place gone either. Because she never wanted to forget this night.

"I heard you have an extra ticket," he said. "To the presentation?"

She surveyed him, with his tired lollipop eyes and anemone hair, and said reluctantly, "I promised it to Legs."

"Ah," Leo said. "Another hot nondate."

"You know it's not like that"—she looked at him meaningfully, tried to communicate it all through her eyes—"*at all*. He's writing a story for *The Siren*."

"Right."

"Wait," she said. "You want to go to the presentation?"

He nodded.

"To protest?"

"Not my style." He'd just taken darts from the board on the wall and handed three of them to her. "Information is power, right? I'm just following your lead." He indicated a line on the floor and nodded at the board.

"No funny business?" She threw a dart and missed the red-and-green board entirely. Her dart hit the wall and fell with a thump to the floor.

Leo held up two fingers with a dart in his hand. "Scout's honor." He threw and hit the bull's-eye, then flashed a smile at Jane.

And flirt. Oh, the woman flirted like a pro.

She said, "You don't strike me as the Boy Scout type."

He froze and looked at her then, and smiled this sort of debonair smile, and she thought maybe *this* was it—finally!—the moment in which he'd kiss her, but then a scurrying sound—undeniable *scurrying*—behind the bar made them both freeze, and then Leo grabbed her hand, headed for the back door, and said, "Let's get the hell out of here."

"Wait." She ran to the bar and grabbed an Anchor postcard before running with him, out into the night.

CHAPTER

eight

A SMALL GROUP OF PROTESTERS marched around the Aquarium parking lot the next night. They held oak-tag signs with marker scrawl that read "Save Coney," "Down with Loki," and "The Future of Coney Island is OURS." There were maybe thirty of them, chanting in a call-and-response—"What do we want?" "Loki gone!" "When do we want it?" "NOW!"—and for no reason she could explain they made Jane sad. Maybe because thirty people didn't seem like a lot. Not enough to save Coney. And what did that even mean anyway? She was less sure than ever.

She kept her head down and followed her father and brother inside and then out again to a tent that had been put up out where the Aquarium faced the boardwalk. It was full of round tables, all covered with white linens and set with white china and too many forks and spoons and glasses. The silver hot trays on the buffet table along one wall still wore their lids, but the tent held a not unpleasant mix of smells. Jane's father stopped to chat and slap backs and shake hands on their way to their table—and introduced Jane and her brother to a few people—but once they found their seats their dad left them to their own devices.

After those silver lids were lifted away by white-gloved, tuxedoed waiters, they filled up plates with Swedish meatballs and lasagna and three kinds of chicken and more. Back at their table Jane and Marcus revived an old game they used to play when dragged to their father's work functions. They acted like they were involved in a very deep conversation, but they were really saying nonsensical things like "Pudding has a bad reputation" and "It's funny you say that, because I've always found it to be the case that letters, when put together, make words."

Marcus said, "The truth of the matter is that ice is quite cold," and Jane said, "It's also frequently the case that fire is hot." Then Legs slid into the seat next to her and the game ended.

Jane looked around the room and saw Leo, wearing a dark gray suit with a white shirt and a skinny tie—looking much older than he really was; sophisticated, even. He looked over at her and straightened his lapels with raised eyebrows. She gave a thumbs-up for the suit across the room and he tilted his chin at her—she was wearing a gray sleeveless dress—and gave a thumbs-up back.

Lights dimmed and silverware clattered and coughs rose and voices quieted, then everyone took seats. A large screen at one end of the room projected the Loki Equities logo and then: THE FUTURE OF CONEY ISLAND HAS ARRIVED.

Jane had been prepared to hate everything about the Loki presentation. Every idea. Every graphic. Every ride.

But she didn't.

As image upon image appeared on that screen, she saw a vision of a place where she might like to spend some time. A place that had a circus tent, water parks, playgrounds, nice restaurants, and more. She saw some grandeur in the new amusement park design, which obviously drew inspiration from the spirals and minarets and crescent moons of the past, and the Tsunami looked amazing in full-color renderings.

For the first time in a long time, when she imagined what it would feel like to ride it, she touched up against a feeling that had more in common with excitement than dread. The feeling of a surfer riding the wave of a lifetime. She got choked up just thinking about how proud she was of her father.

If it hadn't been for the shopping mall built out onto a pier and the complete absence of the Anchor and Wonderland, she might have fallen for the proposal hook, line, and sinker. It was certainly closer to the old Coney she loved than what was here now.

Leo would probably never understand the way she felt about it all now that she'd really seen the whole scale of the Loki plan, and she'd probably never tell him. Even if Jane saw only gray, the world *was* black and white and this entire situation was out of her hands. When the lights came up, Leo wasn't in his seat. It wouldn't surprise Jane at all if he'd bailed, if he'd joined the protesters outside.

After the presentation, Legs led Jane to a tank for tiny seahorses in a darkened corridor, claiming he wanted her help with his story. Jane didn't really think she'd be much help and had never helped Legs with a story before, but then he said, "You're really pretty, you know," and Jane knew it wasn't about the story at all.

"Thanks," she said as she watched seahorses gallop slowly through the water, using their curly tails to maneuver. They were yellow, with round black eyes, and so very tiny and beautiful. She wished she could shrink herself and dive in and escape all this awkwardness.

She cleared her throat and said, "Okay, so what are you going to lead with?"

"That." He bent down on a knee like he had that day so long ago, and he had a funny look in his eyes and then a second later, he was leaning in as if to kiss her. He said, "That was my lead. That you're really pretty."

"Legs—" she said, putting up a hand.

"Sorry." Sadness seemed to shrink his face to a normal size. "But why not? I mean"—he backed off—"we get along great. We spend all this time together."

"I'm sorry." She shook her head. "I can't explain. I'm just happy with the way things are, with us being friends."

He ran a hand through his hair. "I don't need friends."

She said, "But I do."

"Jane," he said. "Give me a break."

It was only then that Jane realized she actually had friends. A bunch of them. Real ones. Maybe for the first time ever. Because even if things never got better for the Dreamland Social Club, she still had Babette and Legs and H.T. and, well, Leo.

Legs said, "Have you ever thought that maybe you are to him what I am to you?"

She took a second to try to parse the words but was still confused. "What are you talking about?"

"Leo. I mean, he must just see you as a friend. Because wouldn't something have happened by now?"

"I've got to go," Jane said, looking into the tank and saying a silent farewell to the yellow seahorses. "I'm sure your story will be great."

She stepped out into the Aquarium courtyard for some air and saw Leo standing by the penguin environment. She clicked over in her heels and he turned. "This is where Dreamland used to be, you know."

She shook her head.

"This penguin palace might have been the Helter Skelter or Midget City or Hell Gate. Preemie's little incubator might have been right here for all we know."

Jane sighed. "You hated it."

"No." Leo stood up straighter, shook his head. He looked so grown-up in that suit, but so sad, too, which was maybe par for the course. Jane wondered whether all of this had made her more grown-up and more sad, too. "I didn't hate it. I wanted to. But no."

"And the Tsunami?"

"If the goal is to scare the crap out of people, I'd say your father pretty much hit the nail on the head."

They stood there in front of fake icebergs and shimmering black water lit from below—a few people walked by, laughing and talking—and then Leo said, "You and I have some unfinished business."

She thought back to the peanuts and the rooftop and the way she was sure he'd been about to kiss her that night, would have if it hadn't been for the situation with Legs. She thought about the night at the Anchor, about the scurrying and what it might have interrupted, and said, "We do?"

"We do." He turned to face her and said, "The Bath key."

"I actually asked your mom about it," Jane said, and she pulled the key from her purse. "But she wouldn't tell me anything except that my mother had a thing for secrets."

Leo was nodding. "She said the same thing when I asked her."

"You asked her?"

"Yeah." He took the key from Jane and studied it closely. "And I've been thinking that when people have secrets they sometimes leave clues."

"True," Jane said. "My mother wrote a note in an old book of mine that said that mermaids were good at keeping secrets, and I did find the keys inside a mermaid. But beyond that, I don't know. 'Bath.' It just doesn't make sense."

"Well, obviously, there's not exactly a perfect trail of bread crumbs," Leo said. "But maybe there's still a crumb or two out there."

"Maybe," Jane said, but she wasn't convinced.

nine

THE FLIERS WERE BACK in the morning and in numbers that indicated great urgency. Jane stopped to read one that said,

dreamland social club
EMERGENCY (YES, AGAIN) MEETING TODAY.
RIGHT NOW. ROOM 222.
She's not dead yet.

Jane hurried upstairs and found most of the rest of the club already assembled.

"I think we should cancel the mermaid funeral," Babette said after the meeting was called to order. "I mean, what's the point anyway?"

"Fine by me," Venus said.

Minnie said, "Me, too."

H.T. said simply, "But Little B, you were so excited." And Jane suddenly wondered what it meant that Babette *let* H.T call her that.

"I just mean, did you see all those suits last night?" She turned to Jane and said, "No offense."

Jane said, "You were there? I didn't see you."

"People rarely see me when I don't want to be seen," she said, then turned back to the group. "All those suits are going to be there on parade day, probably in some ridiculously swank viewing trailer they park in front of Nathan's or something, and the whole thing, putting on a show for them, just makes me feel sort of dirty."

"Seriously," Jane said to Babette, "don't be like this." She *really* didn't want it to be canceled, especially not now that she had the mermaid costume figured out.

"I'm not being *like* anything." Babette threw her hands up. "There's just no point."

"Of course there is," Jane said, and felt a certain power in being able to speak with at least a tiny bit of authority to Babette for once. "There's even *more* of a point."

She looked over at Leo, who seemed to be egging her on with his eyes. She said, "It's a mermaid *funeral* on Coney Island just as all these old businesses are getting shut down."

Rita smacked her gum. "So it's like this metaphor, you mean?"

"Exactly," Jane said. "That was the whole seed of the idea!"

"I don't know," Venus said. "It seems like it's the wrong message to be sending. Almost like we support what's going on."

"Yeah, like we're glorifying it or something," Babette said.

Jane shook her head. "But if it's this awesome and really sad and beautiful thing, people will get it. They'll feel it. That it's about mourning the past."

Leo's silence, by this point, felt conspicuous. All faces had turned to his, and Babette said, "I know you're mad at Jane because of what she said about the rats, but this is something different and you should share some thoughts."

"I think she has a really good point," he said, smiling at Jane. "And it was true, by the way. About my dad not paying his rent and not dealing with the rodent situation."

"Really?" Venus said. "Sucks."

"Yeah," he said. "Sucks. But, well, we have to do something, right? We can't just *not* do the parade."

"All right, then," Babette said. "If everyone agrees."

Marcus walked into the room then and all heads turned. "Sorry, I just saw the fliers," he said, and Babette shot Rita a look.

"Don't look at me," Rita said. "I didn't invite him."

Then eyes went to Jane and she said, "It wasn't me."

Babette started banging on her desk and they all joined in. *"Gooble gobble, Gooble gobble. We accept her. We accept her."*

"Her?" Marcus said.

"Don't worry about it," H.T. said, and Marcus took a

seat next to Rita, who promptly leaned over and kissed him on the mouth.

Babette looked for a moment like she'd been struck by a stun gun, but then she said, "Welcome, Marcus."

"Thanks," he said. "So what is this club anyway?"

Babette rolled her eyes. "Rita can explain, but in the spirit of the club, I'm just going to say that I'm sorry I've been a jerk. It's cool. I'm happy for you. There. I said it."

"Really?" Rita said.

"Really," Babette said, then she looked at Minnie and cleared her throat dramatically, and Minnie stood up. "Fine," she said. "Jane, it was me who filled your locker with condoms. I'm sorry. I was hurt." She looked sheepishly at Legs, then back at Jane to say, "And I took it out on you."

"What about the doll in the noose?" Jane dared.

"No," Minnie said. "That was the Claveracks."

"Okay," Jane said. "Well, apology accepted."

Babette said, "Venus, anything you want to say?"

"No," Venus said. "I'm cool."

"Fine," Babette said. "Adjourned!"

"I'm proud of you," Jane said to Babette when they were alone.

Babette huffed. "Don't get me wrong. I'm jealous and all." Her eyes pooled up. "I mean, who is ever going to like me?"

Jane squeezed her shoulder. "Somebody will!"

Babette blew her breath out through circular lips, pushing tears away. "I mean, look at me, Jane!" She almost laughed.

Jane laughed, too, and said, "I'm looking!"

There was a van parked in Preemie's driveway when Jane got home that day, its back doors open to face the porch. Four huge men wearing thick gloves were trying to coax the Claverack horse off the porch.

Jane's father saw her and waved. "They called and wanted to come right over. I thought it'd be okay."

"Yeah," Jane said. "Of course."

She climbed the steps and stood next to her dad and watched as the horse disappeared into the van amidst a grunted chorus of "Easy"s and "Hold it"s and "Okay now"s. She'd boxed up the rest of the stuff—except for the demon, which she'd just covered in protective paper—and saw that it had all already been moved to the porch. Once the horse was done, the men took the demon, then slid the boxes into the van and soon they were gone.

Her father squeezed her shoulder. "You good?"

The van was backing out of the driveway.

Yes, its a driveway.

"Yeah," Jane said. "I'm good."

"Any word yet?" she asked him after a moment. They had no idea when the verdict about the new Loki plan would come down.

"Nope," he said. "Not yet."

After the van pulled away, she got a black marker out

of her bag and went down to the sign on the driveway and added the missing apostrophe.

Upstairs, she sat down to do some reading for Mr. Simmons's class and found the postcard she'd taken from the Anchor on her desk. After studying the photo on it—a black-and-white shot of the bar's exterior—she turned it over and started to write.

> *Dear Mr. Simmons:*
>
> *There's a writer whose name I can barely remember how to spell who wrote something rather lovely about how everyone has a holy place on earth where their heart is pure and their mind open, where they feel close to truth or God or whatever it is they worship. [Trust me, he said it better.]*
>
> *I think Coney Island might be my holy place, but I can't be sure yet. I just know that I feel closer to a lot of things here. Closer to my mom. Closer to myself. Maybe even closer to fun.*
>
> *Best wishes,*
> *Luna Jane Dryden*

She stepped out into the hall and called out, "Dad!"
His "Yeah?" came from far away.
"Do you have a stamp?"

ten

FRIDAY BLEW BY in a whir—all anyone was doing was counting the hours to meeting up for Wonderland's last night—and Jane found herself bolting out of school at day's end so she could go home and get ready. Not that there was even anything to do to get ready, but everything felt urgent.

Since there was no way to make time go faster, Jane had to find a way to fill it. Sitting in her room, surrounded by that hideous green-and-pink wallpaper, she decided she needed to look no further for something to do. She moved her bed away from the longest wall in the room and then found a loose corner by the bottom edge of the wall and grabbed and started to pull it up and off. Two strips later, she was certain that she was uncovering something significant. There was definitely something underneath, a pattern of some kind. Whatever it was was covered in glue that made it sort of hard to figure out at first, but eventually the mural's scene started to take shape. It was one big oversize doodle of Coney Island as it must have been when her mother had lived in this house.

The Parachute Jump was there, with a picture of a key at its base. The Thunderbolt was there—all overgrown with vines and plants and with a small house underneath—also with a key icon by a gate. Looking for Wonderland, Jane found it—replete with Mad Hatter, and *this* Mad Hatter had a key dangling from one of his fingers.

So Leo had been right about the "Wonder" key after all. Which left "Bath."

When she saw the key drawn next to the picture of the round sea vessel sitting underneath the Cyclone's tracks, she sat and thought hard for a second, about *The Beast from 20,000 Fathoms*—didn't the scientist who went down to find the sea creature get eaten up in one of these little vessels?—and of the postcard her mother had sent Beth— with the mermaid smoking a cigarette on a little round sub. She closed her eyes and let her mind go. In the movie they'd called it a "bell," but there was another word, and she could hear her mother's voice say . . .

There has to be a submarine or a shipwreck or a bathysphere around here somewhere.

Bathysphere.

And here was the map of where to find it.

■   ■   ■

She got changed for Wonderland and walked out onto Steeplechase Pier and inhaled.

So that was that.

She exhaled and took another drag of salty air and closed her eyes as her hair whipped across her face in the wind. She pushed some strands away and thought about screaming into the wind again. It had felt good that one time. It had been cathartic and almost fun. But what would she even say this time?

What am I doing here?

She was actually starting to think she knew.

Why did you leave?

Was it so that Jane would have to come back? To find Leo? To find the bathysphere?

It was there, right where her mother had drawn it; she just knew it. The journal, too. All of her questions would be answered.

"This is your captain!" she finally screamed, and the words seemed to catch the wind and fly. "We are passing through a storm!"

She needed to stop to take another deep breath before she could yell, "We are quite safe!"

A smile had crept into her features, she could feel it. She couldn't shake it the whole way to Wonderland.

eleven

T HE GOAL WAS TO GO ON EVERY RIDE and to play every game before closing time. Or at least that was Babette's goal—and that included all the kiddie rides. So Jane played the part of proud parent as Babette went on silly rides with names like the Frog Hop and Hippo Hat, scaring wailing toddlers and their parents alike with her head-to-toe black clothes and dark eyeliner.

"You don't know what you're missing," Babette said, upon exiting a miniature flying elephant ride.

Jane finally had the nerve to say, "What's up with the goth thing anyway?"

"What do you mean?"

They started to walk toward the grown-up rides, some

of which Babette would be too small to go on. "I just mean, you're not a very good goth."

Babette stopped by a bench and climbed up on it to stand so she could see Jane better. "Honestly, I think I did it because I thought it'd be a distraction, you know? Like people couldn't just say 'Hey look, there's a dwarf.' I thought that if I did the goth thing, I don't know, the dwarf thing wouldn't be my whole identity."

It made sense. Somehow.

"I don't know"—she held out a hand and Jane helped her down—"I think maybe it backfired. And we're all in therapy now and I somehow can't bring myself to go to the sessions as a goth. Analyze that!"

"It just doesn't seem very *you* is all." They were nearing the bumper cars. "But that's good, about your parents and therapy, right?"

"Come on." Babette pinched Jane's leg. "I'm going to bump you so hard that your clothes will come back to life."

Rita and Marcus were already in bumper cars. Legs and H.T. and Leo and Debbie and Minnie, too. Even the Claveracks were squeezing themselves into small seats and then someone threw a switch and the bumper course came to life. Jane hit her pedal hard and barreled across the course to hit Harvey Claverack sideways, and hard, and then backed up, turned, and moved on. She made a straight line for Leo and hit him hard on the side.

"Hey!" she said. He spun around and shot off and then came back and hit her hard head-on.

She had to shout. "I need to tell you something."

But he just rammed her again and said, "Later, gator," and was gone.

She and Babette and Rita hit the Teacup Ride together after walking off the bumper cars, tilting their stiff necks this way and that, shaking out their legs. Jane did most of the spinning of the turntable at the center of the cup when the ride started. She grew tired quickly.

"I could use a little help here, guys." She looked up.

But Rita and Babette just exchanged a look and laughed, so they just let the car spin until it stopped and that was okay. The whole cup was also spinning on a disc and rotating on a larger turntable, so there was still plenty of spinning even without Jane's help. The effect was dizzying. Jane wasn't sure if it qualified as fun.

They went on a Tilt-A-Whirl after that and then took a break from rides to try to knock down three milk bottles with a baseball and shoot out paper stars with BB guns. When they shot water guns into clown faces to explode balloons, Jane thought of Preemie and how very much she felt indebted to him and his attic for making her year what it was. She'd spent enough time looking at enough pictures of him by now that he no longer looked like a clown in her mind's eye.

Finally, as the park's closing neared, Jane found herself sharing a car with Leo—just Leo—on the Polar Express. She wanted to just give her body over to the centrifugal force that was pushing her down the bench seat and into

Leo as the ride gained speed, shooting them around in circles. She'd felt this way pretty much since the second she'd seen him outside the bar that first day—like some invisible force was pulling her toward him, pushing her toward him—so it was nice to not have to fight it for once.

She was watching paintings of polar bears and ice caps whir by in a white blur. *Are you sure I'm not a brown bear?* that baby polar bear had asked, and for the first time, Jane found the joke sort of sad. She herself had been behaving like that baby bear, trying desperately to find a place to fit in.

"I'm sorry I'm crushing you!" she screamed as the ride reached peak speed and her and Leo's hip bones banged up against each other.

"It's okay," he said. Their arms had gotten tangled as they both clung to the bar in front of them, white-knuckled and tense.

"I found some crumbs!" she shouted over the music.

"You did?" he shouted back.

She nodded and screamed, "Do you know what a bathysphere is?"

"Of course!" he screamed back.

"The Bath key," she said, and then she waited for the realization to dawn.

"*Seriously?*" Leo shouted. "Here on Coney?"

Just as a voice came from the ride's control booth—"Do you want to go backwaaaaaaaads?"—Jane closed her eyes and let her head hang back and yelled, "Yes!"

■   ■   ■

Without anyone even specifically suggesting it, they all made their way down to the Anchor after they got kicked out of Wonderland at closing time. Leo went behind the bar and started pouring Cokes. Jane took a seat on a high stool and studied the crowd. There were old people and young people, black and white. Some were well dressed, some barely dressed. And they were shoulder to shoulder at the bar.

"Hey." Jane saw the petition hanging on a clipboard on a nail in the wall behind the bar; the seahorse postcard from Weeki Wachee was back. "I want to sign the petition."

"Re-he-heally," Leo said. "You want to save this rat-infested shithole?"

She smiled and said, "I guess I do."

"Save yourself the trouble." Leo took the petition down, started ripping it up.

"What are you doing?" Jane said.

He just kept ripping. "Loki said it's open to renegotiating a lease for one more season, since it'll take that long for their whole plan to be final anyway, but my dad says it's like negotiating with a terrorist." He threw the paper bits into the trash can behind the bar, then refilled Jane's Coke, which she hadn't even realized she'd drunk. "Technically, the bar shouldn't even be open now, but my father wanted a last hurrah. He's been talking crazy talk about moving all the stuff that's in the bar to a different building overnight tonight. Something to do with Hemingway and a urinal. I have no idea."

He shook his head, then leaned forward conspiratorially and said, "So what's the deal? How did you figure it out?"

"My mother drew a map of it all. It was under the wallpaper in her room. And it shows that there's a bathysphere somewhere right under the Cyclone."

He shook his head. "I would've seen it!"

She shrugged. "It has to be."

He said, "Let's go have a look."

"Now?"

And so they walked down the boardwalk and stopped near the Cyclone and looked. Jane didn't see a bathysphere, but there was a weird little shed that she had certainly never noticed before. "You think it's in there?" Leo asked.

"Only one way to find out," she said, and turned to face him fully. "Two a.m.?"

"Two a.m." Leo nodded. "Bathysphere or bust."

Then he said, "I should get back to the bar." Jane went, too, and after they walked in and Leo went to help his dad serve more drinks, Babette appeared on a stool beside her. "All right," she said. "Spill it."

Jane turned. "Nothing to spill."

"You're still a bad liar," Babette said.

Jane looked around to make sure no one else would hear. "We go out sometimes, late at night. My mother had this set of keys to all these secret sort of Coney places."

"Oh. My. God." Babette said. "He *is* into you. I never would have thought it possible."

"Thanks," Jane said. "Thanks a lot."

"No, I mean, it's awesome. I mean, how often does the nice girl win, right?"

"It's not that simple." Jane felt like she might cry. "I mean, he's never *said* he likes me or anything, but I don't know. This time it just feels different." She got up and started pacing around, suddenly felt like an animal in a cage, like an elephant about to make a desperate swim to escape. "I'm freaking out," she said, still pacing. "I don't even know why!"

"All right, all right." Babette patted her on the leg. "Just be cool. All right, just be cool. Whatever is going to happen is going to happen. Just calm the ef down."

Jane followed the smell of paint and found her father in his bedroom with the furniture covered, rolling pale blue paint onto the walls. There was a glass of whiskey on his desk next to a nearly empty bottle. Some of his paint lines were sort of woozy.

"Dad?" she said, because nothing about the scene indicated whether the drinking was a happy drinking, bad drinking, or just drinking. "What's up?"

"We got word." He kept rolling. "Big fat veto."

"Seriously?" she said, and she plopped down on the bed and felt her world start to spin. Were they going to have to leave Coney? She shook her head and said sadly, "I really thought they'd go for it."

"Well, here's the thing." And still rolling. He'd obviously been at it a while; the room was almost done. "Here we were thinking all of this business was being conducted out in the open, but in the meantime there's been this secret deal being cut."

"What kind of secret deal?" Jane couldn't remember what color the room had been before. He was on his second coat.

"The city is going to buy out Loki."

"What?" She shook her head. "What does that mean?"

"It means that the Loki plans are being scrapped, the city is buying all of Loki's property on Coney, and then the city is going ahead with its own redevelopment plan, which has yet to be determined."

"Wow," Jane said.

"Yeah, wow." He stood back and admired his work. "I've already been approached by someone from the city council. They like my work. Not necessarily the Tsunami, but they want to see something else."

Jane felt the start of a new seed of hope. "Do you *have* anything else?"

"On the desk," he said, and then he set about closing up the paint can and starting to clean up.

Jane walked over to her father's desk and saw his drawing of a small spiral roller coaster, with just a few cars, that itself spun on its own axis like a dreidel or top. "It's like the ride from Luna Park," she said.

Her father came over and pointed things out with painty hands. "Yes, inspired by. But some of the cars go backwards and there are two entwined spiral tracks, not just one. And it can spin both ways on its axis.

"This drawing shows it better," he said, and he pulled out another rendering, where Jane saw the ride's name written in pencil and underlined: <u>Lunacy</u>. "Named after you, of course."

"I love it," she said, and he cocked his head, almost as if surprised, and said, "Me, too."

"So we're staying?" she asked, and her hands went to fists and her eyes shut tight and he said, "Yes, Luna Jane. We're staying."

twelve

J ANE HAD NOTED THE DUMPSTER beside the fence surrounding the Cyclone earlier that afternoon, and so she walked right over to it. They climbed up on top of it—and it sure did smell something fierce, like rotting bananas and souring meat and worse—then climbed over the fence from there without even talking. Jane thought for sure she'd rip a hole in her jeans, or her legs, but navigated the chain links unscathed, finally jumping off backwards to land on the ground again. All this sneaking around and breaking in was getting easy.

Leo had a flashlight and led the way under the wooden beams of the coaster toward the shack they'd seen. "Watch out," he said softly, shining his light on the ground. "Dog doo."

"How romantic," Jane said before she could stop herself, and Leo said simply, "Just calling it like I see it" with a smile.

When they reached the shack, Leo shined a light on the lock. "Try it."

Jane stepped forward and tried the key, and the padlock clicked open. She twisted it and slid it out of the shack handles, then opened the door. She shrieked and ducked—Leo, too—when a bird or bat flew out, and then they stepped into the shack and found it.

It was a big metal ball—like a wrecking ball with a few round windows, a large one on one side, and two smaller ones on the opposite. Jane took the flashlight from Leo and shone it on the far side, where the words NEW YORK ZOOLOGICAL SOCIETY appeared atop the word BATHYSPHERE atop the words NATIONAL GEOGRAPHIC SOCIETY. "Sponsors?" she said.

"Guess so."

Leo circled the bathysphere now, like it was a bull and he a matador, then he reached out and touched it and whistled. "I did some research. This was the bathysphere made by William Beebe, this guy who totally broke records for deep-sea exploration and like *discovered* all these crazy sea creatures that people had never even seen before."

"Unbelievable," Jane said. "And no one even knows or cares that it's sitting right here? I mean, why isn't it in a museum? Or at the Aquarium?"

"Because this is Coney." He reached for the hatch, then

unreached and said, "The lady should do the honors."

Jane reached out and pulled the hatch open, then shone the flashlight inside, shrugged, and smiled. She climbed in. "Come on!" She poked her head out. "Before someone sees."

There was barely enough room for two people in there, so they sat close. Hip to hip. Again.

"Wait." Leo shifted, then lifted an arm and put it around her to make more room. "Okay," he said. "That's better."

Then he said, "I feel as though I'm leaving a world of untold tomorrows for a world of countless yesterdays."

It was a line from *The Beast from 20,000 Fathoms* and it made Jane replay the scene in her mind, where the scientist in the bell—the *bathysphere*—is looking through the small round window for the beast, roving the ocean's bed. She felt a little bit of sympathy for the monster awakened by the bomb, felt like that microscopic explosion in her mother's brain all those years ago had awakened a beast inside her, too. She smiled a little and said, "What kind of idiot signs up for that mission?"

"I don't know." Leo smiled back. "I might've done it."

Jane remembered the film's final, fiery scenes. The whole thing seemed horribly sad, and funny, and for a second she wondered whether she should climb the Cyclone and cry out in a rage like the beast had, whether that would feel good. Whether her mother had wanted to step into the beast's shoes, too. Whether that explained the Dreamland Social Club's inaugural stunt.

She sat back against Leo then, thinking of the moment

she first saw him and had felt that shock of recognition. Maybe it hadn't *really* been the seahorse at all. Maybe it had just been *him*. She remembered the first day they'd talked on the boardwalk, the way she'd imagined climbing into a submarine and telling each other their darkest secrets. A bathysphere would have to do, and then a realization dawned. She pushed Leo aside and said, "It has to be here," and started looking everywhere, in every nook of the bathysphere's small chamber.

"What has to be here?" Leo said.

"Her journal."

"Jane, it's been years."

But she was already standing, though bent, and her knees were pressing against Leo's chest or his shoulder, she didn't know/didn't care, because right then, on a ridge by a seam in the metal, her hand found something.

A notebook.

She pulled it out and then they sat back down again.

Leo was quiet for a moment, then just said, "Wow."

"Yeah." She rubbed her hand across it, knocking off a layer of dust. She sat staring at its cover, a canvas material on which her mother had drawn her name in bubble letters and a few other small pictures, like a Ferris wheel and, yes, another bathysphere. "I think I'm afraid to look."

"Why?"

Jane exhaled. "Because what if it tells me stuff about her that I don't want to know?"

"Rats or excessive fruit flies?"

"Exactly."

She felt his shrug when he said, "I'd want to look."

She held her notebook on her lap and studied its cover again.

"Just do it," he said.

"*Now?*"

"I'll just sit here and hold the flashlight. You know, in case you need me to shoo the rats away."

And so Jane opened to the first page of weird drawings and quotes and the names of bands written in different kinds of print: Bubble. Block. Script. Page after page was covered in doodles and quotes and dates and random scribbling.

"Beth Loves Jimmy"

"SML 5/3/88"

"Warriors! Come out to play!"

"Wherever You Go There You Are"

"Gabba Gabba Hey!"

"OMFUG"

It was endless, with words written in impossibly small print in every available white space. Just page after page of miniature graffiti, with only the occasional actual paragraph or two of writing. When she finally found a solid paragraph beside a drawing of a mermaid, she read:

I talked Beth into coming to Florida with me. We're going to audition to be mermaids and I just KNOW we're going to get it. We're going to have the best summer ever. And as soon as it's official I am going to rub it in the face of the people—you know who you are—who are saying it's a dumb thing to do, that I'll never

*make it. I don't care if people think it's dumb. I'm doing it. So there!
Oh my God, it's going to be soooooo cooooooool.*

She was stunned by how much like a teenager her mother sounded. It only made sense, of course. She had *been* a teenager, but Jane had always thought of her mother as wildly sophisticated and sort of figured she must have always been that way. To discover that she had been just a regular girl came as a bit of a shock. And a relief.

Flipping through more and more pages of sketches and doodles and graffiti, she saw a big, juicy heart with a knife stuck into it, and she stopped and stared. It was familiar, maybe something her mother had drawn absentmindedly when she was talking on the phone or making a shopping list. She read the neighboring paragraph:

Mrs. Mancuso is sick. Like really sick. Like not going to live cancer sick. Beth can't come to Florida.

It took Jane a second to realize that Mrs. Mancuso was Beth's mother, Leo's grandmother, and then she kept reading.

I'm sick about it, too, and sick for Beth. It really makes you think . . . about, well, life. And how you never know what'll get you in the end. And how important it is to really enjoy every day. Which is pretty hard considering how lame school is. Honestly, I don't think I'm going to go to college. I'd rather run off and get married or backpack around Europe or maybe be a mermaid at Weeki Wachee forever than bury my face in books. I know college is the smart thing to do, but what's going to make me happier? I feel awful for Beth. Just awful.

Jane flipped ahead a few pages, found the same heart and a drawing of a gravestone with the name Anastasia Marie Mancuso, then "RIP," written on it.

Leo hadn't moved an inch the whole time.

She flipped through the rest of the book, finding a few random paragraphs that said nothing much at all, and then to the last page to see where it ended. There she found a drawing of a man with a head that shrank toward the top, like the pinheads she'd read about. The only writing on the page said, again, *Gabba Gabba Hey!* Jane flipped through the rest of the pages to be sure that was the last entry, and it was.

Finally, she looked up. "Do you know what 'Gabba Gabba Hey' means?"

Leo turned off his flashlight. "Ever hear of the Ramones?"

Jane shook her head. A determined sliver of light from the street penetrated a gap between shed planks and sent murky waves of light through the round windows.

"Never saw *Rock 'n' Roll High School*?"

She shook her head again.

"Really?" His body tensed with surprise.

"Really."

"Hey! Ho! Let's go!" he said, and Jane said, "Oh!"

He shook his head, like he couldn't believe it. "I'm gonna forgive you for not knowing that that song is by the *greatest band to ever come out of New York City* because we're sitting in *the bathysphere* thanks to you, but we'll have to educate you on that front. And fast. 'Gabba gabba hey' was sort of their catchphrase."

"But what does it mean?" It was her mother's final message, the last thing she'd written in this book she'd kept for years.

"Nothing, really." Leo shrugged. "It's supposedly some variation on the whole 'Gooble gobble, we accept her' thing. I don't know why they made it gabba. I don't think anyone does."

Jane felt sadness creep in. It wasn't a clue to who her mother was. It was more old carny crap. Her voice started to shake and crumble when she said, "I guess I thought it would tell me more about who she was. Or who to be."

Leo squeezed her close as she started to cry, and the sound of it echoed inside the bathysphere, rippled through the air around them as if through water.

"You know what?" The excitement in Leo's voice filled the whole echoey chamber. "You *know* who she is. Or was. But no"—he shook his head—"I'm sticking with *is*. Present tense. Because she's right here. I mean, God, she's not even my mother and *I* can't stop thinking about her. About Trip to the Moon. Elephant Hotel. I want to fast-forward to when I have kids of my own just so I can play those games with them, you know?"

Jane was still wiping tears, and Leo pulled her even closer and kissed her—sweetly, softly—full on the mouth. It only lasted a few seconds, but Jane felt as though the whole world had frozen, the moon lost its pull, the tides halted. When it was done, Leo pulled a few inches away and put on a deep voice. "This is your captain."

Jane felt the start of laughter.

"This is a really bad storm or"—Leo laughed—"whatever it is he says."

She laughed now, too, and imagined them falling and falling, down into the darkest seas, bumping up against silver eels and translucent fish the likes of which the world had never seen.

"You already know who to be, Jane." He sighed and let her fall soft against his chest, and she imagined them floating up and up and up again, then resurfacing, into the light.

Triumphant.

Into countless tomorrows.

thirteen

ONTHS HAD PASSED and still no one but Marcus had seen Jane's mermaid costume. She'd carefully covered it with a trash bag and carried it down to the staging area for the parade.

"Well," Babette said. "Let's have a look."

Jane lifted the trash bag off, and the mermaid's shimmering skin caught the light and nearly blinded them.

Babette studied it. "Holy crap."

"That is awesome." H.T. came closer to inspect the costume as Jane adjusted some of the fabric.

"Nice job!" Babette gave Jane a pat on the back of her leg.

"Thanks," Jane said, and then Rita came over. She was carrying a heart-shaped flower arrangement with an "RIP Mermaid" sash across it and wearing an old-fashioned hat, the kind with a veil that came down in front. She lifted the black mesh off her face to say, "Cool costume."

"And I have to say the boys did a good job on the bier," Babette said, turning to the wagon they'd painted black and silver.

A girl walked over to them then, and Babette looked up, squinting, and said, "Can we help you?"

"It's me," she said. "Debbie."

Jane saw now that she looked almost exactly the same. Just without the hair. It had been a distraction, but it had also been her main identifying trait, and it was gone. "You look the same," Jane said. "I mean . . ."

Debbie nodded. "I know. It's weird. I thought I'd look so different, but I'm still me. Thank God, right?" Jane hadn't actually noticed how pretty she was, had just been too distracted by the hair.

"How'd your mother take it?" Jane asked.

"She'll come around," Debbie said, and Jane thought she saw the start of something in her eyes—tears—but then it was gone and replaced by a smile.

Jane changed into the costume, slipping her tail and fin on under her skirt, then ditching the skirt, then taking off her shirt to reveal the seashell top. She perched a crown of pearls on her head and turned back to take in the scene.

Sea creatures made from papier-mâché filled the air in every direction; one was long and blue with a mouth that could hold Babette. It looked like a snake but had fins that wagged in the wind. A huge gray octopus was being held in the air by nine people—one at the center and one at each of its tentacles. Another monster was green and scaly, like the beast from 20,000 fathoms, and Jane took a quick look around for a bathysphere but found Leo instead.

"Nice job," he said.

"You think?" She felt suddenly naked.

"I think." He smiled crookedly. "Though a true Looky Lou would've just come to watch."

Jane nodded and smiled. The sun was hot right then; her skin, too. "Maybe I'm not a Looky Lou after all."

Leo had to go round up his dirge band, and she felt a sort of tug when he walked away. But everything had changed since the bathysphere. She no longer had to doubt what was there in the space between them.

It just was.

Legs helped Jane, who was coated in sunscreen, up onto the bier, and when she lay down she was grateful that it was at least a little bit breezy, a little bit overcast. And then she was rolling and it was time for them to join the parade. Two of the school band's trombone players started to play Leo's dirge, and they walked down their side street and turned onto Surf Avenue.

At first, the noise of spectators was pretty scattered, but with each block the noise got thicker and thicker, and by the time they neared Nathan's—Jane was occasionally opening her eyes for a split second to steal peeks, plus Babette was giving her updates—it was out of control. Between the noise of the subway, and the crowds, and the dirge—not to mention the buzzing in Jane's ears coming from somewhere inside—it was almost too much. She heard a few people say, "Check out the mermaid funeral," and she heard Leo's dirge, which wasn't entirely sad but somehow full of longing, and not exactly the bad kind. Like the mermaid only wished she could climb up off her funeral bier and dive back into the sea.

Over and over again, she had to fight the urge to smile, to say cheese at the cameras she knew were pointed at her.

It *was* a funeral, after all.

A funeral that took *hours*. She couldn't believe how slowly the whole thing moved, how much time was spent hanging around, just lying there and waiting, but it was what it was.

Finally, they turned off Surf Avenue and headed toward the boardwalk down another side street packed with spectators. Jane stole a peek and saw a blur of sunglasses and cameras and baseball hats and sun hats and smiling faces and it felt like maybe it was what Coney used to be like, back in the day—and maybe would be again.

After an impromptu party on the beach, Jane went home to change back into normal clothes and grab the journal before heading to the Coral Room, where she found Beth sitting at a table by the aquarium, doing some paperwork. There were two women in swimsuits in the tank. Jane stopped and watched their golden hair glimmer in the underwater lights, watched the way they formed a circle with their two bodies, hands touching feet and feet touching hands, backs arched back.

Beth turned to look at the aquarium. "It's mermaid practice."

Jane started to move forward.

"Big show tonight," Beth added.

"They look great," Jane said, then she took her mother's journal out of her bag. "I found this," she said. "I thought you might want to look through it."

"Oh my gosh!" Beth took the book in her hands and then rubbed her palm over the cover. She opened to the first page. "I haven't seen this thing in so long." Her eyes ranged over page after page. "You sure?"

"Yeah." Jane nodded.

"I've been thinking about her a lot," Beth said. "About why she left for art school and never came back."

Jane just waited.

"I can't help but think it was because she wanted more. For *you*." She shook her head, waved a hand dismissively. "I know it's crazy. She hadn't even had you yet. Hadn't even met your father. But maybe she knew she wasn't going to meet him *here*."

"But why not?" Jane had met Leo. She'd met Leo here.

"Most of the smart ones leave." Beth closed the journal. "You'll do it, too."

The blue dress was one of the first ones she'd found in that chest in the attic, but it was so dressy that she'd never found an occasion to wear it. Tonight would be the night. She slipped into its silky blue fabric and felt like she was traveling back in time; in the mirror, her features, too, seemed somehow transformed. More angular, more old-fashioned. But more herself, more *now*, at the same time.

When she walked into the kitchen, Marcus and her father both looked up.

"Wow," Marcus said.

Her dad came over to kiss her forehead. "Lovely." He pulled back, holding her by her shoulders. "And that mermaid! It was spectacular!"

Jane's father and brother were going to the ball, too, but weren't ready yet and Jane didn't want to wait, so she walked back up to the boardwalk, to the roller rink building, where the party was already in full swing. A disco ball was sprinkling light on the crowd, dotting people with pink and blue and green lights like raindrops. Jane saw a tuna roll dancing with a clam on a half shell and thought that maybe next year, instead of a funeral, she'd like to make a float that celebrated something instead of mourned it.

She saw the seahorse first, then the rest of Leo came into focus. The hair on the back of his head was damp with sweat, clinging to his neck in pointy curves, and when he turned, he smiled. "I've been looking for you!" he shouted over the music. There was a band onstage playing some snazzy burlesque song.

"Why?" Jane shouted.

"Because I'm up next."

He disappeared into the crowd then, and the band on-stage finished their number and walked off and Leo appeared in their place. He was carrying a saw in one hand and a stool in the other, and he put the stool down and sat in front of a microphone. From his back pocket, he plucked his bow and held it in his right hand at the ready. He nodded off to the right, and a man came onstage and pulled a movie screen up out of a metal tube and latched it onto a hook. Then Leo nodded to someone at the back of the room somewhere and a funnel of projection light filled the air.

Orphans in the Surf appeared in shaky black-and-white just as Leo's saw started to sing and sway. It sounded like a woman singing a wordless song of longing, like she'd give anything to be with those children—to be able to take them in her arms and tell them they weren't orphans after all—but couldn't. It was wrenching and beautiful and it was coming from *him*. He played with his eyes closed, not even watching the way the saw bobbed and bent, and it made Jane feel like her heart might burst out of her chest. Just when she thought it was over, because the film was that short, it started again. And then again. The effect of showing the footage on a loop was heartbreaking, and Jane only wished that the children had played a game *other* than Ring Around the Rosie, something that would have lifted them up and not dragged them down. Leo's saw seemed to sing *ashes, ashes*, each and every time.

"Something weird just happened," she heard Babette say when Leo had left the stage. "Bend down."

Jane complied.

"H.T. just asked me out."

Somehow this didn't surprise Jane at all, didn't seem that weird. "What did you say?"

"I said, 'For real?'"

"And he said?"

Onstage Jane saw that Leo had returned with his band; the drummer clicked off a count with his sticks.

"He said, 'For real.'"

H.T. appeared and took Babette's hand and led her into the middle of the crowd, and Jane turned to watch Leo. This time it was him—and not his saw—doing the singing.

"Come with the love-light gleaming/In your dear eyes of blue./ Meet me in Dreamland, sweet, dreamy Dreamland./There let my dreams come true."

What's the best thing about being you?

She never had answered that final question for herself or anybody else and now her mind seemed to travel to the tips of all ten of her fingers and all ten of her toes, and up to the top of the Parachute Jump and the Thunderbolt and back. It seemed to climb the Cyclone and scream out in a fiery rage and then dive back down into the bathysphere, passing mermaids and turtles on the way, even saying hello to the bird on Nellie's hat. It shot up to the North Pole and then on up to the moon, where it was serenaded by Selenites, and back. It was searching out an answer that was right there—just not in any way she could verbalize.

And then there was a memory—of a day spent shopping, of a wall of televisions, of the lights and minarets of Luna Park.

Leo had brought buckets and shovels and all sorts of weird plastic gadgets to the beach that night, and together he and Jane started to build a sand castle Coney, even though it was dark. When she found a sun hat among the stuff in his beach bag, she reached out and put it on his head. She said, "What sound makes you happy?"

He was molding sand, but he looked up with a suspicious smirk. "Why do you ask?"

"Just wondering." She shrugged and returned to her own bucket, and after a moment he said, "The sound of you laughing."

Jane's hands were gritty and wet and Birdie's dress was covered in clumpy sand. She wiped them off as she shot him a look.

"I mean it," he said, shrugging and looking away like he was shy, though she knew better by now.

"Okay," she said, feeling a warmth in her heart despite the cold wind off the ocean. "What was the last dream you had that you remember?"

"There were rats in my house. I was trying to escape."

Jane looked up, skeptical.

"I'm serious!"

"Name one thing you want to do before you die."

"Have a kid."

"Wow," she said.

Jane hadn't ever actually imagined having a kid, but thought that yes, someday, that would be nice. Like Leo said, she could play those old games with her child, keep that memory alive.

"Too heavy?" Leo asked.

"I was thinking more along the lines of drink a cocktail out of a pineapple." She asked him, "What's the best thing about being you?"

"I don't know." He stopped and looked around. "I think it might be this. The fact that I grew up here. Makes you not take anything for granted."

He still hadn't built anything that looked anything at all like the Shoot the Chutes. It was dark, but the relative lack of light wasn't the only problem.

"How in the hell did she even do this?" Leo asked as another bucket of sand fell away in a series of small landslides.

"I don't know." Jane was having no better luck with a Monkey Theater. "Maybe I don't even remember it right, you know? Maybe I made it up."

"Don't say that," Leo said. He was kneeling in the sand in his jeans, scooping wildly.

"No, it's okay if I did," Jane said. "I mean, I was really young. Who knows?"

"You could ask your brother."

She thought about that for a second. "Nah," she said. "It'd ruin it."

Leo started to build the Shoot the Chutes again.

"Here." Jane tossed him a smaller bucket. "Try this one."

They worked quietly for a while, then Jane said, "That song you played on the saw at the party, and tonight . . . She used to sing that to me, the Dreamland song."

"Yeah?"

"When I was little and didn't want to go to bed because I wanted to be with her, she'd tell me that she'd meet me in Dreamland, and she'd lull me to sleep. I'm pretty sure she said it right before she died, too. That she'd see me there."

Leo looked up, pushed some hair out of his eyes with sandy hands. "Are you *trying* to kill me, Jane?"

Luna, she almost said. The name's *Luna.*

He wiped sand off his hands and she did, too, and they lay back on their blanket and Leo said, "I forget sometimes."

"Forget what?"

"That it's a beach." He shook his head and laughed. "Seems like an awful lot of fuss over a beach."

CHAPTER
fourteen

"S O," BABETTE SAID AT LUNCH. "Friday. Electric Bathing."

It was the last week of school, and Jane was a little sad that she wouldn't be seeing much of their cafeteria table for a few months. The good news was that she'd be back next year. Talks between the city and Loki were ongoing. Her father was still in the mix, as was his Lunacy ride.

"Are you both going?" Babette asked.

"Definitely," Rita said.

"I don't know," Jane said.

"Oh, you're going," Babette said.

"Hell yeah, you're going," Rita said.

But Jane tried to picture herself swimming in the ocean;

there was more than one problem. "I don't own a bathing suit."

Her friends started laughing then, and at first Jane felt like her cheeks were going to crumble and give way to tears, but then it struck her as funny, too.

Hilarious, even.

Babette said, "You can borrow one of mine," and they all started laughing even harder, and Jane said, "Do you have anything in black?" and they laughed even harder. Then finally, when they stopped, Rita said, "I guess we'll go shopping."

I'm in a department store with my mother and she's looking at big, shiny things. Dishwashers and clothes washers and stoves and refrigerators. I'm looking at my twisted reflection in the stainless-steel doors and looking warped and pushed and pulled and horrific. "Mommy," I say, "I look funny." She crouches down next to me and says, "There are worse things in life than looking funny," and then she goes back to looking at the machines.

Bored, I wander to the end of the aisle, where white lights reflect on the long white path that leads to the mall. I want to run down it the way a plane wants to cruise down a runway and take off, so I start to run but then I see the wall of televisions, all tuned to the same station, all showing some black-and-white movie of a Ferris wheel and millions and millions of people on a beach somewhere far away. I stand and watch and forget about my mother and everything as the lights of the amusement park on the televisions twinkle and glow. A man's voice is narrating the film, saying, "It became known as 'the playground of the world.'"

"Luna!" my mother is screaming.

"Luna!"

But I don't turn until she's by my side, hugging me, holding me, crying. There is a woman standing next to her, a perfect stranger best I can tell, and she says to me that I must never, ever, leave my mother's side, that I must hold her hand and never let go. The woman wanders off, and my mother pulls me up into her lap and sits in a leather armchair in front of one of the TVs. The Ferris wheel spins and spins and spins. . . .

Jane bumped into her brother sneaking out of the house at midnight that Friday. She had her new swimsuit on under shorts and a T-shirt. It felt good to be wearing new things, and Jane thought she'd have to go shopping with Babette and Rita again sooner than later.

"You're going?" Jane said. "Really?"

"Yes, really," Marcus said back. "Since when did you decide you're so much cooler than me anyway?"

"Give me a break, Marcus."

They elbowed each other as they pushed through the front door and onto the porch. The sagging window there seemed somehow to have tightened up, and Jane imagined it was because she'd gotten rid of Preemie's dead weight. The house felt lighter, newer, like it wouldn't be the worst place to spend another year. Or two. Jane had kept the stuff that held meaning for her—the *Is It Human?* poster and framed photos and some of the old books and costumes, even the two-headed squirrel. But that was all.

They headed for the boardwalk and turned left when they got there. Jane saw shadows on the beach, the silhouette of a pole of some kind, and a figure atop it.

Tattoo Boy.

He was stringing up a lightbulb that ran to the Anchor via the world's longest extension cord. The bar had opened up again after the city's purchase of the land went through, and while there were no guarantees, there was hope.

A moment later a small circle of white light cast a glow over a small portion of the surf and the beach. Bunches of people were suddenly in the water, shrieking and splashing. It looked like everyone from school had turned up.

A host of golden daffodils.

Jane picked up her pace, afraid of missing out, afraid that it would be over—shut down by the cops—before she even got wet.

"Hey," Babette said when Jane found her on the group's outskirts. She had a towel around her shoulders but was bone-dry.

Jane looked out at the electric bathers and start to strip.

"You're really going in?" Babette seemed giddy.

Jane nodded. She was a girl on a mission, a mission to claim some little part of the excitement of the park that was her namesake, of that bygone era.

The water was black, like fuel, and Jane tried hard not to think about everything that lived beneath its surface—electric eels and stingrays and big pulsing jellyfish—as she picked up one of the ropes tethered to the light tower and strode into the surf. It was cold, bracing, and the sand curled around her toes but she pressed on, until she was the farthest person out. The water was still only waist-high, but with each swell she wondered whether she was an idiot, whether she should scream for help right then, before she really needed it. Before it was too late.

Looking out over the water, she saw just a few lights—Staten Island—and she overheard someone behind her say, "Do you know how Staten Island got its name?"

Someone else said, "No," and the other voice returned with "The Dutchman who saw it from his ship pointed and said, 'Is stat an island?'"

Jane felt pretty sure that she wouldn't ever have to swim away from Coney in fear for her life but wondered, still, how long she would be able to hold her breath. She imagined that her mother, a mermaid, had been able to do it for a really long time. But what counted as a really long time?

She inhaled and held it and watched her classmates in the water.

She saw Legs with Minnie propped on his shoulders. She saw H.T.'s floating torso next to a dog-paddling Babette and watched Rubber Rita push Marcus under the water and laugh.

They were *frolicking*.

There was no other word for it, as silly and old-fashioned as it sounded. And she closed her eyes for a second and opened them again and it was as if she could see the lights of Luna Park and Dreamland and Steeplechase Park right there.

A double-exposed photograph.

It felt as though the water itself had trapped Coney's history in its molecules and she was steeped in it, soaking it in through her pores, breathing it as if through gills. She thought of all the people who had come to this very place, who had swum in these very waters—millions upon millions—and who had had the time of their life. She had spent the year wishing she could travel back through time and spend just one day there, during the era of the dawn of fun, but that would never happen and maybe that was okay.

Because this felt close.

Something slimy brushed against her leg and she jerked away and started to head back to shore, skin prickling from the cool air and the shock of the reminder of all the murk and mystery beneath the water's choppy skin.

And me without my bathysphere.

Leo was directly in her path.

"Hey, Looky Lou," he said. The lightbulb's glow made his figure a backlit silhouette. It cast silver light on the right side of his wet face as she exhaled.

Someone in the crowd shouted, "Oh, victory! Forget your underwear. We're free."

I'm still in the department store and the strange lady has scolded me and then left. My mother and I are still sitting in the leather chair and the film has ended again. The credits have rolled for the third time, and the salesman comes over and says, "Ma'am. We're closing."

He has been nice to us, playing the film again and again, but he knows we are not buying a TV.

My mother pushes me to get up off her lap and I do so, but then she grabs me and lays me down on the big chair and it turns out it spins and spins and spins and the lights on the ceiling are a swirl of white whipping by.

"Look!" she says. "It's a human roulette wheel."

I don't know what that word means, roulette, but it's fun.

When I get up, I make sure to hold onto her hand. "The lady said to never let go," I say. "Never ever."

My mother pulls her hand from mine, using her other one, and it hurts.

"You can let go," she says, "as long as you stay close."

They were standing face-to-face, wet and breathing hard, and she felt certain that if there were no one else around, Tattoo Boy would kiss her again. Or she'd kiss him.

A different *kind* of kiss, too.

If it didn't happen tonight, it would happen the next day or the one after. She knew that it would as surely as she knew her own name, as surely as she knew that she'd been lost and then found.

"My name isn't really Jane," she said.

Gooble gobble. Gooble gobble.

Tattoo Boy smiled lazily, like he already knew what she was going to say and maybe he did. "You don't say."

"It's Luna," she said. "*Luna* Jane."

He lifted an inky arm out of waist-high water and she

saw the *Gabba Gabba Hey!* tattoo for the first time. Had it been there all along? "Pleased to make your acquaintance, Luna."

She went to shake his hand just as a wave swelled around their bellies and then curled over and crashed hard. They tumbled toward the shore together in a churning funnel of white and black, sand and sea, and then stood up—laughing, and still holding hands.

"I think," Leo said between short, recovering breaths, "that might have been"—another inhale on the tail of a laugh—"Coney's way of saying . . ."

"I know," Luna managed, also struggling for air.

Then she licked her salty lips and found solid footing in the sand and nodded. "It's saying, 'What took you so long?'"

A NOTE ABOUT HISTORY, CONEY, AND DREAMLAND SOCIAL CLUB . . .

The Coney Island depicted in *Dreamland Social Club* is a mix of fact and fiction. The Parachute Jump, The Cyclone, The Wonder Wheel . . . these things actually exist on Coney Island. As did Dreamland, Luna Park, Steeplechase Park, and the Thunderbolt.

But The Anchor, Wonderland, and Morelli's, while inspired by real places, are entirely fictional. The Coral Room is even *more* fictional, if it is possible to be such a thing, and Coney Island High bears no resemblance to Coney Island's Lincoln High School.

Why? Because I wanted to take liberties with certain kinds of locations and did not want to mess with actual Coney institutions while doing so.

The Anchor, just as one example, is very much inspired by Ruby's Bar, a glorious dive bar on the boardwalk that lost its lease just weeks before I sat down to write this note. I adored Ruby's. My husband and I were there on our first date, and celebrated our engagement there some months later. Its closing has been devastating to all who know and love Coney. I created the Anchor as a sort of stand-in because my characters' relationships with the bar needed to be complex and, like the bar's fate, entirely in my control.

The fact of the matter is that there are, in the world, many more qualified chroniclers of Coney Island history than me. Readers who want to know more will be entirely mesmerized by books including Charles Denson's *Coney Island: Lost and Found* and *Coney Island: The People's Playground* by Michael Immerso. There is also a riveting film about Coney Island in the PBS American Experience series. I highly recommend you seek out some of these sources.

One final note: I may have manipulated some details regarding the item linked to *Dreamland Social Club*'s "Bath" key. Interested parties can turn to Adam Green's *New Yorker* article entitled "Deep" (April 11, 2005) for the whole story.

—TA